YOU CAN CALL IT A DAY

YOU CAN
CALL IT A DAY

A NOVEL

by

PETER CHEYNEY

THE BOOK CLUB
121, CHARING CROSS ROAD
LONDON, W.C.2

TO

LAURA

COPYRIGHT
PRINTED IN GREAT BRITAIN
FOR COLLINS CLEAR-TYPE PRESS: LONDON AND GLASGOW
BY WILLMER BROS. & CO. LTD., CHESTER STREET, BIRKENHEAD
1950

CONTENTS

CHAPTER ONE

NARCISSE NOIR

I

VALLON came out of his bedroom ; closed the door ; stood for a moment in the corridor. The scent hit his nostrils— *Narcisse Noir*. Vallon, who had a nose for perfume, wondered when he had last smelt *Narcisse Noir*. He thought it might have been in Paris. He wasn't certain. He walked slowly down the curving staircase into the hotel lounge ; stood at the bottom looking about him, watching the people.

He wore a dark blue, double-breasted suit that had been cut by a good tailor, a cream shirt, a blue tie. He was just under six feet and thin. His face was long, triangular shaped ; his eyes sombre, deepset but with a sardonic light lurking in them. He was dark and his well-kept hair was inclined to wave. He weighed a hundred and seventy pounds and kept his weight well forward on the balls of his feet like a boxer. He looked tired.

Everything about Vallon was quiet. He moved lazily ; talked in a quiet voice with a peculiarly attractive timbre to it. He preferred to remain unnoticed but never succeeded in this. In spite of himself an odd and engaging personality came out of him and affected most people with whom he came in contact. Especially women. Women found him fascinating because he never tried to be like that. He had spent a considerable portion of his life trying to avoid them. With little success.

On the other side of the lounge in the corner was the bar. Vallon looked at his strap-watch. It was nine o'clock. Most of the people in the hotel had finished dinner. The lounge was beginning to fill up. He went over to the bar ; sat on one of the high stools. He ordered a double Bacardi and when it was served sat looking at it. He realised he didn't want it.

Life, he thought, was rather like a Bacardi cocktail. If you wanted one you wanted it like hell ; if you didn't want it it was either too weak or too strong. They'd put too much

7

of this or that in it or left it out. But you still drank it. He thought that drinking Bacardi was rather like making love to women. Or wasn't it? He thought he didn't know. He decided he couldn't care less.

He wondered why he had come to this place. Then he remembered three weeks ago somebody had told him that Paignton was an amusing place; that Devonshire was the best county in England. So he'd come. Now that he was here so what? Devon was a fine county all right. The earth was red and the grass greener than any place he'd seen it. If you got bored with Paignton you could always go to Torquay, and if you got bored with Torquay you could always go back to Paignton. You could be certain of one thing—you'd find a bar in each place. And when all is said and done a bar is a place which helps a man to remember the things he wants to remember and to forget the things he wants to forget.

He drank the Bacardi and wondered whether he was trying to remember something or forget it. He decided he wouldn't know that either; that he didn't care anyway. He smelt *Narcisse Noir* again—just a subtle whiff, but it was there. He finished the drink, closed his eyes and wondered what she'd look like. He opened them and found he was wrong.

She had what it takes in a very big way, Vallon decided. She was wearing a navy blue suit with a skirt fitting so well that it looked as if it had been pasted on her. Under her coat was a blouse that came out of France—a fine hand-made georgette in a faint lemon colour with hand-sewn tucks. Her shoes were hand-made and the seams of her stockings were dead straight up the back of the calf. Vallon thought that she would be about thirty-five. Judging by the rings on her fingers she had money.

He ordered another Bacardi. The bar-tender raised an eyebrow. He had served Vallon with at least twelve cocktails during the course of the evening. He thought Vallon certainly knew how to drink.

He said cheerfully: " You *like* Bacardi, sir? "

Vallon looked at him seriously. " No, I don't like anything." He looked at the woman sideways. She was sticking a cocktail pick in a bottle of maraschino cherries. He watched her put it into her mouth. Her mouth was raspberry-coloured and she had full, promising lips. Vallon

8

thought that she was cute. He thought she was the cutest woman he'd seen since he'd been in that part of the world. He drank some Bacardi.

She said : " It's a lovely evening, isn't it ? "

He didn't know whether she was talking to him or the barman. " If you meant that for me," he said, " I'm not interested in the weather. It doesn't make any difference to me whether the sun's shining, if it's raining or Christmas day."

She smiled. When she smiled she looked very attractive. She said : " You're either very unhappy or very happy."

" Believe it or not," said Vallon, " I'm not either. I just don't care about the weather. Do you mind ? " He smiled at her.

" No . . ." She looked a trifle bewildered ; then she smiled again. " I think you're a unique person. You express yourself very . . . succinctly . . . I think that's the word."

Vallon said : " I think it's a very nice word." He ordered a large Bacardi. " I have a good idea," he went on.

She raised her eyebrows.

He said : " You're sitting too far away from me. You're at least four stools away. If I move towards you you might think it impertinent. So you come here."

She said : " There isn't any question about your originality."

" They tell me my mother said that too."

She asked : " What did your father say ? "

He shook his head. " They never told me, but I believe he wasn't very pleased."

She got off her stool. When she moved he saw her legs. He thought they were very good legs.

She said : " Well, here I am. If you consider it would be impertinent to move towards me, perhaps you think it forward of me to come to you."

" No one who looks like you has to worry about being forward. Have you ever drunk Bacardi ? "

She nodded.

He said : " Drink one with me."

Whilst the bar-tender was serving the drinks, he said : " I smelt you upstairs in the corridor when I came out of my room. You'd just passed. I've got a nose for scent. It's *Narcisse Noir*, isn't it ? "

9

" I'm beginning to be a little scared of you, Mr.——? "

" My name's Vallon. I'm glad you're scared."

She raised her eyebrows. " You haven't told me your first name."

" My name's John, but most people call me Johnny. I've never discovered why."

She asked : " Why did you say you were glad I was scared ? "

" When a woman says she's scared," said Vallon, " she means she might at sometime be interested. Let's do something."

She asked : " What ? "

He pointed with his finger through the open windows of the lounge, across the gardens, to the fair on the sea-front. The three-quarters of a mile of lawn between the road and the esplanade was filled with wagons, coconut shies, round-abouts, and most of the inhabitants of Paignton. The darkness was beginning to fall and the thousand and one lights, from coloured electric bulbs to humble acetylene gas lamps, twinkled in the half light. The scene was attractive, alive but, for some reason, imbued with an odd feeling of unreality.

" I don't believe it's true. Why don't we go out there and see whether the fair really exists, Mrs.——? "

She said : " My name's Gale."

" I'm glad to meet you, Mrs. Gale," said Vallon.

" I'm glad to meet you, Mr. Vallon. Shall I buy you a drink ? "

" Yes, thank you very much. I like being bought drinks."

She ordered one double Bacardi. He noticed she'd scarcely touched her own drink. He drank it. He got off the stool.

" I'll repay your hospitality with a couple of coconut shies," he said. " By the way, what's your Christian name ? "

" A rather peculiar name—Querida. Do you like it ? "

" I think it's wonderful. You'll always be Mrs. Gale to me." He grinned at her. They walked across the lounge, down the steps, through the gardens.

She thought he was the most attractive man she had ever met.

.   .   .   .

It was eleven o'clock when they came out of the South African mystery man's tent after watching that swarthy gentleman eat fire. People milled about them; throwing rings at four for sixpence over gorgeous looking objects which were seldom won; trying to get balls into holes to win a gold watch; riding on the cart-wheel; doing all those things which people do at fairs and imagine they like doing.

She said: " I think this is rather an adventure. I like it. Do you ? "

" I've been to a lot of fairs in America, in France, all over the place," said Vallon. " I came out of a fair once in Avignon, and they were trying to push a large elephant into a very small truck. It took five men to get it in. I asked one of them if he didn't think it was too small for the elephant. He said no; the other elephant was already inside." Vallon looked at her. His eyes were sardonic, yet somehow smiling. " I think that's awfully funny, don't you ? "

She said: " Supposing I don't ? "

" What do I care ? " asked Vallon. He took out his cigarette case; offered her a cigarette. She shook her head.

He was lighting his own cigarette when he saw Hipper.

Hipper was standing at an illuminated table trying to throw rings over watches set out on the mirrored surface. He was obviously a little drunk.

Vallon said: " You wouldn't be tired by any chance, would you ? "

" No . . ." She smiled at him faintly. " Are you trying to get rid of me, Mr. Vallon ? "

He said: " I'm not trying to, I'm going to. You see, I've just remembered something. Go back to the bar in the hotel and wait for me. I promise you I won't be long."

She asked seriously: " Do you mean that ? "

He nodded. " Every word of it."

She said: " Well, thank you for a very pleasant evening."

Vallon asked: " Shall I see you in the bar ? "

She smiled. " Who knows ? Perhaps . . . That depends on how long you are."

She went away. He watched her walking through the crowd. He thought she walked very well.

When he looked round Hipper was gone. Vallon began

11

to walk about the fair-ground looking for him. He thought it was like looking for a needle in a haystack ; qualified it by the thought that if you looked long enough for a needle in a haystack you found it. He found Hipper after thirty minutes' search. Hipper was throwing wooden balls at coconuts.

Vallon came up behind him. He said: " Enjoying yourself, Hipper ? "

Hipper dropped the wooden ball on the ground. It made a peculiar thudding noise. He turned round and looked at Vallon.

He said : " For crissake . . . ! This isn't so good, is it ? "

" It might be," said Vallon. " It just needs a little explanation. Let you and me go and have a drink."

Hipper started to talk. " Listen . . ."

Vallon said : " Shut up. We'll talk in the bar when we find one."

They went to a bar in an hotel along the esplanade. Vallon ordered two whiskies and sodas.

He said : " All right. Now let's have it. And make it good."

Hipper drank some of the whisky. He was a short, fat man. His face was bloated with drink. He had nice eyes but his mouth was pursed up like a woman's. He was inclined to baldness and there was a greasy ring on the inside of the soft hat which he had placed on the stool beside him.

He said : " You've always had it in for me, haven't you, Mr. Vallon ? But I'm human. What the hell ! "

Vallon yawned. " Who told you you were human ? Well, let's have the story, Hipper. What are you doing here ? "

" Look, have a heart," said Hipper. " I got the job done in Somerset. I got everything—the report and everything. It's all right. Every bit of evidence the firm wants will be there. So I thought I'd have a night here and go back to-morrow."

" On the agency's expense account, hey ? " Vallon queried.

Hipper said : " No."

Vallon grinned.

" I tell you it's not on the firm's expense account," said Hipper. " I put the report and the expense sheet in the post before I left Somerset."

Vallon raised his eyebrows. "You don't say! You don't mean to tell me that you came over here on your own money when you could have charged it to the firm. Well . . . well . . . wonders will never cease."

There was a pause; then he asked: "When are you going back?"

"First thing in the morning." Hipper's tone changed. "Look, Mr. Vallon, you don't have to do anything about this. You don't have to, do you?"

"You mean tell Chennault?" Vallon grinned. "You think if I told Chennault he'd sack you. I don't have to tell him. But I could sack you myself. Don't you know that?"

Hipper nodded. "I know it."

Vallon said: "All right, Hipper. I'll forget it. It'll cost you a large whisky and soda."

Hipper grinned. "I always knew you were all right, Mr. Vallon. I'd like to buy you a drink." He ordered the drinks. He went on: "It's pretty nice of you to take this angle on my coming here."

Vallon picked up the glass and drained it.

He said: "That's what I thought. Good night, Hipper." He went out of the bar.

He thought Hipper was a liar.

   .   .   .   .

It was late when Vallon went into the lounge at the hotel. The bar was closed. There were two double Bacardis on one of the lounge tables near to it. There was nobody in the lounge. Vallon went over and sat at the table with the drinks on it. There was a note under one of the glasses written on a piece of telephone message paper in a regular, delicate handwriting. It said: "*Why should I wait for you? Here's your drink, Q.G.*"

Vallon sighed. He drank one of the Bacardis; then the other. He got up; lighted a cigarette; crossed the lounge; began to walk up the stairs. He was going into his room when a door opened down the corridor. She came out.

She was wearing an attractive pink lace and black velvet negligee and satin mules. She had a handkerchief over one eye. Vallon began to walk towards her.

She said querulously: "I don't know what to do. I've got something in my eye. The pain's abominable."

Vallon said : " That's easily dealt with. Go back to your room. I'll be with you in a minute."

He went to his room ; got an orange stick, a soft handkerchief, a small bottle of olive oil. He went back to her room ; opened the door ; went in. She was sitting at the dressing-table, the handkerchief to her eyes.

Vallon said : " Put your head back and take that handkerchief away. I'm not going to hurt you."

He stood behind her ; rolled the eyelid back over the orange stick. He did it deftly with long, nervous fingers. He dropped a little of the oil into the eye. He said : " Now close your eye and keep your fingers away from it."

She murmured : " Thanks . . . you big bully . . ."

After a minute he told her to open her eye. He asked : " How does that feel ? " He held the eyelashes back ; saw the speck ; removed it with a corner of the handkerchief. " It'll be sore for a little while, but that's all. It's a painful business, isn't it ? "

She nodded her head. Standing above her Vallon could see the sheen on her dark hair ; the shape of her slim neck.

She sat looking at the bottles on her dressing-table. He saw the flask of *Narcisse Noir*.

He said : " Good night."

She got up. She asked : " Did you find your Bacardis ? "

He nodded. " I'll buy some for you sometime. Thanks a lot. Good night, Mrs. Gale . . ."

She took a quick step towards him. She said : " You're just a big bully . . . aren't you ? A big bully with an attractive style to you, a lazy walk and God knows what . . . And you don't care a damn for anything or anybody . . . do you ? "

Vallon said : " No . . . not much. So what ? "

She said quietly : " To hell with you, Johnny . . ."

She put her arms round his neck.

2

Vallon stopped the car on the right-hand side of Lower Regent Street. He looked at his watch. It was two o'clock. He locked the car ; stood by the door on the pavement wondering why he was undecided. For a moment he thought

14

about Mrs. Gale, but only for a moment. He decided it wasn't any good thinking about anything. Not even Mrs. Gale.

He began to walk up Regent Street. He was almost on the corner of Jermyn Street when somebody said: " Hallo, Johnny ! "

Vallon turned round. He smiled. " Hey, Strype . . . what do you know about this ? "

Strype said : " Boy . . . what *do* you know . . . ! " You could have cut his American accent with a knife. He went on : " Say, fella . . . the last time I saw you was on the corner of some goddam track on Okinawa, with a Japanese light tank comin' round the corner. D'you remember ? D'you remember what we did to those bastards ? Did I getta kick when I saw that goddam grenade you threw go right through the air-vent at the back. Boy, you made a mess of those guys ! "

Vallon said : " Those were the days."

" Yeah . . . or were they ? I wouldn't know. Maybe we got inta the habit of thinkin' backwards. Maybe bein' in a war does something to you. You're frightened an' pleased. You don't know which, but you never forget it. Whenever you get bored or steamed up with life you think about it. Howya doin', Johnny ? "

Vallon said : " All right . . ."

Strype looked at his strap-watch. " Hey, what about a snifter ? I know a dump near here where they got rye."

They sat at the bar drinking rye whisky, talking about the Japanese.

Then Strype said : " What're you doin', Johnny ? You look good. But you always did, hey ? Are you makin' out ? "

Vallon shrugged his shoulders. " I'm doing all right. Remember Chennault—the guy I worked under after I was wounded—the guy in the U.S. Office of Strategic Service ? "

" Yeah . . . I remember . . . a fat fella with a weak heart. So you're workin' for him ? "

Vallon nodded. " He came over here before I got here. He started a detective business. I work for him."

Strype laughed. " For cryin' out loud ! You in a racket like that—crawlin' around lookin' through key-holes tryin' to find co-respondents. Boy . . . ! " He took a gulp of rye. " Say, Johnny . . . you don't *like* that, do you ? "

15

Vallon said: "No . . . not much. But I like Chennault. He did me a good turn once. He's not really fit to run his business. He has good and bad days, you know, and anyhow I don't have to snoop through key-holes. I'm the Staff Manager. I look after the eggs who do the snooping. I see they do it."

"Yeah?" Strype signalled the bar-tender; ordered more drinks. He went on: "So you're working for Chennault. How's that wife of his?"

"She's all right," said Vallon. "I've only seen her two or three times."

Strype said musingly: "Yeah? Look . . . you tell me something. How does an old mug like Chennault with a weak ticker manage to get himself a frill like that? Is she a looker! Some momma! I saw her once. Some guys have all the luck." He looked sideways at Vallon. "It's goddam lucky for Chennault that he ain't got some good-lookin' mug around the place—somebody who's got what it takes— somebody like you."

There was a pause; then Vallon said: "I told you Chennault did me a good turn, Strypey."

Strype grinned. "You don't haveta get steamed up, sweetheart. I never *said* anything, did I?"

There was another pause. They both drank rye whisky.

Strype said: "Say, what's the matter with you, Johnny? You usta be full of this an' that. Full of pep an' what it takes an' what-have-you-got. You're sorta serious these days. What's hit you?"

Vallon drank some more whisky. He shrugged his shoulders. He didn't say anything.

Strype said: "Maybe I got it. You know, there's a sort of air of depression around this place that you could cut with a knife. I've been all over the world an' I've been here in London plenty. But, boy, is it grim . . . ! You remember Churchill said that England could take it. I reckon that guy was right. But, by God, they're takin' it hard! They don't laugh much an' I don't wonder. What the hell have they got to laugh about? Everybody's sorta walkin' around lookin' as if they've lost their bill-fold an' are wonderin' where the next dollar's comin' from. Me—I don't *like* t."

Vallon said quietly: "Maybe you're right. But they'll

16

pull out." He grinned. " The English take a lot of beating, you know."

" Yeah," said Strype. " *You* don't know a lot about 'em. How many years of your life have you spent here ? Your mother was English, but that was all."

" That's a lot," said Vallon. " I like them. I've been everywhere and done most things." He grinned. " But it's a nice place to come back to. To me it's home, even if it is tough."

Strype said : " Yeah . . . maybe you're right. But give me the U.S. all the time where they still have some bright spots—where you can still go some place on a Sunday— where somebody still has a little dough—where babies are *babies* ! "

Vallon grinned. " Meaning that some girl has given you the air ? I wondered what had got into you, Strype."

" Aw . . . hell . . . ! " said Strype. " I should worry about dolls givin' me the air. There's always another one. Who was it said there's as good fish in the sea as those that came out of it ? " He sighed. " Me—I like women. My old Pa usta say they were the most pleasant of nature's mistakes. But they're hard to get—very hard." He looked sideways seriously at Vallon. " Maybe not for you, because you've got some sorta special line I've never got around to. You're goddam quiet but you get what you want. Maybe you've got something they never told me about."

Vallon shrugged his shoulders. He ordered two more rye whiskies.

Strype said : " Talkin' of mommas do I get a jolt just after lunch to-day ? Boy, did I see a dream walkin' or did I ? "

Vallon said nothing. He paid the bar-tender ; drank a little rye.

Strype went on : " I'm comin' past the Hungaria—the restaurant just around the corner—an' she comes out. For crissake . . . ! I've never seen anything like it. Boy, I wish you coulda seen it."

Vallon sighed. He said wearily : " I know . . . she was a blonde . . . she was buxom with a small waist and good legs. She had what it takes and she threw you a hot look." He grinned at Strype. " Right ? "

" Wrong to hell . . . this one wasn't *my* type. But, boy,

was she *something* ! I'm just passing the restaurant when she comes out. She's wearing a black suit—a coat an' skirt cut by some egg who certainly knew his pineapples. She's streamlined an' she's got legs you dream about an' little feet an' neat shoes. Everything about this baby is wonderful. She's wearin' one of those nifty sorta hats that you get only in Paris an' it makes a sorta frame for her auburn hair. I tell you I could have eat this baby without even usin' the cruet."

Vallon stifled a yawn. " So what . . . ? "

" So just at this moment," Strype went on, " she's gettin' inta a taxicab that the doorman's got for her, an' she drops her handbag, see ? What didn't come out of it was nobody's business—lipstick, keys, bill-fold, a little phial of perfume. . . . So I watch 'em while they stick around collectin' this stuff an' I see something. Some finger-ring has rolled over to my feet. I pick it up. Boy, is it a ring ! I reckon you an' me have seen plenty jade in China, Johnny, but this was the loveliest stuff you've ever seen in your life. A sort of eternity ring with roses carved in the centre an' little diamonds an' rubies set in the middle of each rose. You've never seen such lovely stuff in your life."

Vallon asked. " So what did you do with it—snatch it ? "

" Have a heart. Me—I wouldn't do a thing like that. I picked it up. By this time they'd got all the rest of the junk back in her bag. She's just steppin' inta the cab an' I say : ' Excuse me, lady, but maybe you'd like to have this.' I pick up her left hand—she's got a white kid glove on it— an' I put the ring in the middle of the palm. ' Maybe you oughta give me something for that,' I said."

Vallon asked : " What did she say to that one ? "

" She smiled at me," said Strype. " That smile took years off my age. She said : ' I'd like to give you something for it. I'd like to say thank you. It's very precious to me.' "

He sighed. Vallon thought it was like a whale coming up for air.

Strype went on : " She got inta the cab an' she went away. Me—I woulda liked to know that frill, I'm tellin' *you* ! "

" Do you want another drink ? " asked Vallon.

" Nope. . . . I've turned over a new leaf as the English say. I practically never touch the stuff . . . well, not much . . . maybe a bottle a day . . . never more."

18

Vallon said : " When are you going back, Strypey ? "

" I'm flyin' over next week. I'll be seein' you, Johnny. If you come over, look me up. I'll be in New York."

" I'll do that," said Vallon.

Strype got off the stool. " So long, soldier . . . I'll be seein' you."

" So long . . ." Vallon watched Strype as he walked out of the bar into the sunshine. Then he put his elbows on the bar. He was looking straight in front of him at the rows of bottles set before the mirror behind the bar. He sat there for a long time. The feeling had come again. The peculiar feeling of faintness in the stomach that always came when he thought about her. Or maybe it was the bullet they'd spent such a long time chiselling out of his insides. Maybe both . . .

The bar-tender said : " Another drink, sir ? "

Vallon nodded. " A Bacardi . . ."

He sipped the drink slowly. Watching him, you would have thought he wasn't tasting it. When he'd drunk half of it he put some money on the counter and got off the stool.

He went out of the bar ; began to walk in the direction of the Hungaria restaurant.

.   .   .   .

When the cab stopped outside the apartment block, Vallon got out and looked at his strap-watch. It was three o'clock. He thought maybe he ought to have phoned through to Chennault ; decided it didn't matter. He paid off the cab and a picture of Hipper came across his mind.

Vallon thought Hipper was a damned liar. The inquiries he'd been making in the Somerset divorce case would have carried the costs of his fare to Paignton, his entertainment there, a few drinks and anything else he'd wanted. But for some reason best known to himself, Hipper had put the account in with the evidence he'd collected in Somerset, and then gone to Paignton at his own expense. Which meant that he didn't want anybody to know he was going to Paignton. Hipper had realised that if he'd put the extra amounts on his charge account he might have been asked to explain them. So he left them out and paid them himself.

Vallon shrugged his shoulders. All sorts of people did all sorts of things for all sorts of reasons—most of the time

19

en*irely different reasons from those you thought of in the first place—especially people like Hipper.

As he turned away from the taxicab he thought that the world was like that. Nobody ever really knew what anybody else was doing and what their motives were. Everybody had a private soul. Or had they? He wondered if he had a private soul. He grinned.

The apartment block lay between Lowndes Square and West Halkin Street. Vallon walked up the entrance steps, through the doors into the hall. A porter in a well-tailored grey uniform was sitting in his glass office. Vallon asked him: "Where does Miss Thorne live?"

"The third floor, sir . . . No. 3. Would you like to go up in the lift?"

Vallon said: "No, I'll walk."

He began to walk slowly up the thickly carpeted stairs. There was the same sort of catch under the heart that he remembered from China—the same quickening of the breath —the same faintness inside his guts. He thought it was nice to get excited about something. Then he thought maybe it was a good thing not to get excited before you knew.

A middle-aged maid opened the door after he'd rung the bell.

Vallon said: "I have an appointment with Miss Thorne."

"Come in, sir," said the maid. "I'll tell her. Shall I give her your name?"

"No . . . it doesn't matter," said Vallon.

The maid shut the door; went away. He sat down in the high-backed chair in the large hallway. After a few minutes one of the four doors leading out of the hall opened. She stood in the doorway.

Vallon got out of the chair slowly. He was smiling. His eyes moved over her—from the small, beautifully shod feet to the crown of her auburn head.

He said: "So here I am . . ."

She put one hand against the door lintel. He noticed the length and delicacy of her fingers; the fineness of the lace ruffles over her wrist.

She looked at him for a long time; then she said in a quiet voice: "You heel, Johnny! So you've got the nerve to come here."

Vallon sat down in the chair again. He took out his

cigarette case; extracted two cigarettes; lighted them. He threw one towards her. She caught it deftly. She put it in her mouth, her eyes still steadily on him.

She said: "Well, what about it, Mr. Vallon?"

He got up. He moved towards her. She thought as he approached her that he always looked a little tired and rather lazy. No matter what the business was he always had the same lazy look—always . . .

He asked: "Do we have to deal in explanations? Explanations never mean a goddam thing to anybody, Madeleine. If they're lies they don't matter, and if they're true, so what? If I shoot a story at you, you can either believe it or not. It might be true and it might not be."

She smiled a little. "You Englishman . . .! Any explanation from you would probably be a lie."

"Yes, that's what I thought," said Vallon.

She threw the cigarette into a brass ash-tray on the hall table. She put her arms round his neck. He could see the tears in her eyes. She said: "Oh, Johnny . . . you goddam heel . . .!" She began to cry.

Vallon thought that that was pretty good. He put his arm about her shoulder; held her close. He smelt the light, attractive perfume she always wore—a perfume that reminded you of flowers and sunshine. He remembered it but he'd forgotten the name. She cried for quite a while.

Then he said: "Why don't you call it a day? Or do you want to have red-rimmed eyes and a red nose when we go out to-night?"

She stood away from him. She said: "You'd better come n here."

He followed her into the drawing-room. It was large, luxuriously furnished. He looked about the place; saw everywhere the evidence of her fastidious taste.

She said: "How do you know I'm going to dine with you to-night?"

He grinned. "How do I know my name's Vallon? Somebody told me! Can I sit down?"

She nodded. "If you want a drink there're some bottles in the cabinet." She motioned towards an oak cabinet at the end of the room.

"I don't if you don't," said Vallon.

21

She asked: " What about this explanation ? How did you know I was here ? "

" I had a break. I came up from Devonshire this morning. I left there early. I ran into a Yankee called Strype in Regent Street. I knew him in Japan in the war. We had a drink. He was the one who returned your jade ring when you dropped it this morning outside the Hungaria." He grinned at her. " I'm glad you didn't lose it. I found the taxi-driver who brought you home. Luckily he came off the Regent Street rank. A pound tip did the rest . . ."

She asked: " What were you doing in Devonshire ? " She looked sideways at him. " Some woman I suppose, as usual ? "

" If there was, why not ? " said Vallon. " If I'd known you were here there never would have been any woman. You know that."

There was another pause. She sat down on the settee facing him. She said: " I'm still waiting for the explanation, Johnny."

Vallon sighed. She thought he had the most attractive jaw and mouth she'd ever seen in her life. His teeth were white and even. And behind the laziness was a brain.

He said: " Look, Sweet, maybe this is hard to believe but it's a fact. When I came out of hospital I had to go up to Tientsin. I thought I was coming back immediately. That's why I didn't even bother to say good-bye to you. When I got up there I ran into something—something I don't have to talk about."

" You mean some woman you don't *want* to talk about ? "

" Believe it or not," said Vallon, " it wasn't a woman. Just a job. O.K. I got myself shot up. I was in hospital for sixteen weeks. The first five days I was unconscious. I was very ill for a long time, Madeleine, too ill to write or telephone. Then I got a long distance call to you at the hotel. You were gone." He smiled at her. " Was that kind ? " He looked at her quizzically.

" What did you expect ? You were supposed to be engaged to me. You walk out on me. I never hear anything of you again. For God's sake, Johnny, why don't you behave normally, like anyone else ? "

He said slowly: " I wouldn't know, Sweet. Maybe I'm not normal."

She came across the room and sat on his knee. She put her arm round his neck. She said: " You know what I'd like to call you ? "

He nodded. " That dear old-fashioned word . . . bastard ! But you don't like to say it. O.K. Take it as said. That's the truth. After I left the hospital I kicked around in China for a hell of a time. I tried to get a line on you. I even went and saw the old guy we bought that ring from . . . remember ? Nobody knew where you were. Just another rather good-looking, wealthy, well-dressed American girl chasing her tail and leaving no address behind her."

There was another silence. She asked: " Johnny, have you missed me ? "

" What do you think ? If I were given to poetic phrases I would say it was rather like having your intestines taken out and walking about with an empty inside."

She asked: " What have you been doing—besides drinking rye whisky . . . ? "

He shrugged his shoulders. " Kicking around . . . working a little . . ."

She raised her eyebrows. " So you work ? At what ? "

" Believe it or not," said Vallon, " I'm in a detective agency."

" Wonders will never cease ! You . . . Johnny . . . in a detective agency. What do you do there ? "

" Not very much," said Vallon. " I stick around, look after the staff, smoke cigarettes and drink bourbon when I can get it. The boss is a friend of mine. He was the guy who gave me the job in Tientsin."

She nodded her head. " I know . . . one of those mysterious things where you get shot up and nobody knows what you're doing. And you go to hospital and lose me and never try to use your intelligence to find me. Some detective . . . ! Darling . . . I wonder why I love you.'

Vallon said: " Me too . . . It's just a break for me, that's all, Sweet."

She got up; walked to the mantelpiece, took a cigarette from a box and lighted it. She said: " Well, where do we go from here ? "

Vallon said: " I've one or two things to do. I have to do some work sometime. What about the Hungaria at eight o'clock ? I like that place—only because if you hadn't

23

been there for lunch to-day I should never have found you. Put on a pretty frock and I'll try and find a dinner jacket."

"Supposing you aren't there," she said. "You've stood me up before . . . remember? I don't like sitting at a table by myself or waiting for any man . . . not even Mr. Vallon."

He said: "I'll be there at a quarter to eight. I'll be waiting in the foyer for you. Do you think I wouldn't be?"

He smiled at her. She thought that the slow, rather crooked smile had lost nothing of its charm.

She said: "All right. So we have dinner together at eight o'clock. But I tell you, Johnny, if there's any more nonsense with you . . . you know what I mean . . . I'm through with you. This time I mean it." She smiled at him. "I've stood more from you than I ever thought I'd stand from a man. But I'm not taking any more punishment. See, Johnny?"

He nodded. "I see . . . If you knew what a punishment it has been for me to be without you all this time you'd know I wouldn't take a chance on it."

She said: "And after we've had dinner, what then?"

"They tell me it takes three days to get a special licence," said Vallon. "To-day is Wednesday. So that makes it Saturday. How does that go with you, Madeleine?"

She smiled. "Why should I marry you?"

Vallon got up. He walked slowly across the room towards her. He took her in his arms.

"Why not?" he said. "Maybe I'll think up some reasons."

.   .   .   .

It was four-thirty when Vallon reached his rooms in South Kensington. A telephone message was waiting on the hall table. He picked it up and read it. The time on the message was two o'clock. It said:

"I must see you in the office before four. It's very urgent. Chennault."

Vallon thought that was too bad. He looked at his watch. He thought he could make it by half-past five. He took a shower; changed his clothes. He caught a crawling taxi

24

outside; told the driver to take him to Long Acre. It was five and twenty to six when he went into the offices of Chennault Investigations. As he passed the filing room, on his way to Chennault's room at the end of the corridor, Marvin came out.

Marvin said gravely: " I've some bad news for you, Mr. Vallon."

Vallon thought: No . . . it's not possible to-day. There isn't any bad news. Whatever it is, it's not bad. Not as far as I'm concerned.

" So there's bad news," he said. " Who's done what ? "

Marvin said: " Mr. Chennault's dead. I went into his office half an hour ago. He'd fallen across the desk. We had his doctor round. His heart gave out."

" That's not so good, is it ? " said Vallon. " All right, Marvin."

Marvin went back into the filing room. Vallon stood in the centre of the corridor, his hands hanging down by his sides. He thought it wasn't very good about Chennault. A picture of Dolores crossed his mind. He wondered what she'd think about it. He lighted a cigarette ; opened the door of the filing room. Marvin was sitting at his desk smoking.

Vallon asked : " Has anybody told Mrs. Chennault ? "

Marvin nodded. " I phoned her. I don't think she was awfully surprised. He hasn't been so well lately, you know, Mr. Vallon. I asked her not to come round."

" What's being done about it ? " asked Vallon.

" They're sending the ambulance to take him away. It'll be here in about twenty minutes."

" O.K.," said Vallon. He went back into the corridor walked to the end.

He took a bunch of keys from his pocket ; opened the door with *Mr. Chennault* on it. He went inside ; closed the door behind him ; stood with his back to it, leaning against it, looking at the body.

Chennault had slumped forward from his big chair on to the desk. Vallon went over and looked at him. He thought that Chennault looked surprised. But then, thought Vallon, death might easily be a surprising thing—something you weren't prepared to meet—so that when you did meet it it surprised you. Why not ? He drew up a chair and sat

25

down, his eyes moving slowly over the desk and over Chennault.

On the desk was a copy of the midday edition of the *Evening News*, still folded. Chennault had been doodling across the caption on the front page—"*Holiday Train Collision.*" The pencil that had fallen from his fingers was lying across the paper. On the left-hand corner of the space over the heading he had been writing, "*Vallon . . . Vallon Vallon . . . Johnny . . . Johnny . . . Johnny . . .*" Then he'd drawn some stars. Then he'd started playing around with the letters in the newspaper heading. He'd crossed out the "C" in collision and turned it into a "K." And he'd turned the "I" into a "U." Then his mind had switched to something else. He'd done in ornamental lettering: "*B.B.C. . . . B.B.C. . . . B.B.C. . . . 1 o'clock. . . .*"

Vallon could see that he'd been smoking when he died because the cigarette stub had fallen from his lips and was stuck in a fold of the waistcoat over Chennault's plump belly. The cigarette had been alight; had burned a hole in the cloth. Vallon leaned forward; removed the cigarette stub.

He sat in his chair looking at it, thinking about Chennault. Thinking about Chennault sitting there smoking, waiting for him, Vallon, to arrive, because he wanted to see him about something.

Vallon sighed. Women could be the devil, he thought. They deflected you. You were going to do something or go somewhere and some woman turned up and so you didn't do what you were going to do or go where you intended to go. They were soft and attractive and alluring. They were perfumed, charming and seductive. They were hell!

If it hadn't been for Mrs. Gale he might have left Paignton earlier. If he'd left Paignton earlier he wouldn't have met Strype. If he hadn't met Strype he wouldn't have seen Madeleine; he'd have come to the office. He'd have known what Chennault wanted to talk to him about— whatever it was that was so urgent. Vallon sighed. Everything was urgent to Chennault. He had that sort of mind. Everything was so urgent that lots of people in the office never took him too seriously. Vallon remembered his urgency complex in the old days when Chennault was running a branch of the U.S. Office of Strategic Service on the edge of China and Vallon was working for him.

He took a piece of writing paper from the rack on the desk; rolled the cigarette stub in it. He thought maybe the stub would make a good memento of Chennault—a memento of something anyway.

He picked up the copy of the *Evening News*; folded it; put it in his pocket. He got up; walked out of the office; locked the door behind him. He opened the door of the adjoining office. Chennault's two secretaries were sitting there looking at each other. One of them—Mavis—had been crying.

Vallon said: "Well, it happens to all of us some day, and he had a damned good innings. He wasn't young, you know."

Mavis said: "It's still terrible, Mr. Vallon. He was such a nice man."

"Yes," said Vallon. "He was." He went out; went into the filing office. Marvin was at work on one of the files.

Vallon asked: "What did the doctor say? Is there going to be an inquest?"

Marvin shook his head. "He said he'd certify the cause of death. He had angina pectoris. He was liable to go off like that at any moment."

"O.K.," said Vallon. "When the ambulance comes send him home."

He went to the door.

Marvin asked: "What's going to happen, Mr. Vallon—to the office I mean?"

Vallon looked at him. "How should I know?"

He went out. He went down in the lift; took a cab. He stopped the cab in Regent Street; walked to Jermyn Street; went into the bar where he'd drunk earlier with Strype. He ordered a double rye whisky. He sat there, sipping the neat spirit, thinking about Chennault; thinking about the old days.

.   .   .   .

It was six-thirty when Vallon went back to the office; opened the door of the staff room; nodded to the three operatives on night duty. He opened the door of the filing room. Marvin was still at his desk.

Vallon said: "Come into the office. I want to talk to you."

27

He unlocked the door of Chennault's office; went in. He thought the room seemed strangely empty. He crossed over; sat in Chennault's chair behind the desk.

Marvin came in; closed the door behind him. He was a short, spare man with a lined face and grey hair. He'd been working for Chennault ever since the war. He was an unobtrusive, kindly man. Vallon liked him. Marvin's job was keeping the records and files of cases up to date; collating reports; generally acting as archivist.

Vallon said: "Sit down, Marvin. Have a cigarette."

Marvin pulled up a chair; sat on the other side of the desk. He took a cigarette from the case Vallon pushed across the table; lighted it.

"I'm sorry I didn't get back earlier to-day," said Vallon. "When I went to my rooms I found a message from Mr. Chennault. Apparently he wanted to see me urgently. He wanted me to be here before four o'clock. Do you know anything about it?"

"No, Mr. Vallon. But one of the secretaries might have taken a message on the telephone."

"All right," said Vallon. "We'll ask them to-morrow. Is there any current case that Mr. Chennault was especially interested in? Did he ask you for any documents—anything out of the files?"

Marvin nodded: "He asked for the file on the Gale case."

Vallon pricked up his ears. He thought: This might be very funny. He asked: "What about the Gale case?"

Marvin said: "It was an action brought for divorce by a Mrs. Gale——"

Vallon interrupted. "Where does she live?"

"At Paignton in Devonshire," said Marvin.

Vallon lighted his cigarette. Now he knew it was damned funny. He said: "Go on . . ."

"The usual sort of divorce action," said Marvin. "An undefended suit. The solicitors for the petitioner—Mrs. Gale—were Mullins, Sprague and Drew of Lincoln's Inn Fields."

Vallon asked: "We made the usual inquiries for them?"

"Yes, sir. We got the evidence of misconduct and sent it in some weeks ago. The case is in the undefended list."

"But it hasn't come on?" said Vallon.

28

"No, not yet. The petitioner's solicitors had it put back for a few weeks. We don't know why, but then they wouldn't tell us, would they?"

"No," said Vallon. "Why should they?" He began to think that life was very funny; that sometimes coincidences are extraordinary. He asked: "What was Mrs. Gale's first name? Do you know?"

"I don't remember off-hand, but it was an odd sort of name—sounded Spanish."

Vallon asked: "Would it be Querida?"

"That's it . . . Mrs. Querida Estralita Gale . . ."

Vallon grinned. "You're telling me . . . !" he said.

Marvin raised his eyebrows.

Vallon asked: "Who was the operative who was on the case? Who got the evidence of misconduct against the husband?"

"Hipper handled it," said Marvin.

Vallon thought for a moment; then: "The misconduct didn't by any chance take place in Somerset, did it?"

Marvin nodded. "That's right, Mr. Vallon."

Vallon said: "Tell me something, Marvin—and remember this is between you and me—what was Hipper doing down in Somerset during this last week-end?"

"On another case," said Marvin. "Fellows versus Fellows and Orme. He wouldn't normally have handled it but . . ."

Vallon said quickly: "But what?"

"Jameson was originally put on the Fellows case. He was going down to get the evidence last Friday—the usual hotel stuff—but Hipper asked me if he might do the job. He said he had a friend in Somerset whom he badly wanted to see. You know, Mr. Chennault left it to me, Mr. Vallon, and I thought if it were doing Hipper a good turn . . ."

"Quite," said Vallon. "How long's Hipper been with Chennault Investigations?"

"He's one of our oldest men. He's pretty good. He never slips up. A very clever operative."

Vallon smiled. "That's what I thought." He knocked the ash off his cigarette; regarded the glowing end. He went on: "Get me the file on the Gale case. Let me have it in here. First thing in the morning talk to Mr. Chennault's two secretaries. They take a note of every call. I want to

29

know the name and business if possible of everybody who got through to the office to-day."

" Very well, sir . . ."

" And the names of any callers," said Vallon.

Marvin said : " We can give you the names of callers who went through the usual office process, but very often Mr. Chennault saw people who came straight in through the private entrance." He pointed to the door in the far corner of the office that led through a small passage out into the main corridor.

Vallon nodded. " Let me know the people who came in the usual way."

Marvin said : " I'll have all that for you at ten o'clock, sir." He went out.

He returned in two minutes and put the thick, manilla folder on the desk in front of Vallon.

Vallon said : " O.K., Marvin. You'd better go now."

Marvin went to the door. He said : " You know, Mr. Vallon, I'm awfully sorry about Mr. Chennault. He was very good to me. I liked him."

Vallon said : " He was damned good to me. He saved my life one time. I liked him too. So long, Marvin."

The door closed behind Marvin. Vallon opened the folder ; began to read.

* * * * * * *

At seven o'clock he went out of the office. He walked to Regent Street ; got into his car. He drove out to Hendon. When he stopped by the grass verge opposite the apartment block where Chennault lived he didn't feel very good. He began to think about Dolores. He shrugged his shoulders ; walked across the courtyard.

She opened the door. Her eyes brightened a little when she saw him. Dolores Chennault was a tall, slim, black-haired woman with a good figure. She had a white, oval face, deepset, languorous eyes. Vallon thought she was a looker all right. He wondered why Chennault had to marry a woman twenty years younger than he was.

She said : " Come in, Johnny."

Vallon went into the flat after her. It was large, well-urnished. He walked across the drawing-room and stood in front of the fireplace, his hands in his trouser pockets, looking at the floor.

She asked : " Have a drink, Johnny ? "

" Thank you . . . why not ? " He went on : " This is a tough break for you, Dolores."

She shrugged her shoulders almost imperceptibly. She turned round ; stood with her back to the sideboard. " Is it, Johnny ? " she said. " Why doesn't somebody tell the truth ? I've been nursing an invalid for the last six months. In a way I'm glad he's gone."

" He was a damned good husband to you, Dolores. Don't you even feel sorry that you two-timed him so much ? "

She laughed softly. She said : " Do you ? "

Vallon looked out of the window. " Strangely enough, I do. Do you know what I think I am ? "

She opened the sideboard door ; began to get out some bottles. " Tell me what you think you are, Johnny."

He said : " I'm a son of a bitch. There are moments when I even get annoyed with myself."

She laughed. " You've never been annoyed with yourself in your life, Johnny. Why should you be ? You've got something."

" Like hell," he said.

She began to pour his drink. She brought over a glass half-filled with rye and a tumbler of water—a chaser—in the other hand. She stood in front of Vallon holding the glasses out towards him. He took them.

She said : " I suppose that makes me a daughter of a bitch ? "

He nodded. " That's what *I* think. Let's have a drink on that."

There was a long silence. Vallon asked : " How well off did he leave you ? You're all right, aren't you, Dolores."

She nodded. She mixed herself a whisky and soda ; carried it to the armchair beside the fireplace. She sat down. Vallon thought that she moved very gracefully ; that she had good legs and ankles ; that she knew it.

She said : " Everything's all right. Joe was always a pretty careful sort of man. They gave him a big gratuity when he left the O.S.S. He never touched it. He was always a thrifty man, and the business has been pretty good. You know, Chennault Investigations was really *something*.

So I'm going to be all right." She smiled. " What about you, Johnny ? "

" I've always been all right," said Vallon.

She asked him for a cigarette. He gave her one ; lighted it ; went back to the fireplace. He drank a little of the rye.

She said : " What's got into you, honey ? Is it Joe going like that ? We all expected it. The doctor told him six weeks ago that it was going to be any time now. I think he didn't mind very much. He'd had a good time. He liked life."

" Yes . . . and he was damned fond of you," said Vallon.

She smiled. " Well, that didn't hurt him." There was a pause ; then she repeated : " What's got into you, Johnny ? What's the matter ? What's all the drama about ? "

Vallon shrugged his shoulders. " I wouldn't know. It's been a good day for me. I ought to be happy. Naturally, I'm not pleased about Joe." He smiled suddenly. " A man always has a sort of affection for another man who's saved his life—even if he's lousy enough to make the man's wife."

She said : " What is this—a sermon ? "

" No . . . it's not a sermon. I was saying that it was a good day for me to-day except for Joe."

She snuggled back into the chair. " Tell me about it, Johnny." She screwed up her nose. She looked like a cat. Vallon thought she was just like a cat, with its claws barely hidden under the soft pads.

He said : " I've been around in my time and I've been a bonehead quite some of the time. I've done lots of things I haven't felt so good about afterwards."

" Don't be a damned fool. You've got something, Johnny. And women like you. Is it your fault if——"

He interrupted. " Oh, that doesn't matter. I was stuck like hell on a girl once, in China. I walked out on her because Joe was waiting up at Tientsin with a job that had to be done. You know, one of those things ! I got myself shot up and I was in hospital for a hell of a time. When I looked for her I couldn't find her. She'd gone."

Dolores yawned prettily. " So what ? They come and they go. Don't you like that ? " She threw a quick smile at him. " The man who wrote the song called *Love 'em and leave 'em, Joe* must have been thinking about you. Why didn't she stay ? "

Vallon said : " Maybe she'd heard some things about me.

32

Maybe after she'd heard some of the things they used to say about me in China she thought she wouldn't even wait."

She said sarcastically : " And she was stuck on you ? "

" No, she wasn't stuck on me. She was in love with me. I wonder if you'd know what that means ? There's a difference, Dolores."

" All right," she said. " What's it all about ? Then what happened ? "

Vallon grinned. " I found her to-day—by accident. I went to see her because I had to talk to her. I'm crazy about this woman. That's why I wasn't back in the office to see Joe. I didn't go home and get a message he sent me saying he wanted to see me urgently till it was too late."

She got up ; came towards him ; took the empty glass from the mantelpiece. She went to the sideboard.

Vallon said : " Make it a little one this time."

She looked over her shoulder. She smiled wickedly. " Easing up on rye ? " she asked.

Vallon said : " Yes—and women."

She laughed. " That's what you say, Johnny. Just because you've found your girl it's going to be like that. You're turning over a new leaf. Well, maybe you will and maybe you won't."

She came back with the rye. She put it on the mantelpiece. He sniffed. The perfume she wore was heavy and languorous. He thought it was like Dolores.

She stood there for a moment just in front of him, her head back. " You used to like me, Johnny," she said.

" I still do," said Vallon. " But that's all. Go and sit down."

She laughed. " Certainly, sir." She went back to her chair.

There was a silence. It went on for a long time. Then Vallon asked : " What are you going to do about the business, Dolores ? "

" I'm going to sell out. Joe told me three weeks ago he'd had a big offer from World Wide Investigations. They had taken over a big trade inquiry thing and Joe had a lot of tie-ups in that sort of work. I'll get a good price for the business. Then I'm going to get out."

Vallon asked : " Where to ? " He took the glass from the mantelpiece behind him.

She said : " South America for me. It's warm there and

people know how to live." She smiled slowly. She showed her small, regular teeth. She said softly : " Coming, Johnny ? "

He shook his head. " No, thanks . . . When do you think you'll be going, Dolores ? "

She said : " We'll do this deal for the business in a couple of weeks. I'll get you to handle it, Johnny. You have ten per cent of what we get. Do you like that ? "

He said nothing.

She went on : " In a month's time I'll be gone."

Vallon said : " No . . ."

She looked at him. She raised one eyebrow—a trick she had. It made her look very fascinating. She said : " You want me to stay here, honey ? "

" I don't want you to stay here," said Vallon. " But you're going to stay here."

Her voice was acid. " Meaning what ? "

Vallon said quietly : " Joe didn't die this afternoon. Somebody killed him. And I'm going to find out who, and while I'm finding out who, Chennault Investigations is going on."

She sat bolt upright in her chair. " What the hell are you talking about ? "

Vallon said : " Look, Joe had angina. The story is that he was sitting at his desk this afternoon. He was sitting at his desk and he had a heart attack and fell forward over his desk and died there. When I saw him he was lying with his head sideways on the desk. Understand ? "

She nodded.

" The story is," he went on, " that he was smoking a cigarette when he died. He'd very nearly smoked it ; just the stub was hanging in his mouth. You know how Joe always smoked a cigarette to the last eighth of an inch. It fell into a fold of his waistcoat over that fat belly of his. It burned a hole in the waistcoat, see ? "

" I see. So what does all that mean ? "

Vallon said : " I picked the stub off his waistcoat. It was the stub of a Virginian cigarette—an English Virginian cigarette. You know goddam well that Joe never smoked an English cigarette in his life. He only smoked one cigarette—the ' All American.' He used to have them sent over by the ten thousand. See ? "

34

She said : " What are you getting at, Johnny ? "

" Somebody stuck that stub on his waistcoat after he was dead. Somebody came into the office this afternoon and had a showdown with Joe about something. That's why he wanted me to be there. He'd got a copy of the midday *Evening News* in front of him. He'd been writing on it—doodling with his pencil—'*Vallon . . . Vallon . . . Vallon . . . . Johnny . . . Johnny . .*.' because he hoped to God I'd turn up every moment. Something tough was breaking there. Somebody asked him to do something or not to do something. Or tried to pull something on him. And he wasn't playing. He may have had angina but he was tough all right. So do you know what they did ? "

She said quietly : " No . . . tell me, Johnny."

" Whoever was there pulled a gun on him. They *frightened* him to death. It was a small calibre automatic with a silencer on it. They told him that unless he came across or did what they wanted him to do they were going to give it to him. He told them to go to hell. So whoever it was squeezed the trigger. They shot Joe with a blank cartridge. The wad hit him just above the stomach and burned a hole in his waistcoat. They knew it'd finish him and it did. He died of shock. Because he thought he was shot. So then whoever it was had to do something about the burn in the waistcoat, and whoever it was was smoking a Virginian cigarette. So they stuck the stub on his waistcoat. It looked perfect. Then they went out by the private door that leads into the corridor and got out of the office. See ? "

She got up. She began to walk about the room. " I see, Johnny . . . That's not so good, is it ? But——"

" But what ? " he asked.

" It's not going to bring him back," she said. " It's just going to mean a lot of trouble. His doctor went round there this afternoon and is certifying death from natural causes. Do we want to start a lot of trouble about anything? We can't bring him back, you know."

Vallon grinned. " Anything to get to South America, hey ? "

" Don't be a fool, Johnny." Her voice was harsh. " I suppose in a minute you're going to tell me I did it. I never left this apartment this afternoon and, as you know, I was fond of Joe—even if I have two-timed him once or twice."

35

She looked sideways at Vallon. "But I don't see the good of causing a lot of trouble about this, now Joe's dead. As I've said we can't bring him back."

"Fine," said Vallon. "And what about the guy who killed him? He just goes off, does he?"

She shrugged her shoulders. "I didn't think of that one. What do you want to do, Johnny?"

He finished his rye. He put the glass down on the mantelpiece behind him. He drank a little of the water.

He said: "I'll tell you what I'm going to do. I'm going on running Chennault Investigations because you're asking me to, see? I'm going to find out who killed Joe. I'm going to have him."

"If you say so, Johnny . . ."

"Thanks, Dolores. The business can go on in just the same way. I'll take the same salary. I'll just sit in Joe's chair and run it for him for a bit."

She said: "That's all right with me."

"Now I'll be on my way," said Vallon.

She came over to him. "You're a strange man, aren't you? You're the funniest mixture I ever knew. Sometimes I think you're very clever—very smart—with a hell of a brain and something that women go for. And other times I've thought you were just plain stupid."

Vallon grinned. "Maybe I'm a bit of each. Most of us are. I'll be seeing you, Dolores."

"So you're going just like that?" she said. "Not even a kiss."

He shrugged his shoulders. "What does it matter?"

She laughed. "You're telling me. All right, keep it for the new girl friend—that is if you don't lose her again. I'll be seeing you, Johnny. Any time you want to come in for a drink you'll always find me here . . ."

The telephone bell jangled noisily. She went into the bedroom. After a minute she came back. She said: "Marvin's on the telephone. He thought you might be here and rang up on the chance. He wants you."

"Thanks . . ." Vallon went into the bedroom. The same heavy, languorous perfume greeted his nostrils. He thought with a grin that Dolores always overdid everything. He picked up the receiver.

He said: "Hallo, Marvin. What's the trouble?"

Marvin said breathlessly : " Mr. Vallon, I went back to the office. I remembered I'd left one of the filing cabinets unlocked. Then I went into Mr. Chennault's room through the secretaries' door. I wanted to have a look at it. I was thinking about him."

" I can understand that," said Vallon. " So what ? "

Marvin went on : " Mr. Vallon, somebody's been over the office and searched it since you went out. One of the drawers on the right-hand side of his desk has been forced. That means that somebody's probably got a key to the private entrance. I thought I'd better let you know."

" Thanks, Marvin. I'll come right back. I'll be with you in half an hour."

He hung up the receiver ; went into the hall.

He said : " I'll be seeing you, Dolores . . ."

He closed the door softly behind him.

. . . .

Vallon stood in Chennault's office looking at the third door—the door that led out into the private passageway.

Marvin said : " I wonder where they got the key from. There's only one key to that door, Mr. Vallon. Mr. Chennault had it. When they took him away I took his key-ring. It had the key on it. I locked it in the safe. It's still there."

Vallon swung the door open. He examined the lock. " Look, Marvin, see the scratches. This lock's been opened with a spider. You know what that is ? "

Marvin shook his head. Vallon took out his key-ring. He showed Marvin a spider key—the delicate instrument that can be adjusted by a person who knows his business to practically any lock.

He went over to the desk and sat down in Chennault's chair. The lower right-hand drawer of the desk had been burst open.

Vallon said : " Whoever came in knew what he was looking for and knew where it was. If you're looking for something and you begin to search, you don't start with the bottom right-hand drawer ; you start with the top centre drawer."

" What do you think's going on, Mr. Vallon ? " asked Marvin.

37

" I don't know," said Vallon. " How should I know. But I'll find out." He leaned back in the chair. He gave Marvin a cigarette and lighted one for himself. He asked : " Did Mr. Chennault keep any whisky in the office ? "

Marvin nodded. " He always kept a bottle in his desk in case he had one of his attacks."

Vallon grinned. " I feel like a heart attack myself. And get a glass for yourself."

He leaned back in the chair and began to think. He allowed his mind to wander ; then he took the folded copy of the *Evening News* out of his pocket. He examined Chennault's doodling. . . . " *Vallon . . . Vallon . . . Vallon . . . Johnny . . . Johnny . . . Johnny . . .*" The " C " in the word " collision " turned into a " K "; the " I " into a " U." Then " *B.B.C. . . . B.B.C. . . . 1 o'clock. . . .*"

He got up ; opened the door into the secretaries' office ; looked up the number of the British Broadcasting Corporation. He plugged a line into the switchboard ; dialled the number.

He said : " What would be on the air from the B.B.C. at one o'clock ? I suppose it'd be the ' News,' wouldn't it ? "

He was told yes.

He went on : " I wonder if you'd do me a great favour. Would it be possible for me to send somebody to Broadcasting House to get a copy of the one o'clock news bulletin ? The matter's a little urgent. I wonder if you could help me."

They told him he could have it if he'd send for it.

He went back to Chennault's office. Marvin had poured out the whisky ; found a bottle of water.

Vallon took a drink. He said : " Listen, Marvin . . . you've been in this detective business for a hell of a time. Do you know a first-class man working for some other agency who hasn't any connection with this office ; who's not known in this office ? "

Marvin nodded. " You mean somebody you want to use on this ? " He pointed towards the private door. " A really good man ? "

Vallon said : " That's what I mean."

" There's a man called Trant," said Marvin. " He's pretty good. He works for the Oceanic Agency. I know his record. He was in the Special Branch when the war started ;

was transferred to the Field Security Police. He did very well afterwards. He had an under-cover job in Italy and in the East. When he came back he began work for the Oceanic. They think a lot of him. He handles all their really big stuff."

Vallon asked : " Do you know where you can get him ?"

" I know where he lives," Marvin answered. " He's a friend of mine."

" Listen, Marvin . . . go and get yourself a taxicab and go to the B.B.C. They'll give you a transcript of to-day's one o'clock news bulletin. When you've got it, go and pick up this man Trant ; find him and bring him here. Understand ? You can charge what you're doing to overtime."

Marvin said : " Right, Mr. Vallon. Thank you." He went out.

Vallon sat at the desk, drinking whisky, letting his mind wander on all sorts of things. Disconnected things which were beginning to seem, in some vague way, connected. He thought it was very interesting.

He took the Gale divorce case folder out of the open top right-hand drawer ; began to turn over the widely-spaced typewritten quarto pages. After a while he put the file away. Then he began to think about the day and the day before. He thought the pattern of life was sometimes odd. He'd gone to Paignton because he was bored and because someone had told him it was the place to go to. He grinned. Maybe it had been. Paignton had produced Mrs. Querida Gale— purely by chance—just one of those coincidences. And the inquiries in Mrs. Gale's divorce case had been handled by Chennault Investigations. And Hipper, the operative who'd handled the Gale investigation and secured the evidence, who should have been on his way back from Somerset, was in Paignton getting drunk at the fair. And Hipper had asked to go down to Somerset, taking over another man's work over a week-end too—a time when most men wanted to enjoy themselves—because he said he wanted to see a friend in Somerset. Perhaps it was another coincidence, Vallon thought. Or else . . . !

He looked at the copy of the *Evening News* again. The word " collision " had been changed by Chennault into " kollusion " and " kollusion " was collusion even if you did spell it with a " k."

A straw could change the pattern of life, thought Vallon,

for good or evil. It all depended on the straw. So he'd met Mrs. Gale, who used *Narcisse Noir* perfume—a nice perfume. Who'd bought him some Bacardis; who'd got a speck in her eye. He'd met Mrs. Gale and this and that had happened because, for some reason that he didn't know, that was the sort of thing that always happened to him. He'd often wondered why.

And because of Mrs. Gale he'd been late getting back to London, and because he was late he'd met Strype, and because he'd met Strype he'd met Madeleine! He looked at his strap-watch. It was a quarter to nine. He sighed.

He got out of the chair and went back to the secretaries' room. He looked up the number of the Hungaria restaurant and dialled. He asked for the *maître d'hôtel*.

He said : " Good evening. There's a lady in the restaurant—a Miss Madeleine Thorne. Would you say that Mr. Vallon would like to speak to her." He waited.

When the *maître d'hôtel* came back he said : " I'm very sorry, sir . . . there was a lady waiting here in the foyer. She left half an hour ago."

Vallon said : " Thanks a lot." He cursed softly under his breath. He thought that wasn't so good.

He turned back to the directory ; looked up the number of her apartment block. He dialled the number. When the operator answered Vallon said : " Put me through to Miss Thorne's apartment, will you ? "

There was a pause ; then the operator said : " Sorry, sir . . . Miss Thorne left five minutes ago. You wouldn't by any chance be Mr. Vallon, would you ? "

Vallon said : " Yes."

" Miss Thorne left a note for you, Mr. Vallon. The hall-porter has it. Can we send it to you somewhere ? "

" No," said Vallon. " I'll come and pick it up. Thanks a lot."

He hung up the receiver. He sat down at one of the secretaries' desks and looked at it. He had a peculiar empty sort of feeling in his stomach—the sort of feeling that you have when you haven't had a drink for three days and not much food. He didn't like it.

After a little while he went back to Chennault's room ; sat in the chair. He lighted a fresh cigarette and drank a little more whisky.

At nine-thirty Marvin arrived. He came into the office; another man behind him.

He said: " This is Trant, Mr. Vallon."

Vallon looked at Trant. And liked him. Trant was of middle height; thin with a clean-shaven face. He held himself well and stood well-balanced on his feet. He looked tough and very intelligent.

Vallon said: " Sit down, Trant, and give yourself a drink." He pushed the bottle and Marvin's glass towards Trant. " Marvin, did you get the transcript from the B.B.C. ? "

Marvin nodded. He brought out some sheets of thin paper, closely typewritten. Vallon took them; began to read. After a moment he grinned a little. There'd been a gale warning to all shipping at one o'clock. Vallon tore up the sheets of paper; threw them in the wastepaper basket. He thought Joe Chennault was pretty good.

He said to Marvin: " How would you like to go home ? You've had a tough day. You can tell the staff in the morning that the office will go on just the same as before. I've seen Mrs. Chennault to-night. She's carrying on the business. I shall be running it."

" Thank you, Mr. Vallon. I'm glad of that. I thought there was a chance of our being taken over by somebody."

Vallon said: " Who cares what you thought ? Before you go, Marvin, you might give me Hipper's telephone number. You'll have it on the list."

Marvin nodded. He went away. He brought back the number on a slip of paper. He put it on the desk before Vallon.

He said: " Good night, sir." When he got to the door he turned. " Good luck to you, Mr. Vallon."

Vallon smiled at him. " Thanks . . . You never know, Marvin. I might need it. Good night."

Vallon leaned back in his chair and looked at Trant, who'd finished his drink. He said: " Have a drink ? "

Trant shook his head. " No, thank you, Mr. Vallon. I don't drink when I'm doing business. And I take it I'm doing business."

" You're right. I always drink whether I'm doing business or not." Vallon poured out another drink. He went on: " I'd like you to do a job of work for me, Trant

41

—one of those things. I don't know what I'm doing or where I'm going. Maybe we'll find out. How would you like that ? You can work in your own time. You won't lose anything by it, I promise you."

" That suits me, Mr. Vallon," said Trant. " Excuse me, but aren't you the John Vallon who was working in the liaison tie-up between the United States O.S.S. and our main Intelligence Section on the China border ? "

Vallon said : " Yes."

" I'm glad to meet you," said Trant. " I heard about you."

Vallon grinned. " I hope it was good."

" What's the job, sir ? " asked Trant.

" I don't know," said Vallon. " I have a telephone number here. It's the number of an operative who works in this office. His name's Hipper. I think he's been up to something but I don't know what."

Trant nodded. " It can happen, Mr. Vallon—especially in this sort of business."

" He doesn't know you," Vallon went on. " So what you do is this : You ring him from this office now. If he's at home speak to him. If not, ring later. You tell him that you're a friend of Mrs. Querida Gale of Ladycourt, Marldon, near Paignton. He'll probably be interested and a little careful in what he says. I don't know why, but I think so. You got that ? "

" I've got it, Mr. Vallon."

Vallon went on : " You say that Mrs. Gale has asked you to see him. You make an appointment to meet him somewhere to-night—some quiet pub or a club ; anywhere you like ; somewhere where you can talk. When he arrives you're a little bit mysterious. You say you've been talking to Mrs. Gale and she asked you to see him. Are you with me so far ? "

Trant nodded his head.

" You give him a couple of drinks—he likes liquor. Then you ask him if he's anything to say—any message he'd like to give to Mrs. Gale. He may say something. He may not. He may be scared and shut up and say he doesn't know what you're talking about. Or he might fall for it. He might fall for it if he's had some conversation with Mrs. Gale ; if he's asked her for something."

42

Trant asked : " A little blackmail, you think ? "

" Why not ? " said Vallon. " You've got the general idea ? I'm feeling my way in the dark. Play him like a fish. Get what you can. I'll give you the office number. Ring me through to-morrow. Make a date to meet me, but not here." He took a bill-fold out of his pocket. " There are two fivers on account of expenses. Look after it, Trant, and I'll look after you."

Trant said : " All right, Mr. Vallon. I think I have the general idea. Is that all ? "

Vallon nodded.

Trant said : " Right. Now, if I may, I'll have that other drink."

Vallon indicated the bottle.

" That was a nice job you did in Tientsin, Mr. Vallon," said Trant. " I was around there myself for a little while. They nearly got you that time, didn't they ? It's not often people get over a stomach wound. Does it affect you at all ? "

Vallon grinned. " Not much. It just makes me like whisky. I find whisky keeps it quiet."

Trant put his glass down. " If you don't mind I won't phone to Hipper from here. I think I'd better do it from a call-box."

Vallon nodded. " Maybe you're right. Good night."

Ten minutes afterwards he closed the door of Chennault's office ; went down in the lift, out into the street. He drove westward. A few minutes later he was at Chestnut Court.

He said to the hall-porter : " You have a note for me. I'm Mr. Vallon."

The hall-porter gave him the envelope.

" Thank you," said Vallon. " You wouldn't know when Miss Thorne is coming back ? "

" I don't think she is, sir. She left an address for her baggage to be forwarded."

Vallon said : " If I had that address it would be worth a fiver to me."

" Sorry, sir . . . Miss Thorne said you weren't to have it. She was very definite about that."

Vallon nodded. " The trouble with life is," he said, " that very often people are definite. Good night."

He went out of the building ; sat in the car behind the steering wheel. He opened the envelope.

" Johnny,

" Aren't you a heel ? Do you ever do anything you say ? Do you ever keep your word ? I waited once only in my life for a man—that was you. I waited a long time and you didn't arrive. So I'm not going to wait again.

" I waited sixteen weeks in China worrying about you, wondering what had happened to you, just because you couldn't trust me enough to tell me what you were doing. So why should I trust you ? More especially as during those sixteen weeks I heard a great deal about you, Johnny. You were in love with me or so you said and I believed you. But there were an awful lot of women in China who seemed to think they had some sort of prior claim. They all seemed to know you too well, Johnny.

" To-night waiting for you at the Hungaria restaurant I concluded that you hadn't altered a lot. I wondered who the woman was that had made you late. Do you wonder that I don't trust you, Johnny ? And do you wonder why I ask myself why I should love a man I don't trust ?

" So I'm going to forget you. So long, Johnny. I wish you all the luck in the world.   " Madeleine."*

Vallon put the ignition key in its slot ; started the engine. He tore the note into little pieces ; threw them over the side of the car. The odd feeling was back in his stomach again. He didn't like it a bit. He said : " For crissake . . . ! "

He parked the car in St. James's Square ; walked slowly up Lower Regent Street into the bar in Jermyn Street.

The bar-tender said : " Good evening, sir. Glad to see you again. What can I give you ? "

" A little rye," said Vallon. " Just give me the bottle and some water for a chaser."

The bar-tender poured out a double rye whisky ; put the glass, the bottle, a small jug of water and a fresh glass on the bar in front of Vallon.

He said : " It's been a nice sort of day, sir."

Vallon looked at him. His eyes were blank. The light had gone out of them. He had the odd feeling in his stomach again. He thought vaguely that one day he'd get around to having that little piece of bullet—the piece they'd left in—removed. Or maybe it wasn't the bullet. He thought it might be something else.

44

He said : " Has it ?   I suppose it has.   Why shouldn't it be ? "

He picked up the glass ; began to drink the rye. He sat there for a long time, looking at the shelves on the other side of the bar with their neatly arranged bottles.

The bar-tender said : " Excuse me, sir, but I've never seen a man hold his liquor like you.   You like rye, don't you ? "

Vallon looked at him. When the bar-tender saw his eyes he looked away.

" No," said Vallon, " I don't like rye.   I don't like it a bit."   He poured some more whisky into his glass.

CHAPTER TWO

CŒUR DE CARNATION

1

VALLON sát in Chennault's chair, drawing perfume flasks on the blotter. He thought it would be a nice thing if he could remember the name of the perfume that Madeleine had been wearing the day before. He thought it would be nice if he could buy a flask. Then he thought that maybe he was getting sentimental, and if you were stuck on a woman you didn't get sentimental about her. Not if you'd really got her. You didn't have to be sentimental about something you'd got.   And there weren't any two ways about the situation between any man and any woman. You'd either got her or you hadn't. You hadn't to fight to get a woman or to keep her when you'd got her. She was either yours or she wasn't. And that was that.

He shrugged his shoulders. Life was like the odd and peculiar feeling that he got in his stomach—produced by the remnant of the bullet that maybe was still there. You had it with you all the time. Sometimes it was quiet ; sometimes something stirred it into action. But it was there. You knew it was there and you could not be rid of the thought of it.   That was how it was going to be with Madeleine. He wasn't going to be able to forget her because that was the way it was. And he wasn't going to be able to forget her by playing half a dozen other women. That was out—the technique was beginning to bore him and anyway no woman could ever matter after Madeleine.

He lighted a cigarette. He opened the lower right-hand drawer in Chennault's desk—the drawer that had been forced ; took out the whisky bottle. It was a third full. He put the neck of the bottle in his mouth and took a long swig. He felt a little better. Maybe, he thought, by the aid of this and that, he would succeed one day in forgetting Madeleine. In any event, in the meantime there wasn't anything to be done about it except perhaps to try and remember the name of the perfume she wore so that he could buy a bottle.

There was a knock at the door. Marvin came in. He said : " I've checked on everybody who came into the office yesterday, Mr. Vallon—that is through the outer office in the normal way. It was all quite in order. The callers were people who had legitimate business with us ; whom we know ; people from other agencies ; from a couple of firms of lawyers."

Vallon nodded. " Whoever it is we're looking for came in through the private door." He indicated the door on the other side of the office. " He came in that way because he didn't want anybody to know who he was. He knew of the existence of that door and he knew that if he picked his time he could walk down the passage and come in unobserved. So it was somebody who knew this office or at least knew the geography of the office."

The telephone on the desk rang. Marvin picked up the receiver. He talked ; then put his hand over the mouthpiece.

He said : " It's Trant calling, Mr. Vallon. He says he'd like to speak to you." He handed the telephone to Vallon.

Trant said : " I did that little business last night, Mr. Vallon. I think it's quite interesting. Incidentally, I've got two weeks off from the firm so I'm more or less at your disposal. Would you like to talk to me ? "

" Yes," said Vallon. " There's a bar in Jermyn Street just round the corner out of Regent Street. I'll meet you there in ten minutes' time."

Trant said : " Very well." He hung up.

Vallon said : " I'll be back in an hour, Marvin. If I'm

not just carry on here. You know what's happening, and all about the current cases, don't you ? "

Marvin nodded.

Vallon went on : "You can consider yourself assistant manager to the agency. Maybe I'll be away for a bit now and then. You get a fiver a week more."

"Thank you very much," said Marvin. "I hope Mrs. Chennault will approve of that, sir."

Vallon said : "You don't have to hope. She will."

Ten minutes afterwards he parked his car in Regent Street ; walked round to the Jermyn Street bar. Trant was leaning against the counter drinking ginger ale.

The bar-tender looked at Vallon. "Good morning, sir. Rye or Bacardi ? "

Vallon said : "Rye." He turned to Trant. "Well . . . ? " he queried.

"I think your guess was right," said Trant. "Something's going on. I haven't anything very definite, but I've a series of impressions plus a little information. But perhaps you wouldn't be interested in impressions."

"From you—yes," said Vallon. "Tell me what happened."

Trant said : "When I left you last night I went to a call-box and phoned Hipper. I was lucky. He was in. I told him very politely and quietly that I was a friend of Mrs. Querida Gale ; that she knew I was coming to London and she had suggested that I telephoned him because she thought he might have something to say to me."

Vallon asked : "Was he surprised ? "

Trant shook his head. "Not a bit. He was perfectly easy about it—as if it were a most normal thing. He asked when and where would I like to see him. I suggested The Strangers' Club—a nice little club in St. James's Place. I arranged to meet him there in half an hour. When he turned up I had a look at him. You know him better than I do, sir . . . but he looks to me like a rather indefinite type. Not a man of very strong mental characteristics, if you know what I mean. A little bit weak ; fond of the bottle ; probably quite good at his job as an operative in a detective agency provided the work he has to handle isn't too important."

Vallon said : "You're right up to now. Go on."

"Therefore," Trant continued, "in this thing in con-

47

nection with Mrs. Gale—if it's big or important or serious —I should have expected him to be a little diffident or nervous. He wasn't. Whatever part he's playing in this affair he's damned certain of himself."

Vallon said : " That means he thinks he has nothing to be afraid of and that he can't slip up whatever he does."

" That was the impression he gave me," said Trant. " I asked him what he'd like to drink and he said whisky. I started him off with a treble one. He didn't even notice its strength. Apparently he's drunk a lot of treble whiskies. Then he asked me what I wanted to see him about. I looked a little surprised. I said surely he knew ; surely the fact that I had told him that Mrs. Gale had asked me to see him when I came to London told him all about that. He said yes. He asked what did Mrs. Gale propose to do ? "

Vallon grinned. " That was a tough one for you, Trant. What did you say to that ? "

" I stalled. I said that was rather an odd sort of question to ask me ; that quite obviously what Mrs. Gale did or didn't do depended to a very great extent on what other people did or didn't do. He said that was fair enough ; then he said this—and, by the way," said Trant, " I told him my name was Harper, that I lived at Babbacombe ; that I'd known Mrs. Gale for years. He said that as things were he wasn't dissatisfied with the situation, but he was perfectly easy in his mind about everything ; that so far as he was concerned Mrs. Gale could do what she liked ; that whichever way she wanted to play it suited him. She could do what he'd suggested ; that would be O.K. with him. Or she could do whatever she liked ; that would be just as good as far as he was concerned.

" I didn't know what to say to that one," Trant continued. " So I pretended to consider the matter. I asked him if he thought he was being very fair over this business. Then he said : ' Look here, Harper . . . I've tried to behave like a gentleman over this. Sometimes a man has got to try to do his duty.' When he said this he was grinning at me as if it were something funny. He went on that up to the moment he'd tried on the whole to play the game by everybody ; that he didn't feel that the next step or any approach to it should come from him. Then he said something that mattered. He said : ' When you rang me up to-night and

48

said you'd come from Mrs. Gale I thought she'd decided. I thought you'd come up here to tell me just how she was going to play this. Instead of which you ask me what I'm going to do, as if that depended on me.' "

Trant paused for a moment and drank some ginger ale. He went on : " I thought I'd take another chance. I said : ' Well, Hipper . . . it does in effect depend on you, doesn't it ? If you take the long view.' "

Vallon asked : " What did he say to that one ? "

" He thought that one out for quite a while," said Trant. " Then he nodded his head ; then he said : ' I suppose you're right. I suppose really '—and he smiled when he said this as if he were awfully pleased with himself— ' I dominate the situation. If I were an outsider I'd say I'd got the whip-hand. As it is I only say I dominate the situation. I can do this : I can do that, or I can do nothing at all. And really I don't mind what I do.' Then," Trant continued, " he grinned at me like the cat that swallowed the canary. I thought it was time to ask him to have another drink. He said no . . ."

" So Hipper turned down a drink—when somebody else was paying for it ? " said Vallon.

Trant nodded. " He was afraid to have another drink. He thought he might talk too much. This man Hipper thinks he's on top of the job. Whatever he does, Mr. Vallon, he thinks he's running some situation and he thinks he's safe in doing what he's doing."

Vallon said : " That means he's not blackmailing anybody."

Trant shrugged his shoulders. " There's blackmail and blackmail, isn't there ? You don't have to go to somebody and demand money with menace. You can always write them a letter and say you'd like to talk to them. You can go and advise them or warn them against something or somebody as if you were an ordinary good citizen doing somebody a good turn. And then you go away without asking for anything at all. You're sitting pretty because you've told the person concerned that you know ; that you have strong information about something. If the person concerned wants you to forget it they can always make it worth your while. They can give you something you've never even asked for. That's not blackmail, is it, sir ? "

Vallon nodded. He drank a little of the rye whisky. "I think you've done a good job, Trant. Maybe we've something to work on even if we don't know what it is. Do you know Devonshire ? "

Trant said : " I think it's a very nice place."

" All right," said Vallon. " Hipper thinks you're a Mr. Harper who lives in Babbacombe. Pack a bag and go down to Devonshire this afternoon. Get yourself a room in some apartment house in Babbacombe ; register yourself under the name of Harper. Can you get yourself a fake identity card and ration book ? "

Trant smiled. " That's easy . . ."

" When you get there," said Vallon, " drive over to Paignton and leave a note for me at the Continental Hotel. Tell me what your address is and your telephone number. I'll get in touch with you when I want you."

" All right, Mr. Vallon. That suits me. The air there is very good. I like it."

Vallon said : " Maybe you won't like it so much before we're through." He took out his notecase. He gave Trant eight five-pound notes. " With what you had last night that's fifty pounds on account of expenses. I'll be seeing you."

He finished his drink ; went out of the bar.

When he got back to the office Marvin came in. He said : " Mrs. Chennault's been on the line, sir. She wants to speak to you. She asked if you'd call her back."

Vallon nodded. " Get her on this private line. I don't want the call to go through the office."

Marvin dialled the number ; waited ; handed the telephone to Vallon ; went out of the room.

She asked : " Hallo, Johnny . . . how are you feeling to-day ? "

" Pretty good," said Vallon. " How are you ? "

" Not too bad. Only I'm a little unhappy about Joe. I've called through this morning to the people who were going to buy the business. Naturally, they are a little surprised. I told them I wasn't turning down the offer ; I was just postponing the sale for a bit in order to clear up some private business."

Vallon said : " Yes ? "

There was a pause. " How long is this thing going to take ? " she asked. " How long is it going to be before you find out something, Johnny ? "

" How do I know ? " said Vallon.

She went on : " Well, isn't there some sort of formality about this ? The doctor's given a death certificate. Everything from that angle is in order. They're going to bury Joe on Saturday. If you find that you're right in your supposition they'll probably want to examine the body or something. It seems to me you're making a lot of trouble, Johnny. Whatever you do you can't bring him back."

" That's what you said before. I don't want to bring him back. Maybe he's better off where he is. All I want to do is to get my hands on the man who killed him. That's reasonable, isn't it ? "

She said : " I suppose so. And it's reasonable for me to ask how long you're going to take. I want to go to South America."

" I want to go to a lot of places," said Vallon. " If you want to go to South America, go. If you don't, just be patient."

" Supposing I don't want to be patient ? " she asked.

" What do I care ? " said Vallon.

Her voice was acid. " You're riding me, aren't you, Johnny ? Why do you think you can behave like this to me ? "

Vallon said : " I don't think anything. What's the matter with you—getting hysterical over South America or what ? "

" Don't be damned silly. Maybe I feel a little lonely now that Joe's gone. I felt that way last night. That's understandable, isn't it ? "

He said nothing.

She went on : " What about coming and having a drink with me to-night, Johnny ? "

He said : " No soap . . . I'm going to be busy."

There was a note of sarcasm in her voice. " The new girl friend, hey . . . ? "

" No," said Vallon. " Not the new girl friend."

He heard her laugh.

She said : " You don't mean to say she's taken a powder on you, Johnny ? You don't mean to say she's given you the air ? "

He grinned into the telephone. " Believe it or not, Dolores, that's just what she has done. Now hang up and have a laugh. And make it a good one because that's how it is."

She asked : " You mean that's how it is between you and me ? "

" That's right," said Vallon.

" All right, Sweet . . . go on living on your memory. And be damned to you." He heard her put the receiver down with a bang.

He stubbed out his cigarette ; picked up the office telephone ; called through to Marvin.

He said : " I'm going away into the country. You can get in touch with me at the Continental at Paignton. Don't give my address to anybody. You understand ? "

Marvin said : " Yes . . ."

" And keep Hipper busy. Keep him around here on something that's going to keep him occupied."

" I understand that too," said Marvin.

Vallon hung up the receiver ; picked up his hat ; went out of the office. He drove to his rooms ; packed two suit-cases. He put them in the back of the car.

He took the road to Devonshire.

.   .   .   .

It was eight o'clock when Vallon parked his car in the courtyard at the side of the Continental Hotel at Paignton. He went up to his room ; ordered a whisky and soda ; unpacked. The waiter who brought the drink gave Vallon the note from Trant with his address and telephone number in Babbacombe.

Vallon called the number. When Trant came on the line he said : " Get around and visit any inns or saloons near Ladycourt in Marldon. See what local gossip you can pick up on the Gale divorce case, or Mrs. Gale. If you get anything call me here."

Trant said O.K.

Vallon lay on the bed, smoking, drinking the whisky and soda. He thought that the business of finding Chennault's murderer was not going to be easy. It was as difficult as looking for a needle in a haystack ; it was worse, because this particular haystack seemed to be a very involved haystack.

He began to think about the Gale divorce folder which he had read in Chennault's office. There was nothing extraordinary about it. Mrs. Querida Gale of ·Ladycourt, Marldon, South Devon, had filed a petition for the dissolution of her marriage on the grounds of her husband's misconduct. The name of the co-respondent had been cited—a Miss Evangeline Roberta Trickett. Vallon thought that he liked the name of Miss Evangeline Roberta Trickett. He thought it was a nice name. He wondered what she'd be like. He thought that one of these days if he had time he'd get around to talking to Evangeline. She might be a help. She might be, but he guessed not.

In other words the Gale divorce petition presented no difference from any other undefended suit, because the husband had not entered an appearance and the case had gone into the undefended list. For some reason which nobody seemed to know, it had been put back in the list on the application of the petitioner's lawyers.

The part played by the Chennault organisation had been as simple. They had been informed of the fact that the petitioner believed that her husband Pierce Gale had been associated with Evangeline Trickett. Hipper had discovered the name of the hotel in the country where they had been staying. He'd gone there ; he'd secured the usual divorce evidence, which had been recorded and sent to the petitioner's lawyers.

This should have been the end of the business as far as Chennault Investigations were concerned, except for the appearance of Hipper in court to swear to the evidence he had supplied.

It was difficult therefore to understand why Hipper should attempt to blackmail Mrs. Gale—except from one angle. And that angle would be very easy to understand. Supposing, for the sake of argument, that during the course of the petition Mrs. Gale had herself committed misconduct with somebody else—Vallon smiled to himself at the idea—then it only required a letter to the King's Proctor and she would probably be non-suited on the action. If Hipper knew that Querida Gale had committed misconduct he would certainly be in a position in which he could extract some money from her for his silence.

Vallon took another sip of whisky and thought it all

seemed easy enough. But he couldn't see Hipper playing it like that. Querida Gale was a woman of character. She might not like being blackmailed. If she went to the police ; if she told them that Hipper was endeavouring to blackmail her, Hipper would be for the high jump and the King's Proctor on his part would certainly take no notice of information supplied by a blackmailer.

Vallon thought there was something more to it than that. Trant had told him that everything about Hipper's attitude suggested that he wasn't afraid of anything. Which would mean that Hipper had no reason to be afraid of anything that Querida Gale might do. He knew he was safe in any event. So this supposition could be wiped out. Whatever he'd got on Mrs. Gale was something which would allow him to threaten and yet be safe.

Vallon wondered what the answer to that one would be. He shrugged his shoulders. He swung his feet off the bed ; sat, his hand under his chin, thinking that once again he'd have to play this thing off the cuff. He grinned. Most of his life, in China and elsewhere, he'd been playing situations off the cuff because that was the only thing to do. You threw a spanner into the works and you stood by and saw what happened. You thought that if you threw the spanner hard enough somebody would do something or say something ; give themselves away. Then you'd have something definite to work on. He came to the conclusion that he'd throw a spanner into the works, and there was only one way to do that.

He got up ; went into the bathroom ; took a shower ; changed his clothes. He stood in the middle of the bedroom, holding the half-empty whisky glass in his hand. The pain in his stomach had started again.

He began to think about Madeleine. He thought it wasn't any good thinking about her because it didn't get you anywhere. He thought that so far as she was concerned he'd had it. Yet, for some obscure reason, a vague idea persisted in the back of his mind that in some peculiar way his and her life and the discovery of the Chennault murderer were somehow connected.

Vallon, who was a logical and practical individual, wondered with a sarcastic smile why he should indulge in these fantastic imaginings. He thought the reason might be that because of his seeking Madeleine and finding her he had not been in the office with Chennault. Had he gone straight back to the office and seen Chennault, Joe would be alive to-day . . .

He finished the drink; went downstairs. He started up the car; drove towards Marldon. The evening light was beginning to fade. Vallon thought casually that when all was said and done Devonshire was a lovely county—not that he cared.

A quarter of an hour afterwards he found the house. It stood back off the road in two or three acres of ground. He liked the look of the place—a long, rambling farmhouse which had been converted to the Tudor style of architecture by somebody who knew his business. About the place was an atmosphere of peace and stillness which somehow, Vallon thought, marched oddly with its tenant. He shrugged his shoulders. You never knew with women. Querida Gale had a certain stillness and repose about her, and someone had said that still waters run deep. Vallon knew enough about women to know that they have many facets to their character. He said to himself: You're telling me!

He drove through the iron gates; pulled up in front of the house. He pulled the iron bell handle; waited before the oak door, finishing his cigarette, wondering.

The door was opened by a neat maid.

He said: "My name's Vallon. I'd like to see Mrs. Gale if she's in."

She asked him to come in. He put his hat on an oak settle in the hall; sat down in a high-backed antique chair. The place was big—furnished with many good pieces by someone whose taste was both trained and artistic.

After a moment the maid came back. She said: "Mrs. Gale would like to see you. Will you come in?"

He followed her along the passageway, past the curving staircase. At the end of the passage was a door. The maid opened it. Vallon went in.

Mrs. Gale was standing in front of the fireplace. She wore a superbly cut black velvet dinner gown with a square-cut neck; a dog collar of pearls. There were two diamond clips at her neck. Vallon looked at her with approval from the top of her well-coiffured head to her four-inch-heeled sequin-embroidered shoes.

55

She said: "If you've driven down you'd like a drink, wouldn't you?"

"Thanks," said Vallon. "You're not surprised to see me?"

She smiled at him—a slow smile which showed her small, regular teeth. "Nothing ever surprises me. You'll find what you want in the cabinet."

Vallon helped himself to a whisky and soda. He asked: "Would you like one?"

She shook her head. "I'd like to smoke one of your cigarettes."

He gave her the cigarette; lighted it. He was holding the drink in his left hand. A suggestion of her perfume—*Narcisse Noir*—came to his nostrils. He thought it wasn't a bad scent.

She said: "So you've come all this way, Johnny, and you're not going to kiss me."

"How can I when you're smoking?" said Vallon.

She smiled. "I can always stop smoking." She took the cigarette from her mouth. He kissed her on the lips. She was still smiling. "A rather tardy lover I have," she said.

Vallon shrugged his shoulders. He sat in the big leather armchair on one side of the fireplace. He put the glass to his mouth and looked at her over the rim.

He said: "Even I can be surprised sometimes. First of all I thought you'd be annoyed; that you might not like my coming."

"You mean you thought you wouldn't get such a friendly reception? Why?"

He shrugged his shoulders again. "I've always been taught to believe that you shouldn't kiss and tell or kiss and come back too quickly. Sometimes women prefer to forget . . . some incidents in their lives."

She moved a little. She put one white arm on the mantelpiece. Her smile deepened. "So you consider yourself an incident, Johnny? In other words you think that I make a practice of ' incidents '?" She shook her head. "I'm not like that. Perhaps I was a little foolish about you but" —she shrugged her shoulders almost imperceptibly—" I liked being foolish even if it was dangerous."

Vallon drank some more whisky. He asked "Why dangerous?"

She spread her hands. " For two reasons. What do I know about you ? Nothing—except that you're a very attractive man ; that I felt something about you that I haven't felt before about anybody ; that I wanted to do something about it. That's the first reason."

Vallon asked : " And the second ? "

" I'm divorcing my husband. Have you heard of a gentleman called the King's Proctor ? Supposing by some strange chance the ' incident ' as you call it, at the hotel, became known to that gentleman ? You know that it would kill my divorce ? "

Vallon said nothing. He thought that was very interesting. It meant that he'd been right about Hipper ; that Hipper hadn't got *that* on her. It was something else.

He said : " You were taking a bit of a chance, weren't you ? Or were you ? "

She sat down in the big chair opposite him ; crossed her legs. He noticed the smallness of her foot, the slimness of her ankles. He thought there was something very attractive about Mrs. Gale.

She said : " Don't you ever take a chance, Johnny ? "

He grinned at her. " I've been taking them all my life. They're the only things that make life amusing. Taking a chance is like spinning a penny for a thousand pounds. Sometimes you *know* it's going to come down heads when you call heads—or you think you know. Sometimes you're uncertain about what's coming down. You spin a coin and you take a chance on the result. In spinning a coin it's an even chance for you or against you. In other things the odds are more varied."

She nodded. " Well, I wanted to take a chance so I took it."

" Meaning what ? " Vallon asked. " Are you telling me that you think you're in love with me ? "

She shook her head. " I don't think I've ever been in love with anybody. But there are other things besides being in love. I thought you were very attractive. I don't often think that about men. You've got something."

Vallon smiled at her. " Thanks a lot. There wouldn't possibly be any strings to this, would there ? There wasn't any ulterior motive that might have been responsible for the ' incident ' ? "

"Not at the time, Johnny," she said. "The idea only came afterwards. At the time it was one of those things that just happen."

He was still smiling. "And afterwards you thought of something else?"

She nodded.

He asked: "What?"

She said: "Drink your whisky. Perhaps I don't want to talk about it now." She settled herself back comfortably in her chair. "What made you come down here, Jonny? Are you on a holiday as you were last time, or"—she smiled the same slow smile—"did you want to see me?"

"I wanted to see you," Vallon said.

"So it's like that." She looked at him through half-closed lids. "So you wanted to come back. Does that mean that you're a little interested in me?"

"I'm very much interested in you," said Vallon. "I think you're a most intriguing woman. But there was another idea in this case too."

"What, Johnny?"

He thought a slight note of hardness had crept into her voice.

He said: "I wanted to talk to you about a man called Hipper. Do you know a man called Hipper?"

She did not answer. She sat quite relaxed, her fingers clasping the leather ends of the chair-arms. He noticed those of the right hand tighten just a little.

She asked: "Why, Johnny?"

Vallon said: "When you and I were walking about at the fair I saw Hipper there. He was supposed to be in Somerset. He came over to Paignton to see you. You know, he's not a good type." He smiled at her. She thought that his small, twisted smile was most fascinating. He went on: "You know where you are with a bad man if he's really bad. And you know where you are with a good man. But Hipper comes into neither category. He's cheap, mean and weak. But he came over to Paignton to see you. And he didn't want to ask you what you thought of the weather or how your health was. A man like Hipper doesn't come and see a woman like you unless he has an idea in his head. Tell me about Hipper."

She got up; knocked the ash from her cigarette into an

ash-tray on the mantelpiece. She said : " Why should I talk to you about this man ? "

" I'm not answering questions. I'm asking them," said Vallon. " Be a good girl, and tell me about Hipper."

She sighed. She ground out the half-smoked cigarette in the ash-tray. She went back to the chair. She looked at him.

She said : " I wonder if I was wrong about you."

" Very likely," said Vallon. " Lots of people have been."

She repeated : " I wonder if I was wrong about you. I didn't know very much about you when I met you, but I thought you were quite a man. I'd hate to think differently."

Vallon said : " You think what you like. I don't mind."

" That isn't true, Johnny. You do mind what I think."

" You're being hopeful," said Vallon, " and optimistic. I don't mind what you think. Why don't you tell me about Hipper. I might even be of use to you."

She asked : " What do you think this man's doing ? What do you think *I*'m doing ? You tell me that he came to Paignton to see me ; he didn't come to see me to ask about the state of my health ; he wanted something. Are you suggesting that this man is blackmailing me ? "

" Why not ? " said Vallon. " It's difficult to believe that Hipper would have enough guts to blackmail anybody, but he might if he knew he was absolutely safe in what he was doing ; if he knew that nobody could get him. He might blackmail even you knowing that a woman—especially a beautiful woman like you—can change her mind ten times a day. If he thought he was actually safe he might try it."

She asked : " Do you think he has ? Supposing I told you that this man was trying to help me ? "

Vallon grinned at her. " They often talk like that. They call it helping you. They tell you what they know. They say they want to help you. So instead of paying because you're being blackmailed, you pay for assistance. Is that what he said ? "

" Damn you, Johnny, you have a flair for putting things in a very unattractive way."

Vallon got up. He lighted a cigarette ; began to walk about the room. " You mean I'm right in what I'm suggesting about Hipper. He's told you something. He wants to help you. He knows he's safe in helping you. What have you paid him?"

She said: "Would you like to give me a little whisky and a cigarette?"

He brought her the drink; gave her a cigarette and lighted it. She sat, the glass in one hand, the cigarette between the slim fingers of the other, looking at him. There was a long silence.

Then she said: "I wonder why I don't have you thrown out. I ought to. You're an insolent man. You come here and endeavour to discuss my private affairs with me; to get me to tell you all sorts of things. You do this after I've been"—she shrugged her shoulders—"very kind to you, if I can put it like that. You tell me nothing of yourself; how you profess to know all these things about me. I'm supposed to sit here and answer your questions. What do you take me for, Johnny?"

Vallon said: "I'm not quite certain, but I'll find out." He moved to the fireplace; stood with his back to it, looking down at her. He went on: "It's going to make it a lot easier if you talk. If you talk, and I think you're telling the truth, then maybe I'll do a little talking. If you don't, I might have to be a little tough, you know."

She smiled. "How do you think you could be tough, Johnny?"

"I'd think something up," said Vallon.

There was another silence. She sipped her whisky; inhaled the smoke from her cigarette. Vallon thought that her nerve was all right; that you couldn't push Mrs. Gale into doing something that she didn't want to do, or saying something she didn't want to say.

He said: "I'll tell you what we'll do. Let's go back to the hotel bar. I like it, and it's a nice night for driving. Let's drink some Bacardis. Maybe we'll get very friendly and able to talk to each other. How do you like that?"

"I don't mind. I suppose you think if I drink enough Bacardis I'm going to talk anyway."

"Yes," said Vallon. "You're going to talk even if you only drink water."

She got up. She came close to him. She put the soft fingers of her right hand under his chin. She kissed him on the mouth.

60

She said : " Johnny, I think you're a honey. Will you wait while I get a coat ? Then we'll go and drink Bacardis."

.   .   .   .

The bar-tender began to put the bottles away at a quarter to eleven. Vallon told him : " Two large Bacardis."

The bar-tender said : " Yes, sir." He began to mix the cocktails. He thought that Vallon and Mrs. Gale were two of the toughest drinkers he'd ever met in his life. They'd been sipping Bacardis and talking quietly on and off for a couple of hours. He shrugged his shoulders. He had a duodenal and didn't like alcohol—or rather he liked it but it didn't agree with him. He put the glasses on the table.

Vallon said : " They're going to close the bar in ten minutes' time."

She smiled at him sideways. It was a slow, rather knowing and attractive smile, he thought.

She said : " But you're a resident, Johnny. We can always have a drink in your room."

" I know," said Vallon. " But it looks as if it's costing me a lot of money for nothing."

She sipped her drink. She said : " Why bother ? Shall I order you another one now before they close down here ? "

" Why not ? I like Bacardi. If you drink enough of it nothing matters."

She shrugged her shoulders imperceptibly. " What does matter, Johnny ? "

He turned round on the stool ; faced her. " What matters is Hipper." He sighed. He went on : " Sometimes I think I'm a one-track-minded man. I've an idea at the moment that the track my mind's on is Hipper. He came over to Paignton to talk to you. I want to know what he wanted to talk to you about."

She said : " I've asked you a dozen times to-night why you want to know."

Vallon asked : " Can't you think of any reasons ? "

She smiled again—the same slow smile. " I could think of a few, but one's good enough."

He asked : " What ? "

She moved a little. She finished the Bacardi ; signalled to the barman to serve two more. She put a pound note on the bar.

61

She said: "You've suggested to-night that Hipper, although he's weak and inclined to be frightened, might have been trying to blackmail me when he suggested he was helping me. What goes for Hipper could very easily go for you."

Vallon grinned. "Meaning that I'm doing a little blackmail on the side?"

She said softly: "Why not, Johnny? You've got me where you want me, haven't you?"

He laughed out loud.

The bar-tender brought the new Bacardis.

Vallon said: "So I've got you where I want you? In a way I suppose that's right. What you mean is I could tell you that unless you did this or that I could drop a line to the King's Proctor and inform him that on the night of so and so you spent several hours in a bedroom in this hotel with me. I could tell him that you were petitioning for a divorce against your husband and, the law being the law, he might do something about it. That's what you're suggesting, isn't it?"

She nodded.

"The joke is," said Vallon, "in ordinary circumstances I might threaten to do that."

"Well, that would be blackmail, Johnny, wouldn't it? What would the pay-off be?"

He said: "Believe it or not, it wouldn't be money. The pay-off would be the information I want about Hipper . . . see?"

She smiled. She nodded her head. "You're a very thorough man, aren't you, Johnny? You're quite systematic. You know what you want and you keep on pegging away until you get it."

"That's right," he said. "You're pretty good yourself. You've got a very good head. I've never known a woman drink so much Bacardi as you and keep abreast of the situation."

"I feel I've got to with a man like you. But we're talking in a circle, aren't we? It's a case of the music goes round and round and nobody ever gets anywhere." Now she was laughing.

The bar-tender began to stack the bottles on the shelves. He was thinking of his wife. He wanted to go to sleep. He was tired.

Vallon thought he'd play it another way. He sat, holding his cocktail glass by its slender stem, wondering what the best plan of campaign would be. Then he thought : There's nothing like the truth. Sometimes it can be very efficacious.

He said : " Look, I'm going to tell you the truth, and when I tell it to you you'll know I'm telling the truth. When I met you down here I was spending a holiday here. I'd never been in Devonshire before. They told me it was a very attractive place. I thought it was when you appeared. You remember I got rid of you at the fair and told you to come back here and wait for me ? You thought that was a little rude, didn't you ? "

She nodded her head.

" I wanted to find out what Hipper was at," he went on. " I'd seen him at the fair. He was drunk. You see, I'm the staff manager for the detective agency which employs Hipper." He was watching her like a cat. He saw her eyelids flicker. " Hipper was supposed to be on a case in Somerset. I found him after half an hour's search and asked him what he was doing in Paignton. I accused him of charging up expenses to the firm. He said he'd put in his report and expense account from Somerset. That was true. So he'd paid his own fare over here. That wasn't like Hipper.

" And then I went back to the office and discovered that Hipper was the man who'd handled the inquiries about your husband in your divorce case. See ? "

She moved a little closer towards him. She was sitting on half the stool. She said : " Now I'm beginning to see, Johnny."

" So I knew that Hipper had come over to see you," Vallon went on. " I thought he'd got something on you. I wondered what he'd got. I knew it'd have to be something pretty safe because Hipper isn't made of the stuff black-mailers are made of. So I thought I'd come down and talk to you about it. Don't you think that was nice of me ? "

She finished the Bacardi. " Yes . . . I do. Now perhaps I'm beginning to believe in you, Johnny."

He was still watching her. He thought : Now she's going to give herself a little time to fake up a new story. Now she's got to tell me something. I wonder what it's going to be."

She repeated : " Now I'm beginning to believe in you.

You understand, Johnny, that in the circumstances I was entitled to think what I did think."

"All right," said Vallon. "Let's say for the sake of argument that you were. You see," he went on casually, "I don't want to talk to Hipper about this. I thought I'd rather talk to you."

She made a little gesture with her hands. She said: "All right, I'll tell you. Apparently, all you private detectives know each other. Hipper's no exception. He thought I ought to know that my husband wasn't awfully pleased at the idea of being divorced from me. Hipper had heard that he might make any trouble he could for me. He thought he ought to tell me that. He said he thought I ought to watch my step. He gave me the idea that he'd heard stories about my husband which weren't very nice. I thought he was a decent sort of man. He told me that and I gave him twenty-five pounds. He never even asked for it."

Vallon thought: It's a damned good story, but it's not true. He said: "Now I understand. Could I be curious? You've suggested that your husband doesn't want this divorce to go through. Is he still in love with you?"

She laughed. "I don't think so. But it's quite obvious that he'd rather go on being my husband. You see, I'm not a poor woman, Johnny. I have a lot of money."

He said: "That's as maybe. But even a rich woman doesn't have to give money to her husband unless she wants to. Isn't the story a little bit thin?"

"Not when you know the end of it," she said.

Vallon thought: Here it comes. Here's the thing that she's had time to think up while she's been talking. This is going to be very good.

She went on: "When I married my husband I was mad keen on him. I thought I loved him a great deal." She smiled sadly. "They say that if you make a mistake you have to pay for it. Well, I paid. Because, you see, Johnny, when I married Gale I disliked the idea of a husband who hadn't money being married to a woman who had. So I made a settlement on him. He was to receive five thousand pounds a year while he was my husband. Only two things could cancel the settlement—*his* lawyer drew it and it was pretty good—one thing was death; the other thing was divorce."

64

Vallon thought: Pretty good. He said: "I understand now. I can see why he doesn't want to be divorced. But how can he stop it?"

She shrugged her shoulders. "I don't know, but apparently he's going to try to. That's why Hipper thought I ought to know."

Vallon said cynically: "It looks as if I've misjudged Hipper. Perhaps he's not such a bad sort of guy after all."

"He really isn't. I think Hipper, whatever sort of man he may be, was trying to be decent."

A page boy came over. He said: "Mr. Vallon, there's a phone call for you. Will you take it in the box in the hall?"

"Yes . . ." Vallon got off the stool. He said: "That's the London office calling. Something's turned up, I expect. Excuse me for a minute."

He followed the boy across the lounge; went into the telephone box in the hall. He took up the receiver. It was Trant.

Trant said: "I've been around. I've spent the evening in the locals round about Marldon. I've learned something. It doesn't mean a lot but it might give you a lead."

Vallon said: "O.K., Trant. Drive over and see me here. I'll be in my room." He gave him the room number. "Come over at half-past twelve."

"All right. I'll be there," said Trant.

Vallon went back to the bar. He said: "As I thought, the office. I'm a busy man, you know."

"I bet you are." She pretended to yawn. "I'm a little tired, Johnny. Are you going to drive me back?"

He said: "Yes. Let's go."

They drove half the journey in silence; then she said: "You're satisfied about this Hipper thing, Johnny? You're not worried any more?"

"No," said Vallon. "You must understand that in a business like Chennault Investigations we have to be pretty sure of our operatives. You see, a private detective is often in a position where he can do a little blackmail. We've got to keep an eye on them. I'm the staff manager and that's my job. I was worried about Hipper because he's a very useful man in his way."

She said: "I understand that."

He went on : " Now everything seems to be above-board. I'm quite happy. Let's forget it."

There was a long silence. Vallon swung the car into the courtyard of Ladycourt.

She said : " Are you coming in for a night-cap, Johnny ? "

He shook his head. " No, I think I'd like to sleep to-night. Maybe I'll see you before I go back."

" Johnny, I'm asking you in to have a drink. There's something I want to say to you. Don't be"—she paused, seeking the right word—" ungallant . . ."

He grinned at her. " I won't be. I'd love a drink."

They got out of the car. She unlocked the front door ; led the way into the drawing-room.

She said : " You know where the decanter is. I don't need any."

He went to the sideboard ; poured himself a drink. When he turned she was standing in front of the fireplace.

She said : " Look, I think you're rather a man, Johnny. If I got into any trouble—with Gale I mean—I'd like to have you on my side. I suppose you wouldn't like to work for me ? "

She reached for the cigarette box ; opened the lid ; offered it to him. He took a cigarette and lighted it.

He said : " The idea appeals to me a lot. What's it worth ? "

" You ought to know. I'm not ungenerous, Johnny. I don't think you and I are going to argue about money."

He drank the whisky in one gulp ; returned the glass to the sideboard.

He said : " You're telling me. This is what we do. If Gale starts anything—anything that looks serious—you let me know. I'll do what I can for you."

She sighed. Then she smiled. " That's pretty nice of you. Will you wait while I write a cheque ? "

He nodded. " Surely. I love waiting for cheques."

She went to the writing desk at the far end of the room ; opened a drawer ; took out a cheque book. He watched her while she wrote out the cheque. She looked at it ; blotted it ; folded it ; brought it to him. He put it in his pocket.

He said : " Well . . . I'll be seeing you . . ."

" I told you what my first name is, Johnny. I wonder why you never use it?"

66

" I will," said Vallon. " See . . . Querida . . ."

He took out his pocket book ; extracted a card. " There's the address of the firm and my phone number. Any time you want me, call me. So long . . ."

" Just like that, Johnny ? What's the matter with you ? "

" Nothing . . . I was thinking, that's all." He took her chin in his hand ; kissed her on the mouth. " I'll be seeing you. I can find my way out."

He went out of the room. In the doorway, he turned and looked at her. She was still standing in front of the fireplace. He grinned at her. A moment later she heard the front door close.

Vallon started up the car and drove along the winding road that leads from Marldon to Paignton. Half a mile from the house he pulled the car up on the grass verge. He switched on the interior light ; took the cheque out of his pocket. It was made payable to cash or bearer. It was for two thousand pounds.

Vallon got out of the car. He stood on the grass verge looking at the moon. He took out his cigarette case ; put the cigarette in his mouth : snapped on his lighter. He lit the cigarette. Then he put the flame of the lighter to the corner of the cheque. He held it till it burned away. He got into the car ; drove back to the hotel.

He went up to his room ; took off his coat ; lay on the bed, his hands behind his head, looking at the ceiling. He thought that Mrs. Gale was a very interesting woman.

The phone bell jangled. Vallon took off the receiver. The operator put him straight through to the local exchange.

The exchange operator said : " Will Mr. John Vallon take a personal call from Mrs. Dolores Chennault in London ? "

He said : " I'm Mr. Vallon. Put her through."

She came on the line. She said : " Johnny, I've been thinking about you. I got through to Marvin at his home and told him I needed you urgently."

" Well, you've got me, haven't you ? " said Vallon. " What's the trouble about ? "

She said—and there was impatience in her voice : " I told you I've been thinking about you. I've been thinking about Joe. I've been thinking that there was a lot in what you said. Look, Johnny, you mustn't feel that I'm indifferent

67

about Joe, but I've expected him to go for a long time. It wasn't as if it was a surprise or shock. You understand?"

Vallon said: "I understand."

She went on: "I'm not a bit heartless about it, and I know how you feel, especially after you told me what you thought about Joe's death, so I've been doing a lot of serious thinking. I want you to come back to London quickly."

Vallon asked: "Why?"

She said: "You remember the conversation we had? You remember you told me what you thought had happened in Joe's office the afternoon he died? Well, I think I know who the man was, Johnny."

Vallon grinned. "Now you're talking! I'll be with you to-morrow morning. Good night, Toots!"

She said: "Is that all you've got to say?"

"Listen," said Vallon, "they charge three shillings for three minutes on this line. I'm trying to save you money. Don't you like it? I'll see you to-morrow."

He put the receiver back on its hook. He rolled over on to his back. He lay there until the girl on the switchboard rang through to tell him that Mr. Trant wanted to see him.

He said: "Show him up."

When Trant came in, Vallon said: "Well, what's the news?"

Trant said: "Look, I've been around all the inns in the vicinity. They're all very interested in Mrs. Gale. She has rather a lot of money." Trant smiled. "Everybody likes her."

Vallon asked: "What do they think of Gale?"

"A heel," said Trant. "Everybody's agreed on that fact. They think he's bad medicine. They wonder why she's stood him for so long. They think he spent most of his time two-timing her."

"Interesting," said Vallon. "Who was he two-timing her with—a lot of women or a few or one?"

Trant said: "The idea seems to be that there was one woman—the one who was named as co-respondent—Miss Evangeline Roberta Trickett. But there's another idea that she wasn't the one who really mattered."

Vallon asked: "How come?"

Trant said: "I ran into the egg who used to be gardener

68

at Ladycourt. There's quite an acreage there, you know, and the boy could usually see what was going on. After she'd started this divorce against Gale he came down to see her once or twice. But when he came down he used to park his car about a quarter of a mile from the house in the lane, and go up to the house on foot. When he parked the car he used to leave a woman in it, see ? "

" I see . . . What was she like ? "

Trant grinned. " The gardener was interested in that too. So he managed to get pretty near the car with the hedge in between and have a look at her. He pretended to be doing something or other. He said she was a piece. She helped him on one occasion by getting out of the car and walking up and down. Apparently, she was impatient. She's tall and slim. She knows how to wear clothes. The gardener said her hair was the colour of corn and lovely and, being a gardener, he ought to know what corn looks like. I asked him if he thought it was dyed. He said no, it was the real stuff. He said she had a very attractive face with a fine skin and one of those rather nice noses that look as if they meant to turn up at the end and then decided otherwise. Have you got the general idea ? "

Vallon said : " I've got it. An observant guy, this gardener. He's got everything except her voice. I expect that must have been like a corncrake. The rest sounds too good to carry a voice as well."

" Believe it or not," said Trant, " she's got a voice too. One afternoon she was up there walking about, waiting for Gale to come back, and she broke her string of imitation black pearls. They went all over the road. The gardener said he got through the hedge and helped to pick them up. He said she was cursing in a very attractive and level sort of voice. He said she had a very good command of the language too." Trant put his hand in his pocket. " He kept one of the smallest pearls," he said. " When he was telling me about this he showed it to me and I gave him half a crown for it. I thought it might come in useful to you somehow." He handed the pearl to Vallon.

Vallon tried it on his teeth. He said : " Who told you this was imitation ? This is real. It must have been cheap at half a crown." He swung his feet off the bed. " Let you and me have a drink, Trant. It's been a nice sort of day."

He took off the telephone receiver ; spoke to the night porter ; ordered the drinks. When they came up, Vallon poured them out.

He said : " Look, stick around here. Keep an eye on Ladycourt. Pick up anything you can. I'm going back to London to-morrow early. I'll ring you at the place you're staying at. Anything you've got keep till then."

" All right," said Trant. " Good night, Mr. Vallon."

He put his glass on the table ; went out.

Vallon went to the bathroom ; began to clean his teeth. He stopped half-way and looked in the mirror, but he wasn't seeing his own reflection. He was seeing all sorts of things. He thought, by and large, it had been a very interesting day.

He began to undress. In spite of the amount of liquor he'd consumed the pain in his stomach had come back. That made him think of Madeleine. He wondered where she was ; what she was doing. He thought about the perfume she wore. He wished he could remember the name of the goddam stuff. He thought if he could remember the name he could buy a bottle and smell it. He thought maybe that would stop the pain in his stomach ; that he wouldn't have to drink so much whisky—so many Bacardis.

2

Vallon stopped the car outside the apartment block at Hendon. He got out ; looked at his strap-watch. It was eleven o'clock. The sun was shining and somewhere in a nearby tree a bird was singing. He felt very tired. In the lift going up he began to think about Querida Gale. He thought she was quite a woman. He thought some other things too.

Dolores Chennault opened the door. She said : " Hallo, Johnny. You don't look so good to me."

" I don't feel so good," said Vallon. " I'm tired. I like driving a car but I'm having a little too much of it lately."

He followed her into the drawing-room.

She asked : " Do you want a drink ? "

He shook his head. " What's the big idea, Dolores ? "

She moved across to the window and looked out. He saw a shade of anger cross her face. She turned suddenly.

She said : " You're a hell of a guy, aren't you, Johnny ?
You don't even say good morning or ask how I am. You
wouldn't want to kiss me any more, would you ? "

" All right . . . good morning. And consider yourself
kissed. And how are you ? "

She said : " To hell with you." She turned again to the
window. After a pause she went on : " Don't you think
of anyone else except Joe ? Whatever you do you're not
going to bring him back, you know."

He lighted a cigarette. " Why should I worry about
bringing him back ? I'm not interested in Joe. He's
probably better off where he is. I'm interested in the man
who killed him. So why don't you get it over with ? "

She said : " You mean that you and I are finished finally ? "

" Why not ? Everything has to finish sometime or other.
And this is one of those things that ought never to have
started."

She laughed. " I never expected to hear lectures from
you."

He shrugged his shoulders. " I never expected to go in
for them."

She moved across to the arm-chair ; sat down. She took
a cigarette from the box on the table beside her and lighted
it.

She said : " I've been thinking about what you said,
Johnny. I'm not quite certain that you're right, but you
might be. I'm just as keen as you are on finding the man
who did this thing to Joe if that's how it was."

Vallon said : " So you've been thinking about it, and
you've got an idea ? "

She nodded. " There was a man called Perdreau—not a
bad type."

Vallon asked : " Was Perdreau another of your boy
friends ? "

She shrugged her shoulders. " I suppose so. It was one
of those things. You know how it is." She went on : " Joe
was a funny type. I think he used to think all sorts of
things about me, but he never said anything. He rode it,
if you know what I mean."

" You mean he rode it if he thought the man of the
moment was decent. Maybe he didn't like this Perdreau."

She said : " You're perfectly right. He'd found out

71

something about Tony—something he didn't like. I think he had the idea that I was still seeing him."

Vallon asked : " Were you ? "

" Just occasionally. I liked some things about him quite a lot. He was amusing."

Vallon grinned. " If a man's amusing it covers a multitude of sins."

She said bitterly : " You should talk. You were amusing *once*."

" That was before I grew up," said Vallon.

" Was it ? " Her voice was hard. " What you mean is you've changed your point of view since you found and lost your girl friend."

" All right," said Vallon. " You have it your way. Go on about Perdreau."

" I have an idea," she said, " that Joe had been talking to him on the telephone. I came down to the office one day. I came up the stairs and went through his private door. I heard him talking. I had an idea then that he might have got wise to what was going on. I had the impression that he intended to see Perdreau and tell him where he got off."

Vallon said : " What you're saying is that Joe knew plenty about this Tony Perdreau ; that he didn't like him ; that he sent for him and told him that he'd either got to lay off you or he'd fix him. Would that be it ? "

She shrugged her shoulders. " Possibly ! "

There was a silence ; then Vallon asked : " Anything else ? "

She said : " That's all."

He stubbed out his cigarette ; deposited the end in the ash-tray. He said : " All right. Where does one find Perdreau ? "

" He's got a club—one of those expensive places—in Dorset—a couple of miles beyond West Stour off the main road."

" O.K.," said Vallon. "I'll try to find out what he was doing on the afternoon Joe died. I'll let you know."

He walked across to the door. " If you think of anything else, Dolores, let me know about it, won't you ? "

She said : " O.K. But for God's sake don't be so damned serious. Don't you want a drink. Is that stomach of yours still worrying you ? " She smiled at him suddenly. Sometimes she could look quite charming when she smiled, he thought.

He said : " It always worries me."

" Why don't you get them to take out that bit of bullet or whatever it is ? Maybe then you'd drink because you wanted to drink and not because you wanted to put the pain to sleep."

He said : " Maybe. I'll be seeing you ! "

He closed the door quietly behind him. When he'd gone she sat back in the chair looking straight in front of her. She sat there quite motionless until the cigarette singed her fingers.

Vallon stopped the car in Jermyn Street. He thought it might be an idea to eat some lunch. He went into the bar ; ordered a sandwich. When the bar-tender put the rye bottle and the glass with the water jug on the counter in front o him Vallon said : " Make it ginger ale this morning."

The bar-tender sighed and took the bottle away.

Vallon ate half the sandwich ; then he looked at the clock behind the bar. It was a quarter-past twelve.

He drove to the office ; went into Chennault's room ; sat down behind the desk. He called through on the office telephone for Marvin.

When Marvin came in Vallon asked : " Did Mrs. Chennault telephone for me yesterday ? "

" No, Mr. Vallon. Nobody asked for you."

" Where's Hipper ? " said Vallon.

" He's in the staff-room," Marvin answered.

Vallon got up. " Send him in. I want to talk to him. What job is he doing at the moment ? "

Marvin said : " I've put him on a commercial investigation. You said you wanted me to put him on to something that would keep him busy."

Vallon said : " Get a good, reliable man from some other agency and put him on to Hipper."

" You mean observation on his house ? " asked Marvin.

Vallon said : " Put somebody on his house so that if he decides to go away we have an idea where he goes to. I think he might decide to do that."

" Very well, Mr. Vallon." Marvin went out.

Hipper came in through the staff door three minutes afterwards. He was freshly shaved and looked as if he hadn't been consuming quite so much whisky. He carried his hat in his hand.

He said : " Good morning, Mr. Vallon. You're looking very tired. This must be a worrying time for you."

Vallon said : " You'd be surprised." He was standing with his back to the window looking at Hipper. " Sit down, Hipper."

Hipper sat down.

Vallon said : " You're old enough to know that the truth always catches up with you sometime or other. Let you and me have a little talk, shall we ? And let's not try to tell too many lies."

Hipper sat quite still. He looked quite unperturbed, which Vallon thought was strange. He was at ease.

He said : " I don't know what you're talking about."

" All right," said Vallon. " When I talked to you at the fair at Paignton you'd gone down there to see Mrs. Gale. There's something on between you and Mrs. Gale. You wouldn't know where I was last night, would you ? "

" No," said Hipper. " How should I ? "

Vallon said : " You're a damned liar. You know I was at Ladycourt with Mrs. Gale last night. When she went out of the room to get her coat to come down to the hotel bar to have a drink with me she telephoned you. She told you she was in a spot because I knew you'd been down there to see her ; that I knew there was something on between you two. She didn't know how to handle it. You told her. You told her to tell me that in the course of your investigations in her divorce against her husband you'd come into possession of some information which made you think that Gale might try some funny business with her ; that he didn't like her ; that he was dangerous. You considered that it was your duty to come and tell her—just as any decent man would. You told her to tell me that story. So she told it to me. Where do we go from there ? "

Hipper said : " I don't know what you're talking about, Mr. Vallon. I think you've got a bee in your bonnet. I assure you you're all wrong. I didn't tell her anything like

74

that. If she told you that it's because——" He shrugged his shoulders. " I don't suppose you're going to believe me but it's the truth. When I was working on the Gale case I heard that Gale was going to do anything he could to upset this divorce. I heard that he'd got it in for his wife, and it wasn't any concern of mine, and it wasn't any concern of the Chennault agency. We were employed to get the evidence on him and, as you know, I got it. But it worried me. I knew all there was to know about the Gale case. I knew that Mrs. Gale was a very nice woman. From what I can hear of Gale he's poison.

" I didn't know what the hell to do. Then I was put on that Somerset job. When I went there I hadn't any idea in my head about seeing Mrs. Gale, but after I'd completed my investigation into the thing I was working on down there I realised I wasn't very far from Paignton, so I rang her up. I said I'd like to see her ; that I'd got some information I thought she ought to have. She wanted to see me. She wanted me to go out to her house, Ladycourt, but I said I didn't think that would be a good thing.

" So she took a drawing-room at the Continental. I saw her there and had a drink with her. I told her what I thought. When I'd done that I felt better. Then I went over to the fair and had a few drinks." He grinned. " I had a sort of comfortable feeling that I'd done my duty for once."

Vallon nodded. " You had the comfortable feeling that twenty-five pounds in your pocket always gives a man like you. I bet you were surprised to see me."

" You bet I was," said Hipper. " That's the truth, Mr. Vallon, whether you believe it or not. But maybe you think I'm a liar."

Vallon went back to his seat behind Chennault's desk.

He said : " I don't think . . . I know. . . . O.K., Hipper. That's all."

Hipper got up. " Thank you, Mr. Vallon."

He went out of the office.

Vallon lighted a cigarette. He leant back in the chair thinking about Querida Gale, Dolores Chennault, Hipper ; about Madeleine Thorne ; about himself. He thought that maybe you could think too much.

He picked up his hat. He went back to the bar in Jermyn

Street. He sat there, sipping Bacardi, trying to stop himself thinking about things that he didn't want to think about.

.   .   .   .

The doctor said to Vallon : " It's just one of those nervous things, and it's not much good worrying about it. I looked at the X-rays a couple of days after you saw me the last time.   You can take it from me that when they took that bullet out of you they took all of it out.   You know, the body often remembers a thing, and your stomach is remembering that bullet.   It's a nervous place, the stomach.   People feel hatred and love and all sorts of things in their guts.   Perhaps you're worrying a little about something.   Maybe that brings it on.   Have you noticed that it comes on at any especial time ? "

Vallon said : " Sometimes I go a couple of days without it.   But I can always stop it."

The doctor asked : " Veganin ? That's the best thing for that sort of ache."

" No," said Vallon.   " Whisky or Bacardi.   If I drink enough it goes away."

The doctor smiled.   " So you drink enough.   Whisky of course is a hypnotic, so is veganin.   You'll find veganin is cheaper in the long run."

Vallon grinned.   " Maybe . . . but I don't like veganin." He got up.   " Well, if they got it all out they got it all out. So long, doctor."

He went out of the consulting-room ;   down in the lift. Outside, he got into his car.   He looked at his watch.   He thought he would make West Stour by seven o'clock.   He thought that might do.

.   .   .   .

The Pleasaunce roadhouse was a converted hotel that had been turned by a good architect to look like something very attractive.   It stood in a dip between the hills, off the main road that runs behind West Stour.   The lawns about it were well-kept and in the gravel courtyard in front of the house half a dozen expensive cars and one or two not so expensive cars were parked.   There was a flower garden on the left of the house, and on the right, just behind it, a swimming pool.

Vallon thought it looked rather a nice place. It was restful and had atmosphere. One day, he thought, when he had nothing to do, nothing to think about, he'd come down here and stay for a few days. He wondered what the hell Madeleine was doing; where she was. He wished he could remember the name of the perfume she wore.

He parked the car at the end of the gravel courtyard; walked across; went into the main entrance. The hall was large, oak-lined, well-furnished. There was a reception office with a pretty girl in the corner.

Vallon went across to her. He said: " My name's Vallon. I'd like to see Mr. Perdreau."

She asked : " Have you an appointment ? "

Vallon shook his head. " But you tell him I'm a friend of Mrs. Chennault's; that I'd like to see him particularly."

She took off the telephone. She said : " He might be dressing. We have dinner at eight. I'll find out." She spoke into the telephone ; then she said to Vallon : " Mr. Perdreau would be glad to see you." She rang a bell. " The page-boy will take you up."

They got out of the lift on the first floor ; walked along a thickly-carpeted corridor. The boy opened a door and Vallon went in. The room was the drawing-room of a suite. As the boy closed the door behind Vallon, Perdreau came in through the connecting door from the bedroom. Vallon thought he didn't dislike the look of him.

Perdreau was tall, slim, carried himself well. His clothes were well-cut and of good material. His face was open. He would have been good-looking except for the suggestion of a cast in one eye.

He said : " Good evening. I'm always glad to meet a friend of Mrs. Chennault. What can I do for you ? " He moved a chair forward.

Vallon said : " Thanks." He sat down.

Perdreau said : " We make a very good Martini here—not the sort of warm mixture you usually get in this country. How does the idea go with you ? "

Vallon said : " Very well."

Perdreau took off a telephone ; ordered the drinks. Then he went and stood in front of the fireplace, his hands in his pockets, looking at Vallon.

77

Vallon said: " Last Wednesday afternoon Joe Chennault died in his office. Did you know that ? "

" No," said Perdreau. " But I'm not surprised. He had a bad heart, hadn't he ? "

" That's right—a very bad heart. But I have an idea that he didn't die. I have an idea that somebody killed him. Somebody fired a blank cartridge out of an automatic at him. You get the idea ? "

" You mean the shock killed him," said Perdreau. " In his condition it would. A clever trick, that."

" Maybe," said Vallon. " Well, nobody's got any ideas about this yet. I mean the police haven't. I spoke to Dolores Chennault about it, and she thought at first that the idea was a little far-fetched. Now, apparently, she's inclined to think it might be right. I asked her if she knew of anybody who might have wanted to do that to Joe and she suggested you." He smiled at Perdreau. " She said you might have felt that way about him."

Perdreau moved his shoulders a little. He smiled gently. Vallon liked the way he stood with his weight forward on the balls of his feet like a boxer.

He thought that Perdreau was in pretty good shape, mentally and physically.

" I never had any funny ideas like that about Joe," said Perdreau. " I was sorry for Joe."

Vallon said: " So was I. I guess one or two other people were too. I suppose you wouldn't like to tell me what you were doing on Wednesday afternoon ? "

" Surely," Perdreau answered. " I went to see Joe Chennault."

Vallon asked: " And you went in by the private door— the door that leads out into the side passage ? "

Perdreau nodded his head. " That's right. He asked me to come in that way. He didn't want me to go through the main offices. He was a little bit "—he smiled again ; shrugged his shoulders expressively—" sensitive about me, I think."

Vallon said : " Could I make a guess ? "

" As many as you like." Perdreau reached behind him for the cigarette box. He offered it to Vallon, who took a cigarette and lighted it.

" My guess is," Vallon went on, " that maybe there

was something on sometime between you and Dolores Chennault."

Perdreau said : " Did she say so ? "

Vallon shook his head. " Not in so many words. But I know Dolores and you're her type."

Perdreau laughed. " Well, you know how it is with Dolores. She always knows what she wants and she always makes a certainty of getting it. Quite a person, isn't she ? "

" Yes," said Vallon. " So Joe rang you up and asked you to come and see him last Wednesday afternoon at four o'clock."

Perdreau shook his head. " No soap. I went there at half-past two. I have a flat in London. He telephoned me the week before. He said he wanted to talk to me about some particularly urgent and private business. I told him that I didn't know of any business I had with which he could be connected. He said there *was* some. So I went round. When I got there he told me that he knew all about Dolores and me. He said he didn't like it very much. He said that as he knew, now, it'd got to stop. He was quite nice," Perdreau went on. " He didn't even get excited about it."

Vallon said : " Joe never got excited about anything much. So what happened then ? "

" I told him," said Perdreau, " that there wasn't anything on between Dolores and me. I said that was all washed up. That shook him a little bit. It surprised him." Perdreau produced the same gentle smile. " I always believe in telling the truth on these occasions. It makes it so much easier for all concerned. I told him that Dolores and I had agreed to call it a day about six weeks before."

Vallon asked : " Was he interested enough to ask you why ? "

Perdreau nodded. " He was plenty interested. He asked me why and I told him that Dolores had found a new boy friend—a case of off with the old love and on with the new. That baby certainly gets around. She must have a bicycle!"

Vallon said : " Maybe you're right. Just on a point of interest I suppose you wouldn't know the name of her new boy friend ? "

Perdreau shook his head. " I haven't any idea as to who the new boy friend was. I expect it was one of her temporary affairs. There was only one person she was really stuck on."

"Was there?" asked Vallon. "Who was that?"

"You," said Perdreau. "Wouldn't you know?"

Vallon said nothing. After a while he said: "And so that was all?"

"That was all," said Perdreau. "I was in his office a minute before half-past two. There's a clock on the wall over his desk. It was right in front of me. Our conversation lasted twenty minutes. And then I left. The funny thing is I can prove what I say."

Vallon asked: "How?"

The door opened and a waiter came in with a cocktail shaker and two glasses. Perdreau poured the drinks. Vallon drank some of the Martini. He thought it was very good.

When the waiter had gone, Perdreau said: "Do you keep a register of phone calls in Chennault Investigations?"

Vallon nodded.

"At half-past two," said Perdreau, "a call came through to Chennault. It was a firm called Malinson, Brook & Co. He was speaking to a Mr. Malinson. He was talking about some industrial investigation. Does that let me out?"

Vallon said: "When I get back I'll look in the telephone register. If that call's in it, it looks as if you're O.K. Not that that matters."

Perdreau asked: "Why doesn't it?"

"I don't believe you'd do a thing like that anyway," said Vallon. "You don't look that sort of man. You're certain you don't know the name of the man who took Dolores Chennault away from you?"

Perdreau shook his head. "I wouldn't know. And if I did, why should I tell you?"

Vallon finished his cocktail; got up. He said: "Thanks a lot."

"I'm very glad to have been of any assistance," said Perdreau. "If somebody killed Chennault I hope you get him. Are you sure you wouldn't like to stay to dinner?"

"No thanks," said Vallon.

"Well, have another Martini . . . ?" Perdreau indicated the cocktail shaker.

Vallon said: "Thanks. It's very nice of you." He poured himself out another drink; took it in one gulp. "Well, so long, Perdreau."

"So long, Vallon." Perdreau reached behind him for another cigarette.

When Vallon went down the steps outside the roadhouse the evening sun lit up the green lawns; caused attractive shadows from the trees and bushes. He thought again that it would be a nice place to live in. He walked towards his car.

A woman came round the side of the house from the direction of the swimming pool. She was wearing a black ace dinner gown with a light wrap over it. She was a very good-looking woman with corn-coloured hair. She moved very gracefully. Vallon walked towards her.

He said: "Good evening. My name's John Vallon."

She looked at him. She smiled a little. Her eyes were very blue. Vallon thought she was an attractive piece.

"How interesting." Her voice was musical. "What am I supposed to do about that, Mr. Vallon?"

He said: "I have something that belongs to you. Do you remember breaking the string of your black pearls whilst you were waiting in Gale's car for him to come back from Ladycourt at Marldon?"

Her eyes opened wide. "Of course I do. But why? What——?"

"Did you ever realise that you were one pearl short—one of the smallest ones?" asked Vallon. "The gardener who helped you to pick them up thought they were imitation and I suppose he kept this one as a tip given by himself."

Vallon put his fingers into his waistcoat pocket and produced the pearl. He held out his hand, the pearl in the middle of his palm, towards her.

She moved towards him and a whiff of the perfume she wore came to his nostrils. He recognised it. It was a sweet-smelling, heavy scent—*Cœur de Carnation*. He thought it wasn't a very attractive perfume; that it was too heavy.

She said: "How did you know it was I who lost it?"

Vallon grinned. "The gardener took quite a shine to you. He told me all about you and what you looked like. I bought the pearl off him for half a crown. I'd a vague dea that you and I might meet one day."

She said: "I wonder why you thought that."

He shrugged his shoulders. "Maybe it was just a hunch."

" Hunches are amusing things sometimes, aren't they
Mr. Vallon ? "

He nodded. " I've just been having a drink with Perdreau.
I won't keep you. He's finished dressing and I don't want
you to be late for dinner."

She threw a quick sideways glance at him—an all embrac-
ing glance. " I think you're very kind. Good evening
to you."

Vallon said : " Good evening."

He walked over to the car ; started up the engine. He
took a last look at the Pleasaunce roadhouse ; drove on to
the main road. He stopped the car, undecided which way
to go—London or Devonshire. He spun a coin. It came
down heads which meant that he went back to London.

He turned the nose of the car towards Devonshire.

CHAPTER THREE

FLEUR DE LILAS

1

VALLON stopped the car at a little inn on the west side of
Fairmile. Now the shadows were darker. The summer
evening was beginning to fade. He thought it was a good
time of the day—if you worried about what the day was like.
He went into the inn ; bought himself a whisky and soda ;
drank it slowly. He wondered what he was going to do.
After he'd finished the drink, he drove on. He stopped the
car and pulled on to the grass verge a few miles farther
towards Paignton. He sat behind the wheel, smoking, still
wondering what he was going to do.

Life, thought Vallon, was essentially a matter of what
you were going to do. If you were one of those people who
never had to worry about what you were going to do, you
led a dull routine existence ; the pattern of your life was
stale, flat and unprofitable. It was either like that or you
were a person who wondered what you were going to do
and then decided and did it.

He began to think about Joe Chennault. Joe, he thought,

had been a very good egg. Quite a man in his way—*quite*
a man. A tough, hard personality who was straight ; who
believed in meeting life as it came ; who wore his weak
heart like he'd worn anything else ; without talking too
much about it, or even thinking too much about it, which
is even harder than not talking about a thing. Vallon, who
was himself a tough, hard man in his own peculiar way,
realised that he was wondering what he was going to do
about himself. Life at the moment seemed not to present
many interesting facets, apart from the one concerning Joe.
That was the interesting one and that was the thing that
mattered, and that was what he was wondering about.
Existence, he thought, was rather like the investigation he
was making into Joe's death. It was one of those things.
You went on. You met people. You talked to them. You
thought about them. You tried to come to conclusions. If
you came to the right conclusion you might get somewhere.
But it was just as easy to come to the wrong conclusion.
He shrugged his shoulders. What did it matter ? Not very
much as long as you eventually got somewhere. And you
had to be wrong sometimes.

Certain salient facts were available. He checked them
in his mind. The first fact was that he had met Mrs. Querida
Gale because she'd had an appointment with Hipper. He'd
run into her at the bar at the Continental Hotel soon after
Hipper had left her.

Hipper was the first fact. Hipper, who was the man who
had carried out the investigation for the Chennault agency
into Pierce Gale's misconduct. Somehow, somewhere,
during the course of his investigations he'd come across
something which made it necessary that he should talk to
Querida Gale. Vallon had been told about that. He'd had
two explanations—one from Mrs. Gale and one from
Hipper. He believed neither. The idea of Hipper being
an altruistic or even a decent man, going out of his way to
warn a woman for her own good without any hope of reward,
was so much damned nonsense. And Mrs. Gale was lying
because she *had* to lie. She couldn't do anything else.
Probably she thought that she couldn't trust him—Vallon.
That was O.K. by him. Why should she ? She wasn't
certain of him. She didn't know what he was doing. She
didn't know what he was trying to get at. He'd told her

he was merely interested in checking up on Hipper—one of the Chennault operatives. Well, that wasn't true. All he was interested in was finding out who killed Joe Chennault.

Then—in a rather extraordinary manner—other people had come into the story. Dolores Chennault—a seductive woman who hadn't loved her husband ; who had two-timed him when she wanted to. One of those provocative women who think they can do what they like with life ; who have little sense of responsibility or duty ; who never admit that they've been wrong ; that they've ever done anything that wasn't quite so good. A woman with always a first-class, ready-made excuse for anything she did ; who covered a multitude of sins by persuading herself that she was interested in people ; who persuaded herself that, in spite of everything she did, she was fond of her husband.

Vallon wondered what she was at. Certain things were obvious to him. First of all she hadn't really been interested in trying to find Joe's killer. The doctor having given a certificate of death, the matter was closed so far as she was concerned. All she wanted to do was to get to South America. With whom . . . that was the question ? Vallon knew that Dolores did not intend to go to South America alone.

Then afterwards she discovered that she *was* interested in who killed Joe. She had an idea. She had an idea that it might be Perdreau. She had this idea, according to her, because she'd heard Chennault talking to him on the telephone sometime in the past. Vallon lighted a cigarette. The interesting point was, he thought, how she'd known that Perdreau was going to see Joe Chennault on the afternoon of his death. Because she *had* known. If she hadn't she wouldn't have put Vallon on to him. She certainly did know. Yet, according to Perdreau, he had gone to Chennault's office because Chennault had asked him to go and discuss some important business, and in the circumstances it was certain that Chennault would never have told his wife about this conversation which he intended to have, because Joe was that sort of man. It was one of the things he wouldn't discuss with his wife.

So Dolores knew that Perdreau was going on that afternoon, by some means outside Joe. And it was hardly likely that Perdreau, who had already been given the air by her because of the new man who had come into her life, would tell her that he was going. Vallon grinned. He thought he had the answer. Dolores herself had suggested to Joe that he had a talk with Perdreau. She did this because she was tired of Perdreau ; because she wanted to be rid of him and because she wanted Joe to know that it was all over. She knew that when Chennault accused Perdreau of having an *affaire* with his wife Perdreau would say that it was all over ; that there was nothing further to worry about.

But it was important to her that she put Vallon on to Perdreau ; that she put the idea into Vallon's mind that Perdreau might be the man responsible for Joe's death. And she had to do that quickly. So she telephoned him at Paignton and told him that she'd got his telephone number and address from Marvin. This was a lie. Marvin had never given her the number or the address. So she'd got it from somebody else, and that somebody could very well have been Hipper or Querida Gale.

He began to think about this new man who had come into Dolores Chennault's life. He couldn't quite understand about him. He thought she wasn't very keen on this new man. He thought this because he knew Dolores . . . too well. She was a " one-man-at-a-time " woman ; and because she had seemed still as keen on carrying on with him—Vallon—as she had been in the past it was obvious that the new man wasn't very important in her life.

And there might be an answer to that one. It might be that Dolores was using him for a purpose. Just as she used every man for something or other besides love. Just as she had used Vallon for something else and then discovered that she was really keen about him when it was too late ; after Vallon had become tired of something that had bored him—something that began in boredom and finished in the same state.

He drew on his cigarette ; watched the shadows creeping across the white dust of the road.

But he liked his guess. Vallon liked this. It fitted in with one or two things in his mind.

Now the next coincidence. The next coincidence was the fact that Perdreau knew the woman who used to wait in Gale's car when he went to visit his wife at Ladycourt—the woman whose black pearls had broken. What was the connection between Gale and this woman ? They were obviously close together but not close enough for her to be the co-respondent in the Gale divorce case. That honour had been reserved for Miss Evangeline Roberta Trickett. Vallon thought he must get around to Evangeline sometime or other. Meanwhile there was this other piece—this woman who waited so impatiently for Gale whilst he went to visit his wife and who, oddly enough, was a friend of Anthony Perdreau—the man who had been Dolores' lover—the man who had visited Joe's office on the afternoon of his death.

So what ! Vallon shrugged his shoulders. When you had two or three things that you thought were facts and they added up to mere theories—disjointed theories at that—what did you do about it ? It was all very well to talk about throwing a spanner into the works and seeing what would happen, but when you'd thrown the spanner and the works were all gummed up, it wasn't any good ; something had to emerge from the chaos. And up to that moment nothing very much had emerged except that Mrs. Gale had given him a cheque for two thousand pounds to work for her in case Pierce Gale became difficult, she having learned from Hipper that such a process was likely.

Vallon thought that maybe it would be a good idea if he talked with Pierce Gale. It *might* be a good idea. And yet some instinct told him that the moment had not arrived for this purpose. It could wait.

He threw the cigarette stub out of the open window ; lighted a fresh one. He thought he was smoking too much. He grinned. He was smoking too much and drinking too much. He was doing these things because there was nothing else that mattered particularly ; nothing to make him want to stop.

And there *was* nothing to make him want to stop. Vallon smiled to himself. He thought that there was a certain philosophy of life contained in those words. People, especially men, always did what they wanted to do. Whatever they said about it, and however much they disagreed with the idea, they always did what they really wanted to do. If they drank too much it was because they were trying to forget something or trying to remember something—something they *wanted* to forget or remember. Vallon thought people worked subconsciously towards their main

86

desires all their lives, and the fact that a man's—or a woman's—life was good, bad or indifferent, depended on what their desires were. Or did it? Who in hell cared anyway? But the idea was amusing.

He wondered why, after he'd spun the coin and the result had shown him that he should go to London, he had decided to drive to Devonshire. He wondered if this was instinct. He wondered if there *was* such a thing as instinct, or whether you did something that you wanted to do and then deluded yourself that you had an instinctive reason for doing it. He grinned to himself. Somebody had once said that when you were in doubt the thing to do was to deal with the nearest thing to hand in the most simple way. Vallon, like most direct people who spend their lives following their noses—believed in listening to people talking. You can always discover the truth about people if you listen to them talking long enough. There were exceptional types of course who talked one way and *did* another way, but the truest indications of most people came from what they said when they were talking and off their guard, or alternatively when they were so much on their guard that they were being careful to say the right things, and in the process of doing so made it obvious to the listener what they were trying to avoid.

He started up the car; let in the gear. He pulled on to the road and drove fast. At ten o'clock he arrived at the Continental. The night porter gave him a telegram which he said had been delivered two hours before. Vallon put the telegram in his pocket. He didn't bother to read it. He thought it would be from Marvin. Anyhow, it could wait.

He ate supper; went to his room; took a shower; went to bed. He was tired out and when you were tired the obvious thing to do was to sleep.

He woke up with a start; looked at his strap-watch. It was one o'clock in the morning. He felt rested and his mind was clear. He thought it was funny what a little sleep could do for you. He rang down to the night porter; ordered a large whisky and soda and some black coffee. He got up and began to walk about the bedroom in his pyjamas. He thought for a while about Mrs. Gale. Then he remembered the telegram. He took it out of his jacket pocket and opened it. He had been right in his guess. It was from Marvin. It said:

" Cannot understand situation here stop Have received visit from Acme Investigation Agency stop According to them and their statement verified by properly negotiated deed of transfer signed by Joe Chennault Investigations was sold to them for cash ten days ago stop Cannot understand this as I believed negotiations were pending between World Wide Investigations and Chennault for the purchase of this business stop Have informed nobody and requested Acme Agency who expected to take over business in three months time Chennault having asked for that time lapse not to discuss this affair until instructions received from you stop Mrs. Chennault as you know is under impression that the sale of this business is proceeding with World Wide Investigations and that payment is to be made in respect of it on completion stop What do I do

Marvin."

Vallon lay down on the bed, the telegram in his hand, and looked at the ceiling. This, he thought, was a good one. He wondered what Joe had been playing at. Joe, apparently, had opened up negotiations with the World Wide Investigations for the sale of the business ; the negotiations had been brought to a conclusion, but the deal had not been definitely fixed. Then, quietly, without saying anything to anybody, he'd sold out to the Acme Agency and taken cash for it. He said nothing to anyone.

Vallon grinned at the ceiling. He wondered what Joe had been playing at. It had certainly been *something*—and something *definite*. Joe was like that. Vallon wondered why he'd told Dolores all about the original negotiations with World Wide Investigations and then quietly sold out under her nose. Vallon wondered whether Joe had been fed up with the whole set-up : whether he'd intended to cash in and get out. He wondered why Joe had said nothing to *him* about it. He wondered if Joe was so fed up with his wife that he'd decided to take a run-out powder on her and leave her flat. He wondered if there was a tie-up between the interview with Perdreau and this other business. He shrugged his shoulders. He thought the business was becoming more interesting at every moment.

He picked up the telephone and rang through to Marvin at his private address. When Marvin's sleepy voice came on the line, Vallon said : " I've got your wire. It's very interesting, isn't it ? "

" You're telling me," said Marvin. " What the hell was Mr. Chennault playing at, Mr. Vallon ? We all knew that he'd made the arrangements for selling out to World Wide Investigations. A draft agreement of sale had been drawn up. It had been approved by Mr. Chennault but not signed. So it wasn't fixed. Then in the meantime, and some time after the draft had been sent to us, he makes a deal with Acme and sells out for cash, and by what I can hear from the Acme people he sold out pretty cheaply too."

Vallon asked : " What did he sell out for ? "

Marvin said : " I'm not certain but from what the Acme people said I think somewhere in the region of ten thousand."

" What was the figure mentioned in the original draft agreement with World Wide Investigations ? " asked Vallon.

Marvin said : " Twenty-five thousand."

" All right," said Vallon. " Keep what you know under your hat. You understand ? "

" I see, sir. I'll speak to nobody."

Vallon went on : " You're certain that Mrs. Chennault doesn't know anything about this second deal ? "

" I'm absolutely certain," said Marvin. " She believes the business is going to be sold to World Wide Investigations."

" All right," said Vallon. " I'll be back soon. If not, I'll get in touch with you. Just play things along and don't talk."

" I never do, Mr. Vallon. You know that."

Vallon said : " I'm going to send Trant up to London. He'll probably be with you sometime to-morrow afternoon. Give him any information he wants. Have you got that ? "

Marvin said he'd got it. Vallon hung up.

Here was more food for thought. So Joe had lost fifteen thousand pounds by selling out for cash. That only meant one thing. He wanted a quick deal and he wanted to get out. He didn't want to sell to World Wide Investigations because the deal was going to take a little time to go through —according to Dolores only a month, but that was too long for Joe. Joe had had it, and wanted to take a powder on everybody and everything.

89

Vallon yawned; swung himself off the bed; lighted a cigarette; picked up the telephone and told the night porter to ring Trant's number at Babbacombe.

When Trant came on the line, Vallon said: "I'm over here at the Continental. Has anything happened?"

"Not a thing," said Trant. "Everything at Ladycourt seems to be very quiet. I've done a round of the local pubs again, but I haven't anything new."

Vallon said: "O.K. Pack your bags in the morning, Trant, and get back to London. Ring up Marvin and make a date to see him somewhere outside the office. Tell him to bring the Gale divorce file with him. You're interested in Miss Evangeline Roberta Trickett. Understand? She is the co-respondent with Gale. You will get the address mentioned in the petition from the file. Get on to this baby and let me know what you can about her. I'll be back to-morrow or the day after. I'll ring you when I get to London. Understand?"

Trant said: "O.K."

Vallon put the receiver back on its cradle; sat on the edge of the bed. He smoked the cigarette to its end. He thought nothing was really very involved. There was nothing that couldn't be worked out. You just sat on your backside and let things happen. If you were *that* sort of person they happened. He thought things were going to happen.

He got into bed; went to sleep. He was interested and in some vague way exhilarated. He even forgot the tray with the whisky and the black coffee which stood on the table at his bedside.

. . . .

Vallon awoke suddenly. He sat up in bed, wondering why for no reason at all you should wake up. Somewhere a church clock struck with a peculiarly cracked note. He looked at the illuminated dial of his strap-watch. It was just after four o'clock.

He yawned and reached out for the electric light switch. Standing on the bed-table was the tray with the whisky and the cold black coffee. Vallon got out of bed; drank the whisky; drank a cup of the coffee. He thought it tasted like hell, but it was better than nothing.

He began to walk up and down the bedroom. He began to think about Hipper. There was one thing about Hipper,

90

Vallon thought, that intrigued him. Hipper, according to Mrs. Gale, had come down to Paignton to tell her that her husband—Pierce Gale—was going to be difficult about the divorce. Vallon wondered why he should be. Here was a man who was receiving five thousand a year under a settlement made by his wife—a settlement terminated only by death or divorce—who had in the first place apparently agreed to be divorced, inasmuch as he had gone off and committed misconduct with Miss Evangeline Roberta Trickett, and then afterwards, for some reason, suddenly changed his mind. Vallon thought it might be very interesting to know why.

He did a little more walking. His eye fell on the telephone on the table by the side of the bed. It was a quarter-past four and that was the time, he thought, when most people weren't on the top of their form. They were tired. Perhaps they wouldn't find it so easy to invent lies.

He took off the telephone receiver; asked the night porter for the Ladycourt number. There was practically no pause before Querida Gale's quiet voice said: " Hallo . . ."

Vallon said: " You'll be getting tired of me in a minute. This is Johnny Vallon. I'm at the Continental. I think I'd like to talk to you."

" Would you ? Why not, Johnny ? " Vallon thought she seemed not at all surprised. She asked: " Has something happened ? "

Vallon stalled. " You employed me to work for you if Pierce Gale became difficult. I have an idea in my head that he's going to become a little difficult."

She asked: " Have you found something out, Johnny ? "

" I think so," he answered. " I'd like to talk to you."

She said: " Come up. . . . Just a moment . . . it's nearly twenty-past four. It'll only take you ten minutes to drive up here and I'd like to do my hair first. Will you be here at five ? Come to the side entrance—the door on the right-hand side of the house. I'll leave it open for you and the light on inside. You'll find a stairway at the end of the passage in front of you. Go straight up. My room is facing the top of the stairway. If you like, when you've reached the top of the stairs, you can turn off the light in the hall below from the switch on the wall. Is that clear, Johnny ? "

He said : " Yes. I'll leave here at ten to five."

He hung up the receiver ; dressed very quickly. He thought it rather peculiar that Mrs. Gale should be thoroughly awake at a quarter-past four : even more peculiar that she should want to do her hair before he arrived. He thought that her hair would look very attractive even undone.

He went down the stairs three at a time ; got his car from the garage. He drove quickly ; reached Ladycourt just after the half-hour. He pulled over to the right on to the grass verge that bounded the road ; drove the car in to the hedge ; switched off the lights. Keeping in the shadow of the hedge he walked up the road ; crossed quickly ; slipped through the main entrance gates. He moved round in the shade of the shrubberies to the side of the house from which he could watch the side and the front entrances.

He stood there, an unlit cigarette in his mouth, his hands in his pockets. He was relaxed. He felt almost happy. At a quarter to five the side door opened. Somebody came out. The man walked quickly, placing his feet carefully on the gravel path so as not to make too much noise.

It was Hipper. Vallon grinned. He moved round the side of the shrubbery ; allowed Hipper to get up to the main entrance ; went after him.

He said quietly : " Hipper . . ."

Hipper stopped and turned round. He said : " Good evening, Mr. Vallon." He did not look very happy.

" It isn't evening, Hipper ; it's morning. Come over to the car."

" O.K. . . ." Hipper's voice was subdued.

They walked down the road to the spot where Vallon had lef his car. Vallon sat on the wing ; took out his lighter , lighted his cigarette.

He said : " Well, what about it ? "

" What's it to you, Mr. Vallon ? " asked Hipper.

Vallon said nothing. He got up. He hit Hipper in the face. Hipper went down on to the grass with a crash. He lay there looking at Vallon.

Vallon said : " Get up and talk, baby. I'm sick of you. What's the big idea ? What are you doing around here ? If you don't talk I'm going to work on you."

Hipper got slowly to his feet. " Look, Mr. Vallon . . .

sometimes a man finds himself in a bit of a spot, see ?
Sometimes he tries to do his duty like I have, and all he
gets is a punch in the face."

Vallon said : " For once you're right. And there's more
where that came from. What are you doing here ? You're
an operative employed by the Chennault agency. You
investigated Mrs. Gale's divorce. There was never any
reason why you should see *her*. To say the least of it "—
Vallon grinned to himself at the use of the word—" your
conduct is unprofessional and unethical, and I'm going to
black-list you in every agency in London."

Hipper produced his handkerchief ; tried to staunch the
stream of blood that ran from his nose. " Look, Mr. Vallon.
. . . I've only done my job. Chennault Investigations were
employed to get the evidence of misconduct against Pierce
Gale and I got it. The agency paid me for that. Well,
O.K. . . . supposing for the sake of argument I found that
there was some irregularity about those proceedings—
nothing to do with the agency but something that Mrs.
Gale ought to know. What's my duty ? I don't have to
talk to the agency about it. It's got nothing to do with
them. They'd done their job when the report and evidence
went to the Gale lawyers."

Hipper went on : " I've been thinking about this for a
long time. When you told me in the office yesterday that
Mrs. Gale had rung me and told me you were with her,
and asked me what she was to say to you, you were right.
I told her. I tried to advise her for her own good."

Vallon said : " And you've been giving her a little more
advice for her own good ? At four o'clock in the morning.
You were with her when I telephoned. It looks as if it
might have been pretty urgent, doesn't it ? "

" It is urgent," said Hipper.

Vallon asked : " How urgent ? "

" That's my business."

Vallon shrugged his shoulders. " So it's like that, is it ?
You're sitting pretty—so pretty that a white-livered blackmailing skunk like you doesn't even have to be frightened.
For once you must be on the right end of the stick. All
right, Hipper. On your way. But before I'm through with
you I'll fix you. That's a promise."

Hipper said : " You think you're bloody clever, don't

you ? Maybe I'll fix you before you can fix me. And good morning to you."

He walked off down the road.

Vallon opened the door of the car ; sat in the passenger seat. He finished his cigarette ; lighted another one. He inhaled deeply, burning the cigarette quickly. He sat there for five minutes, thinking about Hipper and his newly-found courage—a courage which meant that Hipper, who had always been afraid of everything, now knew that he was safe.

Vallon got out of the car ; threw the cigarette stub away ; walked quickly down the road. He turned into the entrance gates of Ladycourt ; walked quickly round the house to the side door ; opened it. Before him was a thickly carpeted hallway. At the end a flight of stairs.

He went quietly up the stairs. At the top was a double electric light switch. He turned off the light below ; tapped softly on the door opposite ; turned the handle ; entered. He closed the door and stood with his back to it, admiring the scene which was, to say the least of it, attractive.

The bedroom was exquisitely furnished and appointed. The walls were a peculiar pinkish white which made a superb setting for the sea-green curtains, hangings and rugs. On the right, in the centre of the wall, was a canopied bed and in it, wearing an attractive *eau-de-nil* bed-jacket over a lacy nightgown, was Querida Gale, her dark hair tied with a ribbon.

She said : " Good morning, Johnny.   This is a little informal, isn't it ? It seems that you and I are fated to have to hold our conversations in bedrooms. Would you like a cigarette ? " She indicated the box on the table by her bedside.

Vallon walked over ; took a cigarette ; offered her one. She refused. He lighted his own ; stood looking at her.

She said : " Johnny, do I always have to ask you to kiss me ? "

He bent over ; kissed her on the mouth. " Do I always have to go on kissing you ? " He grinned at her.

She said : " I think that smile is a little cynical. Don't you want to, Johnny ? Lots of people would like the chance."

" I'm not lots of people," said Vallon.   " I'm only me."

She said : " Pull up a chair and sit down. I want to talk

94

to you. I was delighted when you rang through just now.
I was thinking about you. I was thinking it would be nice
if you were here. I'd just concluded this interesting thought
when the telephone bell rang. Somehow I knew it would
be you."

Vallon said : " I wonder if you wanted to talk to me
about the same matter as the one I wanted to talk to you
about ? "

" I don't think so. . . . You tell me your story first."

" I haven't got a story," said Vallon. " I haven't any
facts to work on. I've only ideas and theories. But I've
been thinking about Hipper. It's not very easy for me to
talk to him . . . you understand ? But you might be able
to help. Hipper would talk more freely to you than he would
to me. What does he think your husband is going to do ?
What does Hipper mean when he says that Gale is likely
to be difficult ? How can Gale be difficult ? He's committed
misconduct. The case is set down for trial. You'll get your
divorce. There's only one way in which Gale could be
difficult. That is if he had some information about you
which would enable him to get you non-suited by the King's
Proctor. What else could he do ? "

She shrugged her shoulders delicately. " I don't know.
It might be difficult for you to understand, because you
don't know Pierce. He's a very peculiar man and he has
quite a brain in his head." She sighed. " He has a way of
making himself extremely nasty to people he doesn't like,
and usually he gets away with it."

" I see . . ." said Vallon. " What does he look like ? "

She put her hands behind her head. She looked at the
ceiling. Vallon thought that like that she was a very
attractive—a very alluring woman."

She said · " He's tall—just over six feet—and broad, and
very fit. He's forty-four years of age. He drinks a great
deal but it never seems to affect him. He takes lots of
exercise. He's one of those people who, after being up all
night, can take a bath and shave and look as if he'd spent a
week in bed. He has an unlimited reserve of energy. He
has a brain as quick as a flash of lightning." She sighed
again. " Pierce can be a very attractive man when he wants
to. The trouble is he knows he's attractive and he's always
—shall we say—experimenting. He's the sort of man who

gets a trifle bored with a wife after a little while, just because she is his wife, and he's got her. So he's inclined to lose interest in her. What really amuses him is seeing what else he can collect."

Vallon said with a wry smile : " Reduced to a minimum, that means he likes women."

" You put it very succinctly, Mr. Vallon. . . . Would you like to kiss me again ? "

" O.K.," said Vallon. He kissed her. " Now do you mind getting on with it ? "

She went on : " You said that merely meant that he likes women. I suppose that's true. Yet, strangely enough, there's always some material object in Pierce's *amours*. There always seems something connected with any *affaire* which he begins which somehow reacts to his own financial advantage in the long run. Do you understand what I mean ? "

Vallon nodded. " What you mean is he likes women and uses them."

She sighed. " Johnny, I wish I had your aptitude for reducing descriptions to a few words. But, being a woman, I like to talk."

He said : " I'm not stopping you. What sort of women does Gale go for ? Just anybody who can be of use to him in some way ? "

She shook her head. "I wouldn't say that. He's inclined to be selective. He prefers what are usually called nice women. I don't think I've ever known him to be interested in a woman who was ordinary or at all common, uneducated or without some sort of culture. He seems to have a flair for finding women who come up to his standards of beauty and intellect and who also can be of use to him."

Vallon said : " The boy seems to have quite an instinct about the feminine class, doesn't he ? "

She smiled. " You're not feeling jealous by any chance, are you, Johnny ? I've no feeling at all for Pierce now. Any love I had for him died a long time ago."

He said : " I never get jealous of anybody. I think jealousy is a non-constructive and redundant emotion." He smiled at her. " I've always considered it to be a sign of an inferiority complex."

He thought that Querida Gale was much more clever than

appeared on the surface. He admired the way she steered the conversation right away from Hipper. She still hadn't told him what definite thing Hipper knew about Gale. Quite obviously, she didn't intend to.

He asked: " What have you been doing to-night, Querida ? "

She said : " I dined here alone. I took the car ; drove into Torquay. I went to the Imperial ; had one dance with an old boy friend I found in the bar, one small whisky and soda, and drove back again. I was in bed by eleven o'clock."

" And you haven't been asleep ? You've been lying awake from eleven o'clock until four in the morning thinking about whatever it is you wanted to see me about."

She said : " That's right."

" That's a lot of thought. You can think an awful lot in five hours," said Vallon.

She nodded. " Some subjects require much more than five hours' thinking about. I found this matter rather intriguing and not unattractive." She smiled at him—a slow, delightful smile. " In point of fact I liked it so much that I went on thinking the same thing over and over again. It amused me. That's why I was so delighted when the phone bell rang. My instinct told me that the subject of my thoughts was somewhere in the neighbourhood."

" The subject of your thoughts being either Hipper or me ? "

She said : " I certainly shouldn't be amused by thinking about Mr. Hipper, nor should I consider the subject attractive. I told you what dealings I'd had with him. He thought he'd done what he considered to be his duty and that was that."

Vallon said : " I see . . ."

She said softly : " Johnny, don't you want to know what I was thinking about you ? "

" If you want me to know, you'll tell me," said Vallon. " Lots of people think all sorts of things about me—some of them not so good."

" You can take it from me," she said, " that I was thinking the nicest things. I was thinking that it might be a lot of fun, Johnny, to be married to you."

" You don't say ? " said Vallon. " Is this a proposal ? "

" Why not ? " she asked.

" What do you know about me ? " he said. " Do you always take chances like that ? Haven't you learned anything from your marriage to Gale ? "

She laughed. " That was my first marriage. That was different." She smiled at him mischievously. " And I wasn't suggesting that I proposed to allow you five thousand a year, Johnny."

He made a face at her. " I thought there'd be a catch in it somewhere."

She turned towards him. " There's something about you that's very intriguing, Johnny, and I don't quite know what it is. But I think you're quite a man. I think you've got a brain in your head and I think, if you married a woman, you'd look after her." She smiled again. " Whether she wanted it or not. In point of fact, I think you're quite a person. This divorce with Pierce ought to be through fairly soon. My lawyers say that the decree nisi might be granted next month. They handle these things very quickly these days. That means that six weeks after that, if all goes well, I shall be a free woman."

" You'll like that," said Vallon, " won't you ? What did you mean by ' if all goes well ' ? "

She shrugged her shoulders. " I don't know . . . it's just an expression that one uses. In spite of Mr. Hipper's warning I don't see any serious reason why everything *shouldn't* go well."

" All right," said Vallon. " So six weeks after the decree nisi you're going to be a free woman. And then ? "

" Do I have to say it all again ? " she asked. " I was suggesting that six weeks after the decree nisi you might like to consider proposing to me *after* I've already proposed to you."

Vallon asked : " Why ? "

" I'm not unattractive, am I, Johnny ? I've got money. You have quite a lot of brains and with my money and your brains we could go places. You could start in something that is worthy of you. I know you'd be successful."

Vallon said : " There isn't any other reason, is there, besides my attraction and my brains ? "

She raised her eyebrows. " What other reasons could there be ? "

98

Vallon shrugged his shoulders. " Maybe you think you're going to need a bodyguard even after you're free from Gale. Maybe you think that he could still be ' difficult ' after the divorce. Maybe you'd like to have somebody hanging around." He smiled at her. It was a cynical smile.

She looked at him for a long time. Then : " You've quite an instinct, haven't you, Johnny ? But this time I don't think it's working very well. When I'm free of Gale I shan't be concerned about him. Why should I be ? "

He said : " Meaning that you're rather badly concerned about him now ? "

" Yes . . . in a way I suppose I am. He's a man who does the oddest things, who plans the oddest things and seems to go through with them successfully. I've told you what the position is. Under the settlement he gets five thousand a year from me until he is divorced. I've told you that I don't think he likes the idea of losing that amount of money. It's quite a lot, you know."

Vallon nodded. " Quite a piece of money. The thing that intrigues me is that Gale apparently agreed quite willingly to this divorce ; that he provided the evidence ; that he did everything you asked him. It seems to me that only since the action has been started has his attitude changed. I wonder why, Querida?"

He looked at her. He was smiling. She thought when he smiled in that way—only with his mouth and not with his eyes—he looked a little frightening.

She shrugged her shoulders again. " I don't know," she said.

" Don't you ? " asked Vallon. " Well, why don't you ask Hipper ? He has to know something, hasn't he ? He couldn't just receive a message out of the blue that Gale was going to be difficult. He must have got some sort of information from somewhere. You're not telling me that Hipper came all the way from Somerset to meet you at the Continental, at his own expense, just to tell you that he had some vague idea that somebody might somehow be difficult some time. Why don't you talk, Querida ? My instinct's not so bad sometimes, you know, and my instinct tells me you're lying like hell."

He got up from the chair ; stood looking down at her, still smiling the same slow, twisted smile.

She said : " I think you're being very unpleasant, Johnny. I don't think you're being nice to me."

" I'm not trying to be nice to anybody. I'm trying to do a job of work."

She said : " I hoped it wouldn't be an unpleasant job. You can't say I've been ungenerous."

" Oh, you mean the cheque ? " said Vallon. " Thank you for that. I assure you the money will be very useful." He went on : " Do you know what I think ? "

She looked away from him. " No . . . I'd like to know, Johnny."

He said : " I think that your proposal of marriage to me is tied up with the fact that you're scared about what Pierce is going to do. I think you have an idea in your head that if I agreed to marry you when this thing is over, you'd talk. But until you feel you've some sort of hold over me you're not going to trust me. Because this thing between you and Gale—whatever it is—is sufficiently tough to make you want to keep it to yourself—not to tell anybody unless you know that they're safe. And you don't *know* that I'm safe. You only *think* I am."

She said : " Johnny, I don't like you in this mood. I don't like your frame of mind."

" No ? You mean you only like me when I'm doing what I'm told. You only like me when I'm believing everything you say and agreeing to do what you want." He went on : " I think you're a very nice woman, Querida. I like you a lot, but I don't have to marry anybody just because she wants to get some sort of hold over me so that she knows she's safe. If I marry a woman it'll be for a lot of other reasons besides that."

She said acidly : " I should have thought the other reasons might not have been unattractive, Johnny."

" You're telling me ! " said Vallon.

He walked away ; moved towards the door. " I'll put the light out downstairs when I go out. Do you know what the Americans mean when they say ' talking turkey ' ? "

" Yes . . . it means talking hard sense or the truth, doesn't it ? "

" That's right," said Vallon. " Any time you feel like talking turkey you ring me up and we'll have another meeting. Until then *au revoir*, my sweet. I'll be seeing you. If I find out what you're thinking first and what it's all about, maybe I'll ring you. So long."

He went out. He closed the door softly behind him. She heard his footsteps descending the stairs very quietly. She put her hands behind her head; lay there for a few minutes looking at the ceiling. Then she turned over and buried her face in the pillows. She began to sob bitterly.

2

The doctor said: "You're losing weight and I think your nerves could be better. Perhaps you've been taking too little veganin and too much whisky."

"Maybe," said Vallon.

The doctor pushed a box of cigarettes over to Vallon. "You'd better have another one. How many are you smoking a day?"

"About seventy I should think," Vallon answered.

The doctor sat back in his chair. He said: "Remember yesterday?"

"Yes . . . I remember yesterday."

"What did you eat during the day?" the doctor asked. "I never eat in the morning. I always have coffee," said Vallon. "I had half a sandwich for lunch. I was given some chicken in the evening, but I didn't like it. I made up on whisky and Bacardi."

The doctor smiled. "What is it, Johnny—money or a woman?"

Vallon said: "Be your age! Those are two things I never worry about."

The doctor shrugged his shoulders. "If you don't eat, and you smoke and drink as you do, even if you're not worrying about money or some woman, even a man as tough as you are is going to come up against it some time. Are you getting any sleep?"

"Yes," said Vallon. "Sometimes . . . not very often."

"Why don't you take a holiday?"

"It's a hell of a good idea. I think I will," said Vallon.

"Do that . . . get away to-morrow. Stay away for six weeks. Get plenty of sun and air and food."

Vallon grinned. "I wasn't thinking about to-morrow. I

101

was thinking about next year maybe. All this is very good but it doesn't help the pain in my guts. That worries me, you know. Anything else ? "

The doctor said : " When you stop worrying about *something* maybe you'll get rid of the pain in your stomach. That's just a reminiscent pain brought on by mental strain. You understand ? "

" O.K.," said Vallon. " You eggs must make a lot of money like this." He grinned at the doctor. " I'll be seeing you."

He went out.

.   .   .   .

Vallon sat on a high stool in the bar in Jermyn Street ; lighted a cigarette.

The bar-tender said : " Believe it or not, sir, we've got a bottle of ' Old Crow '—the finest bourbon in the world."

Vallon smiled. " That's made my day. Give me a lot of it and some water."

He drank some bourbon ; sat looking at the row of bottles behind the bar, thinking about the broken drawer in Joe Chennault's office. It was sticking out like Brighton pier, he thought, that whoever had come to see Joe, whoever had killed him, had wanted something—something that was in that drawer. That was the only drawer smashed. Whatever Joe had put in the drawer was something that was special because in that drawer he only kept a bottle of whisky. So he'd put something in there that he didn't want mixed up with anything else. That would be a document or paper of some sort—maybe a letter. Whoever had killed Joe wanted the letter or the paper or whatever it was. They'd known where to look for it.

Vallon drank some more bourbon. He began to think about the day on which Joe had died. He thought it was pretty tough that he had to meet Madeleine on that day. If he'd gone straight back to the office he wouldn't have met Strype. He wouldn't have gone to the bar in Jermyn Street. He wouldn't have heard Strype describe his meeting with Madeleine and talk about the jade ring. He wouldn't have found Madeleine. If he'd gone straight back to the office and seen Joe, Joe would probably have been alive and because he *hadn't* gone back to the office Joe had died, and because Joe had died and he'd wanted to do something about it, forgetting everything else, he'd lost Madeleine. He thought that was damned funny. He thought life was like that. Then he thought that thinking like that didn't get you anywhere . . . much.

He remembered his meeting with Madeleine at her apartment. He remembered the perfume she wore ; the feel of the soft ruffles at her wrists when they pressed against him when she put her arms round his neck. He remembered going into Joe's office and seeing Joe slumped over the desk, with the *Evening News*, on which Joe had been doodling, lying on the desk in front of him. A mental picture of the folded newspaper came to his mind, and Joe's doodling : " *Vallon . . Vallon . . . Vallon. . . . Johnny . . . Johnny . . . Johnny. . . . B.B.C. B.B.C. B.B.C. . . . 1 o'clock . . .*"

He sat up with a jerk. Collusion even with a " K "—the word Joe had doodled out of the *Evening News* heading— " *Holiday Train Collision* "—meant the same thing in every language, and it meant a hell of a lot in a divorce action. Vallon whistled softly between his teeth. Now he was getting somewhere. So maybe there was evidence of collusion somewhere—*the one thing that would certainly non-suit a petitioner in a divorce case*. Maybe somehow Joe had got a line on it. He had evidence of it—proof of it—so he'd stuck it in the bottom drawer. Somebody had to have it—somebody who wanted the divorce to go through— because evidence of collusion would stop it going through. Who would that be ?

Vallon grinned to himself. That might be an easy one ! The person who wanted the divorce to go through was Querida Gale. The person who didn't want it to go through was Pierce Gale.

Vallon got up. He paid his bill ; lighted a cigarette. He thought the cigarette tasted like brown paper. He went out ; got into his car and drove back to the office. He went into Chennault's room ; sat at the desk ; rang for Marvin.

When Marvin came in he said : " I've had a report on Hipper's movements after he left here yesterday, Mr. Vallon. He——"

Vallon interrupted. " That's all right, Marvin . . . I know where Hipper went." He went on : " You've got a good memory, haven't you ? There's damned little you forget. Take your mind back to last Tuesday—the day before Joe Chennault died. What happened around here ? "

Marvin shrugged his shoulders. " Just the ordinary routine."

Vallon asked : " Where was Hipper ? "

" He was in Somerset," said Marvin, " making inquiries on a case. He came back on Wednesday."

" That's right," said Vallon.

" Mr. Vallon . . . what's in your mind ? " asked Marvin. " If you told me maybe I could help you."

Vallon sat back in his chair. " All right. Can you remember anything funny—any incongruity—any odd thing that happened in this office during the two or three days before Joe's death ? "

Marvin said : " Yes . . . I can. . . ."

" In connection with what ? " asked Vallon.

" With Hipper . . ." Marvin thought for a moment. " Hipper went down to Somerset on that job last Friday. He came into the office at eleven o'clock. He went into the staff-room. I went in there to tell him he could go down to Somerset. While I was talking to him he was taking off his coat. He was going into the lavatory to wash his hands. I came out through the connecting door ; walked through the main office into my own room. When I was going through the main office Mr. Chennault passed me. He stood at the door of the staff-room. He was waiting. He waited for a few moments ; then he went into the staff-room."

Vallon grinned. " You mean he was probably waiting for Hipper to get good and busy washing his hands before he went in ? Is that it ? "

Marvin said : " Perhaps. I never thought of that."

" The point is," said Vallon, " that Hipper left his coat hanging up in the staff room while he went to wash his hands. Joe Chennault passed you in the main office ; gave Hipper time to start washing before he went into the staff-room."

Marvin said slowly : " Yes . . . that's about it."

" O.K. . . ." Vallon sat back in the chair. He smoked for quite a while. " All right," he said. " On that particular day and until Joe died what was every member of the staff doing ? Go and get the register."

Marvin went out. He returned in a few minutes with a time register—a big loose-leaf, foolscap book. He began to read through the names of the operatives—the work on which they were employed—the times they went out and the times they came in—the cases on which they were engaged. When he'd finished Vallon said:

"What about Lipscombe? His name's not down there."

"No, it wouldn't be, Mr. Vallon. Lipscombe was on a special job. He was working for Mr. Chennault—something confidential that wasn't to go through the books."

Vallon asked: "Where's Lipscombe?"

"I don't know. He hasn't been in since Mr. Chennault died. For all I know he may not even know he's dead."

"I see," said Vallon. "Put a man in a cab and send him round to Lipscombe's private address. Tell him to pick Lipscombe up and bring him back here. Find him. I want to talk to him. And make it snappy."

"Very well, Mr. Vallon." Marvin went out.

Vallon lighted another cigarette. He began to think about the doctor. He thought it was a hell of an idea to give up smoking and drinking. He thought maybe smoking and drinking upset the stomach, which was a sensitive sort of place, and knocked you for the loop. One day he'd get around to that. He'd give up smoking and drinking and everything else, including living. He thought that might be just as amusing.

The telephone bell jangled. The girl on the office switchboard said: "A Mr. Trant to speak to you, Mr. Vallon."

Trant came through. He said: "Good afternoon. I'm in a very attractive bar called the Carousel in Piccadilly. The Bacardi's very nice here."

Vallon said: "O.K. I'll be with you."

He picked up his black, soft hat; walked into Marvin's room. He said: "If you find Lipscombe keep him here till I come back."

Marvin asked: "Do you know what time you'll be back, Mr. Vallon?"

Vallon said: "How the hell do I know? I don't know anything."

Ten minutes later he pulled up in Piccadilly by the Green Park gates. He crossed the road; went into the Carousel.

Trant was sitting at a sofa table, drinking. Vallon went over. He ordered a large Bacardi.

Trant said: "You're not looking so well, Mr. Vallon. You look tired."

Vallon said: "O.K. I look tired. Somebody once told me that if enough people tell you you look tired you die. We'll count you as number one. What goes on?"

Trant said: "Miss Evangeline Roberta Trickett. It wasn't difficult."

"Tell me," said Vallon.

Trant went on: "Miss Trickett is a rather attractive woman. She looks very nice. Maybe she's a little common but she's very easy on the eye. She's got an apartment in St. John's Wood—quite a nice apartment. She seems to make out very nicely, and she wears some very nice clothes."

Vallon asked: "How does she get the clothes?"

"It's funny," said Trant. "I had a bit of luck about this baby. I met a man I knew. Did you ever hear of a firm called Sulkin & Frash?"

"No . . ." said Vallon. "Should I have heard about them?"

Trant said: "You'd be surprised! They call themselves a detective agency, and they specialise in finding lady co-respondents for gentlemen who want somebody to sleep with so that they can get a divorce. Got it?"

"I've got it. They find the co-respondent and then they find the evidence. They have it both ways. Does Trickett work for these people?"

Trant grinned. "She is Sulkin and Frash. She owns the business. I think she's very good, don't you!"

Vallon thought for a moment; then he said: "Listen, supposing somebody wanted to engage the services of Miss Trickett, what's the form?"

"That's easy," said Trant. "The form is this: Somebody wants a divorce. Mrs. X is fed up with Mr. X and wants a divorce. So Mr. X has to go and commit misconduct somewhere. Maybe he hasn't got a co-respondent and maybe be doesn't know one, so usually he's put on to Sulkin & Frash by somebody or other. So he rings through to Sulkin & Frash and he talks to somebody there. He makes an appointment and he goes round there. While he's having his appointment Miss Trickett is looking through a hole in the wall and if she likes the look of the proposition, it's O.K. It costs fifty guineas plus expenses. And there you are ! "

Vallon said : " I see. Mr. X and Miss Trickett have an appointment at some hotel somewhere as man and wife, and then Sulkin & Frash come in the next morning and pick up the evidence. Right ? "

" That's right," said Trant.

Vallon asked : " Have you got the Sulkin & Frash address and telephone number ? "

Trant nodded. " Here's their address and telephone number and here's her address and telephone number."

" O.K., Trant. Stick around."

Trant said : " I'm still on leave from the firm, so I'll stick around at home in case you want me." He handed Vallon a card. " My private address and phone. Any time you want me. I'll be around."

" O.K. I don't think you're through yet, Trant. Go home and wait for a call. I'll pay for your drink."

Trant said : " Thanks." He got up. " I'll be seeing you, Mr. Vallon." He went out.

Vallon finished the Bacardi. In the left-hand corner of the lounge was a telephone box. He walked over to it. He dialled Sulkin & Frash's number.

After a moment a man's voice came on the line.

Vallon said : " Good afternoon. Your firm has been recommended to me by my lawyers—a country firm. I'd like to come along and see you sometime."

The voice asked : " In connection with what ? "

" In connection with a divorce," said Vallon " My name's Lennox—John C. Lennox. When can I see you ? "

" Any time this afternoon," said the voice. " How would three o'clock suit you, Mr. Lennox ? "

" That would be very nice. I'll be with you."

Vallon hung up ; went back to the sofa seat ; ordered another Bacardi.

* * * * * * * *

It was two minutes past three when Vallon went into the waiting-room at Messrs. Sulkin & Frash in a small street off Clerkenwell. He thought the pictorial decorations on the wall were good. One was " The Stag At Bay " and the other was a flowered text which said " Love Makes Our

107

Home." Vallon thought that " The Stag At Bay " in connection with " Love Makes Our Home " was a pretty good indication of the mentality of Messrs. Sulkin & Frash.

At the end of three minutes an anaemic young woman with a wart directly on the end of her nose poked her head round the door and said : " Will you come in, Mr. Lennox ? "

Vallon went in. This was a smaller office. There was a cheap desk at one end of it ; a few chairs. Sitting behind the desk was a broad-shouldered individual with a florid complexion and a bulbous nose.

He said : " Pleased to meet you, Mr. Lennox. What can we do for you ? "

The anaemic looking girl went out and closed the door.

Vallon said : " Look, I suppose this is confidential, isn't it ? "

" I'm Mr. Sulkin," said the man. " I'll give you my word that nothing that happens in this office goes outside these four walls." His tone was almost dramatic. He went on in a lower tone : " What's the trouble, Mr. Lennox ? You can talk to me as if I were your father."

Vallon said : " I'm having a spot of trouble with Mrs. Lennox. She thinks I've been a bad boy, so she thinks we've been married long enough."

" It's a great shame," said Sulkin. " It's a very great shame, Mr. Lennox. When distrust sticks its ugly nose into the home anything can happen. But that's life, isn't it ? "

" I suppose so. The point is that I think if Mrs. Lennox were to catch me out she'd put a petition on the file. I don't think I'd mind that."

Sulkin scratched his nose. " I take it your wife has a firm of solicitors who work for her ? "

Vallon said : " Yes. Their name's Medbury & Hollick of Caterham."

" I see . . ." said Sulkin. " And you think that if we were to get in touch with Messrs. Medbury & Hollick and say that we had a little information for them and notify them that we'd like to see them, and if we told them that we had the necessary evidence that you'd committed misconduct, your wife would go on with this. Right ? "

" That's right," said Vallon.

Sulkin made a note of the address on a pad. He said:

"Our charges for a little matter like this would be sixty guineas. Is that all right, Mr. Lennox? Sixty guineas cash!"

"That's all right by me. Does that include the co-respondent?"

Sulkin grinned. "That includes the co-respondent."

Vallon said: "I hope she's very attractive."

"You need not worry," smirked Sulkin. "You want a divorce, don't you? You're not starting a harem, I take it, Mr. Lennox?" He grinned archly.

Vallon said: "I'll bring you sixty-three pounds inside an hour. But I've got to have speed with this, see? I want to move before Mrs. Lennox begins to change her mind. You know what women are?"

"Yes . . . yes indeed," said Sulkin. "Excuse me for a moment." He opened the door behind his desk; went out. He returned in three minutes and said: "That's all right. We can get moving as soon as you like providing we have the cash as you said."

"I told you the money would be here in an hour. Can you fix this for to-night?"

Sulkin nodded. "When you bring the cash round I'm going to give you the address of a very nice little hotel—one of those quiet country places, you know. They've got a bar and everything, and the liquor's good. It's thirty miles outside London. Is that too far for you?"

"That suits me very well," said Vallon.

"All right. When you come back with the money I'll give you the address. If you go there at nine o'clock to-night you'll find that Mrs. Lennox is already registered there. She's arrived with her baggage, registered in the hotel and told them her husband's joining her between nine and ten. The number of her room will be twenty-four on the second floor. That's your girl friend. We'll be along to-morrow or the next day and pick up the evidence. Will that suit you?"

Vallon said: "Perfectly. This is a very efficient organisation." He got up.

"We try to make it so," sighed Sulkin. "Glad to see you in an hour's time, Mr. Lennox."

Vallon went out. As he walked down the stairs he thought

that it was very true that half the world didn't know how the other half lived.

. . . .

Vallon was drinking tea in Chennault's office when Marvin brought Lipscombe in.

Vallon said : " O.K., Marvin . . . Sit down, Lipscombe." He indicated the chair on the opposite side of the desk. He pushed the box of cigarettes over to Lipscombe ; took a long look at him. Lipscombe was a lean-faced, greying man of fifty. He wore a dark grey suit, a neat tie. His linen was fresh ; his shoes well cleaned. Vallon liked the look of him.

He said : " Lipscombe, for some little time you've been doing a job for Mr. Chennault What was it ? "

There was a pause. Lipscombe looked at the end of his cigarette. " It was a personal job for Mr. Chennault. He told me I wasn't to discuss it with anybody. I don't see how I can, Mr. Vallon."

" All right," said Vallon. " Maybe I can help you. You're the oldest operative working with this firm. You were one of the administrative clerks in the office of Strategic Services in China. You worked with Joe Chennault then. He liked you and he trusted you. That's why he put you on that job. He asked you to watch his wife—Dolores Chennault—didn't he ? "

Lipscombe smiled. " You seem to know all about it, Mr. Vallon. It's not much good my arguing. In any event, I know what Mr. Chennault thought about you. I know you were his best friend."

" All right," said Vallon. " Shoot. Why did he want to have his wife watched ? "

Lipscombe shrugged his shoulders. " I don't think he was very happy about Mrs. Chennault. He hadn't been for two or three weeks. He put me on to this about ten days ago. I think he had some sort of idea in his head."

Vallon asked : " What gave him the idea ? Can you make a guess ? "

Lipscombe nodded. " He told me a certain amount. He didn't like doing it either. He was a proud sort of man, you know, Mr. Vallon."

Vallon said : " I know. Well . . . ? "

" I have an idea that Mrs. Chennault got herself in a spot

110

with some man," said Lipscombe. " A man called Perdreau. I think she was a little worried about Perdreau and she'd spoken to Mr. Chennault about him. I think the idea was that when this Perdreau came to London Mr. Chennault was going to get in touch with him ; have a talk with him."

" And scare him off ? " said Vallon.

" Something like that," said Lipscombe. " That's what I understood."

Vallon lighted a cigarette. He finished the cup of tea ; pushed the cup away from him. He asked : " Do you know anything about Joe Chennault seeing this Perdreau ? "

" Yes . . . I think he was interested to know when Perdreau was coming up to town, and I think he relied on Mrs. Chennault for that information. He went home on the morning of the day he died. I think he went to see her about something. When he came back I was in the office. He gave me Perdreau's number and told me to ring through and see if he was in. I got the number on the private line from this office. Perdreau was in and Mr. Chennault spoke to him. I don't know what he said. I'd left the room."

Vallon said : " That's good enough. I suppose you'd been keeping tabs on Mrs. Chennault in the evenings ? "

Lipscombe nodded.

" What did she do ? " asked Vallon.

" She's been very difficult to tail," said Lipscombe. " As you know, Mr. Vallon, tailing a person is a difficult job for one man. I've always believed in using three or four operatives in a thing like that. But apparently Mr. Chennault didn't want anyone else in the office to know about it. Mainly, she used to go a club in the evenings—down the river near Chertsey—a night club. Sometimes she'd get there about six and stay till ten. One or two nights she went there late, arriving about eleven o'clock. Those nights she left at two or three in the morning."

Vallon asked : " Did you ever get inside the place ? And what was it called ? "

" I never got inside. I couldn't very well ; she knew me of course, and if she'd spotted me it'd have been all up. She'd probably have guessed what was going on. The place is called the Mandrake. It looks quite a decent sort of place. The people who go there seem fairly good-class people. The cars parked outside are expensive cars.

"Was there anything funny about the place?" asked Vallon. "Do they specialise in anything or is it a straight drinking club?"

"I think it's straight enough," said Lipscombe. "All the inquiries I made about it pointed to that. People go there to have dinner—they tell me the food is pretty good—and dance. I think a lot of drinking goes on."

"I suppose it closes at midnight," said Vallon.

Lipscombe nodded. "It closes at midnight, but as I've told you sometimes Mrs. Chennault came out at two or three in the morning."

Vallon asked: "When she came out—on the late nights I mean—how did she look?"

"A little tight, I should say. I never got very close to her. There were two entrances to the club—the main entrance in the front and a smaller exit at the back. I think that led direct to the offices. There's a little bar between the offices and the main restaurant. Maybe she used that. I used to stand in the shrubbery at the side of the house, from which I could watch both entrances. I never got very close to her but one night—one of the late nights—she was definitely very high. She nearly fell over when she was getting into the car."

"Whose car was it?" asked Vallon. "Did she use a taxi?"

"Never a taxi," said Lipscombe. "I should say by the look of the driver it was a hired car. It hadn't a Hackney Carriage plate on it but it looked to me like a hired car. You can always tell them. You know what I mean?"

"Yes, I know. Did you ever see her with any man there? Did any man ever come out with her?"

"No," said Lipscombe. "I thought that was funny. You'd have thought somebody would have come to the door with her; seen her into the car. Nobody ever did."

Vallon looked at the end of his cigarette. He asked: "What sort of woman do you think Mrs. Chennault is, if you know what I mean?"

"I know what you mean, Mr. Vallon. Personally, I don't think she's so hot, if you understand me. She likes getting around. I don't think she's a bad piece "—he smiled a little wryly—" by that I mean I don't think she intends to be bad. I think she gets carried away by circumstances. She's a very attractive woman and maybe she got bored a little with Mr. Chennault. I think he thought that too. I found it very difficult to keep tabs on her. It isn't as if we'd had someone inside the flat who could listen to telephone calls and when she made dates. Mr. Chennault helped me as much as he could by creating situations by which he could send me round to the apartment suddenly without notice to fetch something ; to deliver a note or look up one of the files he kept in his own room in the apartment. But I never got on to anything."

Vallon asked : " When was the last time you went round there ? "

" The day after Mr. Chennault died," said Lipscombe. " She rang up and asked me to go round." He smiled again. " I think she likes me. She knew I'd been with her husband for a long time ; that we were friends in a way."

" What did she want you for ? " asked Vallon.

" It was about disposing of some of Mr. Chennault's things. She'd got them all laid out—clothes and his watches and tie-pins, and things like that. She said she couldn't bear the idea of selling any of them and she was going to give them away. She gave me a tie-pin and his wrist-watch because I'd been with him so long. I'm wearing the watch now. It's a good watch."

" And his clothes and other things ? " asked Vallon.

" She'd already had a parcel made of his clothes," said Lipscombe. " I think she said she knew somebody that he liked—someone who was about his build—a big man. I had the idea she was going to send the clothes to him. I wondered about that."

Vallon asked : " Why ? "

Lipscombe spread his hands. " Well, you know Mr. Chennault wasn't particular about clothes. He wasn't a dressy man. He only had two or three suits and used to wear a suit right out before he got a new one. It seemed funny to send things like that away. Maybe the man she sent them to was friendly enough to be sentimental and would like to have them. But I just wondered."

Vallon said : " Anything else—anything that you can put your finger on—anything that you think might help ? "

" If I knew what was in your mind, Mr. Vallon, I might

get an idea, but I don't know what you're thinking of. I don't even know why you're interested."

"All right," said Vallon. "I'll tell you. I think somebody killed Chennault. He had angina pectoris. He'd nearly passed out with it half a dozen times. It's my belief that somebody who knew how he was physically came round here and took a shot at him with a blank cartridge out of an automatic with a silencer on it. They knew damned well the shock would kill him."

Lipscombe whistled. "That's not so good, is it, Mr. Vallon? And it's a funny situation. They're burying him to-day. The death certificate's in order. His own doctor signed it. If you're right, it means a lot of trouble."

"Does it?" asked Vallon. "You mean an exhumation?"

Lipscombe nodded.

Vallon went on: "What the hell's the good of it if they do? Why dig him up? He died from shock. But nobody's going to know what caused the shock. The doctor said he died from angina which is practically the same thing. There are no marks on the body."

Lipscombe said: "Well, it's going to be very hard to make a murder charge stick. The circumstantial evidence, if there is any, will have to be very good."

Vallon said: "Circumstantial evidence can be damned good. Unless somebody's tried to get rid of it. All right, Lipscombe, you can lay off Mrs. Chennault." He grinned. "Joe wouldn't be interested in what she's doing, now . . . well . . . I shouldn't think so. I'll tell you what you can do—get down to Chertsey or wherever it is and make a few inquires. Find out who owns the Mandrake; whether it's a limited liability company or whether it's owned by some individual. Get me the names of the habitués of the place."

Lipscombe got up. "O.K., Mr. Vallon. I'll have that probably by to-morrow. That shouldn't be difficult. Good day, sir." He went out.

Vallon rang for another cup of tea. He drank it slowly. He thought it was a very stimulating fluid, but not so good as either whisky or Bacardi. It didn't do anything to quieten his stomach down.

When he'd finished the tea he drew sixty-three pounds from the office Contingency Account. He spoke to Marvin;

went down to his car ; drove to the offices of Sulkin & Frash.

He gave Sulkin the sixty-three pounds. In exchange he got a slip of paper. On it was written : " *Room 24, The Mayfly Fisher's Hotel, Strete, Near Guildford.*" Vallon put the piece of paper in his pocket.

Sulkin said : " Any time to-night after nine-thirty will be all right, Mr. Lennox. What time do you think you'll be leaving to-morrow morning ? "

" I wouldn't know," said Vallon. " Possibly that depends on the lady."

" You'll find she's first-class and a very nice woman—cultured too, Mr. Lennox."

Vallon grinned. " What's her name—apart from the fact that she's now Mrs. John Lennox for twenty-four hours ? "

Sulkin said : " She's got a pretty name. It's Evangeline Roberta Trickett. A very nice girl. Very discreet. I take it you'll be away from the hotel by eleven to-morrow morning ? "

Vallon nodded. " I certainly shall. I'll probably leave earlier than that."

" All right," said Sulkin. " I'll have a man in there at twelve o'clock. He should be back here with the evidence by three or four. Then I'll somehow get a message through to Mrs. Lennox's lawyers and they can get cracking."

Vallon said : " Thanks. So long."

" Good-bye, Mr. Lennox," said Sulkin heartily. " And the best of luck to you."

Vallon went out. He thought maybe he was going to need it.

He drove to his rooms. He had some more tea ; sat looking at the empty grate. He was thinking about Madeleine. He was thinking that if she knew what was breaking she'd be vaguely amused. He wondered what she'd think about Miss Trickett. He decided that if he went on drinking tea he would have no desire to drink whisky or Bacardi. He thought that was a good idea. He poured himself out another cup of tea ; looked at it ; went to the sideboard and mixed a large whisky and soda. As he drank it he thought that man was a contrary sort of animal.

.   .   .   .

The Mayfly Fisher's Hotel was one of those " Olde

Worlde " places, set in a remote part of the countryside, that never seem to have anybody staying in them. They exist somehow from year to year looking attractive and remote and peaceful. They make money somehow. Nobody knows how and nobody seems to care. Maybe Messrs. Sulkin & Frash could supply the answers.

It was nine-thirty when Vallon stopped his car on the edge of the main road and took a long look at The Mayfly Fisher's. He thought it was a nice place. Most of the places he visited these days seemed nice. He thought perhaps it was his imagination or perhaps it was because they looked quiet and peaceful. Maybe, he thought, what he needed was a spot of peace. He thought that might be nice.

The hotel stood off the main road inside an attractive white paling fence. There was a well-kept lawn in front and rhododendron bushes set about the place in profusion.

Vallon started up the car, drove through the wide gate in the white fence and pulled up on the right-hand side of the hotel. Behind the place was a well-kept kitchen garden and shrubbery, with a garage over on the left.

He took his suitcase from the boot and went into the hotel. There was a reception office in the imitation oak-lined hall, and a grey-haired woman sat inside it, knitting what looked like a jumper.

Vallon walked across and leaned on the counter. He smiled at her. He said : " My name's Lennox. I believe my wife has already arrived ? "

She put down her knitting ; got up. " That's right, Mr. Lennox. She's had dinner—and she registered for you both. Your room is No. 24—bath and a small sitting-room attached. Shall I send your bag up ? "

Vallon shook his head. " I'll carry it. Did Mrs. Lennox order any drinks ? "

" She had a gin and lime," said the woman. " Would you like something sent up ? "

He nodded. " Send up a bottle of whisky, some soda water and ice," he said.

He walked over to the wide staircase ; up the carpeted stairs. He was thinking of Evangeline Roberta Trickett and her reactions.

He thought he wouldn't have to worry about the reactions. Not after he'd outlined the situation generally. Miss

116

Trickett, he thought, would have to play ball whether she liked it or not—and that she would *not* like it was a certainty.

He walked along the corridor to No. 24. He opened the door and went in. The room was a small, prettily furnished sitting-room with chintz curtains and chair covers. The place was neat and attractive. In the left wall, in the far corner, next to the bay window, was a door. Vallon tapped on it, opened it, and went into the bedroom.

He said : " Hey . . . Evangeline ! " He closed the door behind him ; stood, his suitcase in his hand, looking at her.

He thought she was worth it !

Evangeline Roberta Trickett was a young woman of twenty-seven or eight years of age, of middle height, with an extremely attractive figure, a complexion like Grade " A " milk, an exceptionally fine pair of legs, and a lot of light chestnut hair that fell delightfully over her shoulders.

She was sitting at the dressing-table doing things to her mouth with a lipstick. She wore black lace underclothes, with a gold wrap, worked with black Chinese dragons, over them. She wore the sheerest silk stockings and black satin pumps spangled with gold stars. Miss Trickett was a " looker " and knew it.

She said : " Hallo . . . Pal ! " Her voice, Vallon thought, was the nearest approach to the call of the corncrake that he had ever heard. It rasped. He thought that anyhow it would be impossible for a woman who looked as good as Evangeline to have a soothing voice as well as the other things. It would have been too good to be true—almost an embarrassment.

Vallon walked across the room ; put his suitcase on a chair with his hat. Then he sat down on the bed, looking at Miss Trickett's attractive back.

She spun round on the cushioned stool. She smiled at him—a long, languorous smile. She said : " Well . . . I'm glad to see you, and it's not the first time I've seen you, Mr. John C. Lennox. I s'pose that surprises you . . . hey, baby ? "

He said : " No . . . you were looking through a hole in the wall when I saw Sulkin this afternoon. Right ? "

She raised her eyebrows. " How the hell did *you* know that ? "

117

Vallon grinned. " A girl like you is too good-looking and too nice to take a chance on a man until she's had a look at him."

She pushed a tendril of hair back into place. " You got brains. Brains an' personality. D'reckly I saw you I said to myself, I said : Here's a guy with brains *an'* personality, I said. An' in nine hundred an' ninety cases out of a thousand, little Evangeline is right. Only you don't have to call me Evangeline. It sounds just like some bleedin' shepherdess. My pals all call me Bobbie . . . see ? "

Vallon nodded. " I see . . . Bobbie . . ."

She smiled ; stretched, her hands behind her head. She said : " Don't you think a drink's indicated ? I always say have a drink an' get to know each other. There's nothin' like a spot of the old alk for making acquaintances into friends—if you get me . . . see ? "

" I've ordered a bottle of whisky and some ice." He listened. " That's the waiter bringing it into the sitting-room now. Let you and me go and have a little drink."

She got up. In the process she managed the wrap so perfectly that it showed just enough leg.

Vallon said : " Did anybody ever tell you that you've got lovely legs ? "

She smiled at him. He thought that if, by some occult means, her mouth could be permanently closed, she would be almost perfect.

" They told me," she said. " Plenty. But I'm a woman, see ? And you can take it from me, baby, that if a woman's got good legs she likes to hear about it—all the time. Just so's she'll have some memories when her calves go back on her an' her under-pinnin's look like drain-pipes all the way up, see . . . ? " She yawned. " Let's go and have that drink."

She led the way into the sitting-room. The waiter had drawn the curtains ; switched on the lights. The shades were rose-pink. An attractive glow reflected on the chintz furniture. On the table was the whisky, ice bucket, glasses and a siphon.

Vallon poured out a drink. He took it to where she sat, almost curled up in one of the large chintz arm-chairs, a pair of attractive silk-clad knees demurely showing.

She said : " You know, baby, you're a funny one, aren't

you ? You're not like the usual run of men that I meet professionally. I think I like you."

Vallon grinned. " Yes . . . I've got personality ! Right ? "

They both laughed.

Vallon drank a little of the whisky. He began to walk up and down the room. He said : " Look, Bobbie, you and I might as well have a showdown. My name's not Lennox, and I don't want to commit misconduct with anybody, and I don't want a divorce. I'm not even married."

She shot her legs from under her ; sat bolt upright in the chair. Her eyes narrowed. She said in her rasping voice : " What the hell's going on around here ? *What is this ?* "

Vallon said : " Take it easy. There's no need for anybody to get excited. This is just a little professional conversation between detectives, see ? "

" What the hell does that mean ? " she asked.

" My name's Vallon—John Vallon. I'm running the Chennault agency. Ever heard of it ? "

She said : " You bet I have. You mean Joe Chennault—the one that died ? "

He nodded. " That's right. I'm glad to meet somebody in the same line of business. I know all about it, Bobbie. You own Sulkin & Frash. You're the works. The stooge in the office is just somebody you employ to front for you." He grinned. " You're the world's best-looking co-respondent and, believe it or not, I like you."

" Thank you for nothing," she said. " Well, what goes on ? "

Vallon took out his cigarette case ; gave her a cigarette ; lighted it. He said : " I never believe in threatening pretty women, but you know what I mean by a collusive divorce case—that is a case where there's collusion between husband and wife to get a divorce ; where the man goes off and commits technical misconduct in order that his wife may have the necessary evidence to issue a petition. You know all about that. I think you're going to agree, Bobbie, that it's not going to do anybody any good if it's known what Sulkin & Frash are doing. A firm, purporting to be an inquiry agency business, doing nothing but provide a very good-looking co-respondent—you—if she likes the man. It wouldn't be so good for you and it would be the end of Sulkin & Frash."

She said: " What the hell do you care ? What's Sulkin & Frash to you ? " There was a note of fear in her voice.

" Sweet nothing," said Vallon. " Why don't you finish your drink and have another one ? "

" You're telling me . . . I need it. I knew there was something goddam funny about you the first time I saw you. You know what I think ? "

He said: " You tell me . . ."

" You're too good to be true," she said. " You're one of those men who's got something. I wondered why the hell you had to come to a firm like ours. I should have thought you could find co-respondents anywhere, free gratis and for nothing."

He shrugged his shoulders. " Bobbie, I'll tell you what I'll do. I've paid your firm—that is you—sixty-three pounds for this conference. I'll make it up to a hundred. That's fair enough, isn't it ? I want a little information—a little information in confidence between you and me. But I want the truth, the whole truth and nothing but the truth." He smiled at her. " You know that's the legal oath, and I think you'd prefer to tell me the truth, the whole truth and nothing but the truth here rather than tell it in the witness box."

He refilled the glasses.

She asked: " Meaning exactly what ? "

He said: " That Gale divorce case is collusive. Not only is it collusive but its repercussions are going to be pretty good. Do you know what repercussion means ? "

" I can make a guess, baby. You mean there's going to be plenty trouble."

" Right," said Vallon. " Plenty trouble. You wouldn't like to get tied in on a murder case, would you ? "

She grabbed the arms of the chintz arm-chair. " My God . . . ! What goes on around here ? "

He said: " It doesn't matter. If you don't stick your neck out you'll be all right. You won't come into anything and Sulkin & Frash can go on for ever as far as I'm concerned."

" The joke is I believe you," she said. " This don't look so good to me. How do I *not* stick my neck out ? "

" Just answer a few questions. Don't let your imagination run riot. Just give me the works and nothing else."

She settled back in the chair. She took a gulp at the whisky and soda. She said : " O.K. I'll play ball. Shoot."

He said : " You were the co-respondent in the Gale divorce case. Did Gale come to Sulkin & Frash and engage your services in the usual way ? "

She shook her head. " No . . . I met him. I met him at a night club, see ? " She smiled and bridled a little. " I went for Gale," she said. " He's a hell of a guy, *I* think . . . some man ! He's got something—you know, personality ! One night we were dancing and he told me he needed a co-respondent. I said that was O.K. by me. I said the same thing I just said to you that I should have thought he could get plenty of co-respondents without paying for one. He said : ' I know, but I want to keep somebody out of this.' "

Vallon said : " I know that. He wanted to keep a very good-looking woman out of it—a woman with corn-coloured hair who wears a black pearl necklace. Right. . . . You know what her name is ? "

She nodded. " Her name's Ansteley—Claire Ansteley." He noticed the tone in her voice.

He said : " You don't go for her a lot ? "

She shrugged her shoulders. " Why the heck should I ? I don't think a hell of a lot of her."

Vallon asked · " Why not ? "

She drew on her cigarette. " I'll tell you. I'm in a funny sort of racket, and maybe it wouldn't sound so moral to a clergyman. But I got my standards, see ? Business is one thing, but when you're in love with a guy, that's another."

Vallon nodded. " I know. . . . So what ? "

She said : " This dame Ansteley is in love with a guy named Perdreau. She's stuck on him, see ? She's going to marry him. An' this Perdreau is a nice guy. He's all right, but just now and then he has a wandering eye. He has some sort of quarrel with this Ansteley baby. So he thinks he'll show her where she gets off. So he gives some girl a tumble, see ? An' the Ansteley dame thinks she'll teach him a lesson. So she meets Pierce Gale and Gale falls for her. Well . . ." she smiled cynically—" as much as he falls for anybody. They have a right royal time together." Her voice rose a little. The rasp became shriller. " I don't think she even liked him. What she was trying to do was

121

to get Perdreau good and annoyed. I think she did it, too."

Vallon said: " All right. She was trying to put some other woman's nose out of joint—the woman that Perdreau was getting around with. She wanted to get back at him. Who was the woman ? "

She shrugged her shoulders. " Search me. I don't know. I never found out."

Vallon asked: " Where did you get all this information from ? "

" From Pierce. He used to talk to me sometimes. We got around for quite a bit, you know."

Vallon said: " Did you know that when Pierce Gale used to go and visit his wife at Paignton—she's got a house there called Ladycourt—he used to take this Ansteley girl down and leave her in the car ? I suppose this was at the time that the divorce was being arranged."

She said: " Yes, I knew about that. He never worried about making any secret of it."

Vallon walked up and down the room. After a little while he asked : " What else did he tell you ? "

" Not a lot. I asked him how he liked the idea of this divorce. He said he liked it a hell of a lot. He said he was fed up with his wife. She's what they call a nice woman. I believe she has a funny name—Querida. She had the money and I don't think he liked that because I think Pierce is a man who could always make a little money for himself —one way or another."

Vallon said: " You mean he wasn't too particular as to how he made his money ? "

" Maybe not. . . . But I don't think he liked her having the money. She sort of patronised him, see ? When they were married she made him an allowance—a pretty good one, I think. When he got a bit out of hand she used to let him know all about it. She used to remind him of it. I don't think he liked that. You wouldn't have liked it, would you, Johnny ? "

He grinned. " No, I shouldn't have liked it. And I take it if Pierce Gale is divorced he will lose the allowance his wife is making him ? "

" That's right," she said. " He told me he had a settle-ment, but it could be cancelled by death or divorce."

" Did he mind that ? " Vallon asked.

She smiled. " No . . . he didn't give a damn. Why should he ? He'd got Mrs. Querida Gale where he wanted her."

" Had he ? " said Vallon. " How ? "

She shrugged her shoulders again. " I wouldn't know. He never told me. I tried to find out, but no soap. If Pierce wanted to talk, he talked. If he didn't want to talk, he didn't talk. This time he didn't want to talk."

Vallon asked : " What else ? "

" That's the book. I don't know any more. Give me another drink." She looked at him. Her eyes were veiled and resentful.

He said : " Maybe I can prompt your memory. When did you hear of Joe Chennault ? Joe was running a first-class investigation and research agency. He handled divorce, but most of his business was commercial—one of the best and most reputable agencies in this country. You've never done any business with them. How did you know about Joe ? "

" Oh that . . ." She laughed shrilly. " I forgot to tell you that. I didn't think it mattered. After a while Pierce got fed up with the Ansteley baby. He wanted to ditch her, see ? He'd had it."

" Why did he want to do that ? " asked Vallon. " He liked her in the first place. They weren't together for very long."

She said : " That's right enough, but this guy Perdreau that he took her away from is quite a feller, see ? Perdreau's no push-over. He didn't like Gale for taking his girl away and he got on to his tail."

Vallon said : " So Gale was scared of Perdreau ? "

She shook her head. " No, he wasn't. Gale wasn't scared of anybody. He isn't that sort of egg. But I think, just about this time he didn't want any trouble of any sort. He'd got something pretty big on. He was going abroad some place when the divorce was over, and I don't think he liked the idea of any trouble from anywhere. I think he had the idea this Perdreau was hanging around trying to get a line on what Gale was at. So Gale fixed him, see ? "

Vallon said : " Nice work. How did he do that ? "

" Well . . . if you work for the Chennault agency you know Dolores Chennault—Joe Chennault's wife. A pretty

123

hot number, that one, I should think, and good-looking too·
Is she ? "

Vallon nodded. " A very attractive woman," he said.

She went on : " She used to go and dance at the club
where I met Gale."

" The Mandrake Club, I take it," Vallon interposed,
" near Chertsey ? "

She nodded. " That's right. How did you know ? " She
went on, not waiting for the question to be answered : " So
this Dolores Chennault has fallen for Perdreau, see ? She
likes him. She goes for anybody who looks like Perdreau.
In fact," she said with a smirk, " I should think she goes
for anybody who's presentable. She's like that. So Pierce
thinks he'll have one at Perdreau before Perdreau has a
chance to have one at him. So he writes an anonymous
letter to Joe Chennault and he tells Chennault that his wife
is getting around with this guy Perdreau. This way he
thought he'd fix Perdreau."

" What happened then ? " asked Vallon. " What did
Chennault do about that ? "

" I don't know. That's all I heard. It was soon after
that I got my own marching orders from Pierce." She
sighed. " He was a gentleman if ever there was one," she
said. " We had a drink and he said thanks for the memory,
baby, and he gave me this brooch." She pointed to a
butterfly diamond brooch on the lapel of her wrap. " So
we just said so long and that was that."

Vallon lighted another cigarette. " All right. That's
good enough."

" So you've got what you wanted," she said. " I suppose
you know what you're doing."

" Meaning what ? " asked Vallon.

" If you're going to get up against Pierce Gale, watch
your step, mister."

He smiled at her. " I suppose you think I wouldn't have
a dog's chance ? "

She looked him over carefully. " I wouldn't know.
You're one of those surprisin' fellers. Nobody would ever
know what you might or might not do. But I tell you
something. A guy who knew Pierce Gale pretty well told
me one time that he'd sooner start something with a rattlesnake than start something with Pierce."

Vallon said : " So what ! " He finished his drink. " Well so long, Bobbie. I don't think you have to worry. To-morrow I'll send you thirty-seven pounds in notes in a registered envelope to the offices of Sulkin & Frash, addressed to the firm."

" Not a bad pay-off . . . ! What next ? " she asked.

" I'll get my suitcase and scram," said Vallon. " You can tell them in the hotel I've just remembered something—an appointment I'd forgotten. You can pay the bill when you go in the morning. It won't be much. And if I were you I'd phone through to Sulkin and tell him he needn't worry about making any inquiries here to-morrow."

She got up. She put her glass on the table. She watched him as he walked into the bedroom ; came out with his hat and suitcase.

She said : " Well, it's been nice meeting you. So long ! It was nice while it lasted."

" That's what I think," said Vallon. " So long, Bobbie ! "

He was at the door when she said : " Well . . . any time you're at a loose end for a dancing partner or somebody to take out to dinner or anything else like that, you know the phone number."

He asked : " Why ? "

She spread her hands. " I don't know. In my business you meet a lot of funny eggs and you don't like most of them. I don't mind you. You're strange but you got something." She laughed ruefully. " Maybe," she said, " you mean to keep it. Good night, feller."

He went out ; closed the door behind him. She stood looking at it for a few moments ; then she shrugged her shoulders. She went to the table; poured herself another drink.

CHAPTER FOUR

FOUGÈRE

1

VALLON said: " Give yourself another drink."

" Thanks . . ." Trant poured out some more whisky. He looked out of the window to the street below. He said: " By God, Mr. Vallon, this is a hell of a story, isn't it ? The question is, can you make it stick ? "

Vallon asked : " Why not ? "

" There's not even any real circumstantial evidence," said Trant. " There's motive ; there's opportunity if somebody was there at the time, if they could be proved to be there. Nobody saw him come into the office. It's certain he'll have some sort of alibi. Another thing, you've got to find that suit." He repeated : " You're going to have a hell of a job to make it stick."

Vallon grinned. " I'll make it stick. Although I think you're right. There's really no evidence. The only person known to have seen Chennault on the afternoon of his death is Perdreau, and I'm perfectly certain that Perdreau didn't kill Chennault. He's not a killer and he had no motive for killing him. Why should he ? He didn't want anything."

Trant said : " The motive for killing Chennault was to gain possession of something—a letter or document—which would stop the divorce going through—a letter or document that proved collusion. So the person who wanted that document was somebody who *wanted* the divorce to go through." He looked at Vallon. " There's only one person wanted that and that was Mrs. Gale."

" That's what it looks like," said Vallon. " I don't believe it."

Trant asked : " Why not ? "

Vallon shrugged his shoulders. " Never mind . . ."

Trant finished his drink. He asked : " Is there anything else I can do ? "

" No, not at the moment. If I want you I'll call you. When this thing's over I'll give you a cheque."

"Thanks a lot, Mr. Vallon. It sounds odd, but in a way I've enjoyed this."

Vallon grinned cynically. "So have I—like hell . . . !"

Trant picked up his hat. He said: "Well, I'll be seeing you."

Vallon nodded. Trant went out. Vallon listened to his footsteps going down the stairs.

He got out of the chair and stretched; looked at his watch. It was three o'clock. The afternoon sun was bright. Out in the street he could see some children playing on the corner of the nearby gardens. They were laughing. Vallon thought that was the time to laugh—when you were a child —when everything was an adventure and everything was something to laugh about. When you grew up you lost the ability to laugh. That was all that was the matter with age —or was it? He thought he wouldn't know and didn't care.

He began to think about Dolores Chennault. An extremely strange woman, he thought. A very odd one. Nobody knew what made Dolores tick over in the way she did. She was a mixture of decency, violent desires, utter recklessness and a certain ability to take life as it came without making a song and dance about it. But she was not the sort of person to murder or to be associated with murder. Definitely not that.

So what? Vallon metaphorically shrugged his shoulders. What he thought of her wouldn't save her if it came to the showdown. Anything—even the giving away of an old suit of Joe's—would seem evidence against her. In spite of the fact that anyone who knew Dolores would know that once a man—even her own husband—was gone she would give anything away that reminded her of him. Even if it was of value to her. Juries, thought Vallon, could not be expected to understand the curious *nuances* of mind of a woman like Dolores. And why the hell should they? Their business was to find people guilty or not guilty, and not adventure into the ramifications of minds of women who, being unhappy, idle and unsatisfied, played life off the cuff and kidded themselves that they liked the process.

He went into his bedroom; put his suitcase on the bed; put some things into it. He went downstairs; got into the car. He thought he was sick of the car. One time he'd liked driving. Now he was getting tired of it. Driving about the countryside, talking to people, chiselling bits of information out of people ; trying to make somebody tell the truth, or tell such an untruth that it was an obvious one.

He lighted a cigarette. The pain in his stomach was worse than it had been for days. He let in the gear. Outside London he put his foot down hard on the accelerator. He drove very fast.

He stopped the car outside the Pleasaunce roadhouse behind West Stour at twenty-past six. He went into the hotel and asked the pretty girl in the reception office if Mr. Perdreau was in.

She went to the telephone ; came back and said : " Mr. Perdreau will see you, Mr. Vallon, if you'll go up. You know your way ? "

" Yes . . ." said Vallon. He took the lift ; got out at the first floor ; walked along to Perdreau's room. He went in. Perdreau was standing in front of the fireplace. Claire Ansteley was sitting in the arm-chair opposite him.

Perdreau said : " Good evening, Vallon. I'm glad to see you. Would you like a drink ? "

" Thank you," said Vallon.

The woman got up ; went to the telephone ; ordered the drinks. Vallon stood in the middle of the room looking at them—from one to the other.

He said : " You two are pretty stuck on each other, aren't you ? "

Perdreau smiled. " Why not ? " he asked. " We're being married next month."

" Congratulations . . ." Vallon smiled at the woman. " In spite of the fact that you've been a little unkind to each other ; that you've tried to make each other jealous, you're still *for* each other, aren't you ? "

Perdreau said : " That's perfectly right. The course of true love never did run smooth." He smiled amiably.

Vallon thought he didn't dislike Perdreau. He said : " You wouldn't think I was sticking my nose into your private affairs would you ? But you know what I'm worrying about, Perdreau. First of all I want to find the person who killed Joe Chennault, and secondly in the process of doing that I don't want you to run into any trouble."

Perdreau said : " I know what you mean. You mean that I was one person who was known to be in Chennault's office the afternoon he died."

"Yes," said Vallon. "But you were there at two-thirty —although that fact doesn't let you out, because the interesting point is not the time you went in but the time you came out. But you told me when you left and I believe you. Somebody came in after you."

The woman had gone back to her place in the chair. There was a knock at the door. The waiter brought in the cocktails. He put them on the table and went away. Perdreau handed them round.

Vallon said : "Miss Ansteley, I expect Perdreau has told you what all the trouble's about."

She nodded.

"I wondered if you'd like to answer a few questions," Vallon went on.

"If I can . . ." she said.

Vallon asked : "When you were getting around with Pierce Gale I take it that he thought he was fond of you . . . ?"

She shrugged her shoulders. "He may have been or it may have been an act."

Vallon said : "Why? Were there some other strings to it ? "

She nodded. "I owned a club called the Mandrake Club near Chertsey. A man that Gale knew was the manager. Business seemed to be pretty bad. Gale bought the club from me for a very small sum. Then, strangely enough, things improved amazingly. I believe he's making quite a little money out of it."

Vallon said : "You probably mean that the man he knew cooked the accounts, or there was some funny business so that Pierce Gale could make a cheap deal with you. Is that it ? And in order to pull that off he made love to you ? "

"Yes . . ." She looked away. "I shouldn't have taken very much notice of that at the time," she said, "except that I was very angry with Tony here."

"I understand that," said Vallon. "But that doesn't matter. The thing that does matter is this. Did Gale ever talk to you about his divorce ? "

"Yes, he was rather amused at the idea of the divorce. He never seemed to take it seriously. Whenever he spoke about it a quizzical sort of expression used to come over his face. I wondered about that."

Vallon said : "You know that when she married him

Querida Gale made him an allowance of five thousand a year, don't you ? You know that if she divorced him he was going to lose that ? "

She shook her head. " He wasn't going to lose everything. I had an idea he'd got her where he wanted her. Oh, yes, he said he was going to lose the allowance, but one night when he'd drunk a little he said that wasn't worrying him ; that there were more ways than one of killing a cat."

Vallon said : " Meaning that even if he was going to lose the allowance, he was pretty certain of making some money out of Mrs. Gale by some other means."

She said : " That's obvious. It was obvious to me that he was going to make her pay somehow for the divorce. He wasn't going to lose that five thousand a year and say nothing about it. Gale isn't that sort of man, I assure you."

Vallon grinned. " I didn't think he was. Did he ever tell you exactly what sort of hold he'd got over Mrs. Gale ? "

She shook her head. " He only told me what I've told you. He implied this and that, but I might have been wrong in my guess."

Perdreau said : " What's in your mind, Vallon ? And give yourself another drink."

Vallon helped himself to a cocktail out of the shaker. He sat down in the other arm-chair.

He said : " It's sticking out like Brighton pier. Querida Gale gets fed up with Pierce Gale gallivanting. She tells him she wants a divorce. This suits him. At this time he's getting around with you, Miss Ansteley. Actually, he wasn't particularly interested in you except in so far as he was interested in getting hold of the Mandrake Club. So he made some sort of deal with Mrs. Gale. I imagine that he told her he'd consent to being divorced if she paid him a large sum of money down to make up for the allowance he was going to lose. She agreed to this. It's my belief that she gave him a letter saying that if he agreed to the divorce, when the decree nisi was granted she'd pay him the money, or something like that."

Vallon took out his cigarette case ; lighted a cigarette. He went on : " Then Hipper came into the story. Hipper was the operative in the Chennault organisation who secured the evidence against Gale. The co-respondent in the Gale divorce case was a woman called Trickett. It's my belief

130

that Hipper, who probably knew Trickett, met and talked with Gale while he was getting the evidence. It's my belief that Hipper put Gale up to a big idea—an idea by which he could make a whole lot of money. I'm only guessing but I think my guess is right. This, I think, was the connection between Gale and Hipper. Hipper pretended to be a good friend to Mrs. Gale ; pretended to have found out what was going on ; went to see her first for the purpose of starting the little plot that they'd laid against her, and secondly to get a little money on the side and to protect himself by giving her certain information.

" Hipper thought he was safe anyway. That's why he's never been scared of anybody in this game. The whole thing hinges," Vallon went on, " on some document, some letter, some confirmation of the fact that Querida Gale was going to pay Gale a sum of money after the divorce, and somehow that evidence found its way into Joe Chennault's possession. He put it in the bottom right-hand drawer of his desk. Somebody knew it was there. And that somebody knew that you, Perdreau, were going to see Chennault on that afternoon. They knew that Chennault had a motive for disliking you. They knew you'd been getting around with his wife. They thought that here was a very good motive for a quarrel between you and Chennault. So that somebody was waiting outside the building to see you come out, and when you came out they went in.

" Chennault was killed, the drawer was broken open and the evidence—whatever it was—taken out. The killer then got out. He only made one mistake. If he'd taken a cigarette out of Chennault's own case—an ' All American,' the only cigarettes that Joe ever smoked—and stuck a stub of one of those cigarettes on his waistcoat I'd never have guessed the truth. But when Joe fell over the desk dead, and when the killer saw that the wad from the blank cartridge had burned a hole in his waistcoat, he had to do something. So he stuck the stub of the cigarette he was smoking on to the burn." Vallon grinned. " That is the little mistake that murderers always make—the thing you read about in detective books. Then he went out. He was on a good wicket. Nobody would be surprised that Joe Chennault had died. Everybody expected him to die and death from angina pectoris is death from shock. Nobody saw the killer go in. Nobody saw him come out. There's no evidence. He could even get away with it now."

Perdreau said: "What about the cigarette burn? If that suit is produced . . ."

"We can't produce the suit," said Vallon. "The suit's disappeared. If we could, I've got the cigarette stub. I've kept it. But what's the good? You can't go round to the authorities and say that somebody did this; that you know who it was; that you think you know why they did it. A jury has to find a prisoner guilty beyond reasonable shadow of doubt. On the evidence we've got nobody's going to be convicted for killing Joe.

"Or if we try, you're going to be yanked into this, Perdreau. It's going to be proved by somebody or other that Chennault rang you up; that you went to see him on the afternoon of his death. He had good cause to be angry with you, and you with him. In other words you're going to be a red herring. But it's known *you* went to the office. Even you admit it. There's not enough evidence to convict you—you're just a red herring. There's not enough to convict anybody. But you confuse the issue, see?"

Perdreau said: "This killer, whoever he was, was no mug."

"You're telling me!" said Vallon. "And he was well helped too." He got up.

The woman said: "So he's going to get away with it, Mr. Vallon?"

Vallon picked up his hat. "No . . . No, he's not. Maybe I'll have to take justice into my own hands. I think it's going to be amusing. Well, thanks for answering the questions, Miss Ansteley. So long, Perdreau." He went out.

When he'd gone, Perdreau said: "I think that egg is quite a man. Maybe he'll get what he's after. I hope he does."

She thought for a moment; then she said: "Tony, he looks pretty ill to me. Maybe he's worrying about this. I wonder why he's worrying so much?"

Perdreau said: "He was Dolores Chennault's boy friend at one time. You know what she's like. I don't think he liked it a lot, because Chennault was his friend. Chennault saved his life fighting the Japanese, see? He's got a snake in his guts. All he wants to do is to find the man who

132

killed Joe. He thinks if he does that maybe he'll even up the ledger account just a little bit."

" I see ..." She sighed. " You men are strange creatures, aren't you ? "

" You're telling me," said Perdreau. " Why don't you have another cocktail ? "

.   .   .   .

Vallon went into the bar of the Continental at Paignton at a quarter to nine. Mrs. Gale, demure in a black silk coat and skirt with a fluffy blouse, was sitting on the high stool at the end of the bar. Vallon went over and sat beside her.

The bar-tender said : " Good evening, Mr. Vallon. Bacardi ? "

Vallon said. " Two large ones. . . . Well, how is it, Querida ? "

She looked at him. She smiled. It was a cold little smile. " Still following me around, Johnny ? "

He nodded. " Just like a dog," he said. " I went up to Ladycourt. They told me they thought I'd find you here."

She asked : "What is it this time, Johnny ? You said that if you got wise to something you'd ring me up. You thought it better to make a personal call ? "

He said : " Why not ? You're not liking me very much to-night, are you, Querida ? "

She shrugged her shoulders. " I like you a lot, Johnny. But you worry me. You're too consistent. You're like a dog looking for a bone. I think you might make a lot of trouble. I don't like that."

He said softly : " You'd be surprised ! " He drank some Bacardi.

Quite two minutes passed before she said : " Well, what is it ? Are you trying to make me nervous ? "

He shook his head. He dropped his voice. " How much did you agree to pay Pierce Gale down for standing for that divorce and losing five thousand a year ? And what did you give him to let him know he was safe in going through with the divorce ? Gale isn't the sort of man who's going to take your word about anything. Did you write him a letter ? "

She flushed. " What the hell has tha to do with you, Johnny ? "

He said : " Plenty. You remember once I told you I'd make you talk. Take a tip from me, Querida, be careful. You're skating on thin ice. This thing has turned into something more than a divorce case. This thing's turned into a murder job."

She spun round on the stool. She said, in a low, controlled voice : " What do you mean by that ? "

Vallon said : " Whatever the thing was that you gave Gale —the thing that made him sure of getting his money—that thing fell into the hands of Joe Chennault, my boss. Joe had angina, you understand—the worst sort of heart disease ? He was due for the high jump any time. Somebody came into his office and shot him with a blank cartridge. The shock killed him, as they knew it would. Then they burst open the drawer and took the letter or document and got out. I give you ten guesses who it was."

She said : " My God . . . ! "

There was another pause.

Vallon said : " See what I mean, Sweet ? It's not so good, is it ? How would you like to find yourself with no divorce and tied up to a murderer ? "

" You mean Pierce did it ? "

" Who else ? " said Vallon. " Now I know why Hipper was such a good friend of yours. Can't you guess what happened ? "

She nodded. She said in a low voice : " I've been a fool, Johnny."

" You're telling me ! How much were you going to pay Gale ? And what was the confirmation ? "

The bar-tender came back to their end of the bar. Vallon ordered two more Bacardis.

When the man had mixed them and gone away, she said : " I had a talk with Pierce. I had several discussions about this. I told you he was getting five thousand a year. He said he wanted to get away. He'd got some property— a club that he was going to sell. He proposed to leave the country. He said he wanted some capital—fairly big capital —to start something somewhere else. He said that he'd sell out his allowance and agree to the divorce for forty thousand pounds. He said that was a good deal ; it was only an eight years' purchase at five thousand a year. I asked him how I was to know he'd go through with it. He laughed at me.

134

He said that wasn't worrying him. He was fed up with me. He'd be glad to get away from me. He said I was too snooty for him. He said the thing that worried him was how did he know I was going to pay? I didn't know what to suggest. He said the best thing for me to do was to write him a letter saying that on the day after the decree nisi was granted, in consideration of his consenting to the divorce, I'd pay him forty thousand pounds."

Vallon grinned. "And you wrote the letter and gave it to him?"

She nodded. "Do you think I was a fool, Johnny? What else could I do? It obviously wasn't to his advantage to show that letter to anyone. He wanted the forty thousand pounds. He wanted to get away."

Vallon grinned. "You ask me if I think you were a fool. There's one born every minute, my dear. You know Gale. He's an expert in having his cake and eating it. That's what he intended to do with you."

"Johnny . . . all this sounds terrible. What am I going to do?"

He got off the stool. "What can you do? You do nothing. You finish your Bacardi and go back to Ladycourt. Go to bed and try to go to sleep. You won't. But you can still try. You'll have lots of time to think about what a fool you've been. But don't do anything. Don't talk to anybody. Don't see Hipper no matter what stories he may have to tell you. If he comes round here, tell him the next time you see him you'll hand him over to the police. You'll find he'll never come after that."

She said: "I wonder what you think of me, Johnny?"

He shrugged his shoulders. "I'm not thinking anything about anybody. Why should I? I know what I'm trying to do."

She said: "How do I know you're telling me the truth? How do I know you're not playing some game? How do I know you're not a blackmailer? You've taken two thousand from me anyway. You might easily be that."

He grinned at her. "Get your statement from the bank to-morrow and see if the cheque's been cleared. I burnt it ten minutes after you gave it to me. What do you think I am? Good night, Querida."

He moved away.

135

She said : " Johnny, I'm sorry I . . ."

She stopped talking when she saw that he was gone.

2

Vallon said to the girl in the perfumery shop : " It's a very light, flowery scent—very attractive. I've never smelt anything like it."

" And you don't remember the name, sir ? " She smiled at him. She wondered whom he wanted the perfume for.

He said : " No, I can't think of the name. It was a peculiar name—not the sort of name that is usually associated with perfume. You wouldn't have an idea, I suppose ? "

She shook her head. " I'm very sorry. I can't help you."

Vallon said : " Thank you." He went out of the shop.

He got into his car ; drove to the offices. He threw his hat on to a chair ; sat in the big seat behind Chennault's desk.

He rang through on the office phone for Marvin. He asked : " Is Lipscombe there ? "

Marvin said he was there.

" Come in—both of you," said Vallon. He leaned back in the chair and lighted a cigarette.

When Lipscombe and Marvin came in, Marvin said : " Good morning, Mr. Vallon. You look very tired. I think you're taking a lot out of yourself."

" Maybe . . ." Vallon opened the bottom right-hand drawer of the desk ; took out the tumbler and the whisky bottle. There was still one tot. He poured the whisky into the glass ; drank it neat.

He said to Lipscombe : " Have you got anything on the Mandrake Club ? "

" Yes, sir. The place used to belong to a Miss Claire Ansteley. It seems as if she lost money over it. She sold out not very long ago to Pierce Gale. He's turned it into a limited liability company. They're doing very good business."

Vallon said : " O.K. You go off, Lipscombe, and hang around. I'll probably want you in a minute."

Lipscombe went out of the office.

Vallon said to Marvin : " Do you know what Mr. Chennault did about his will ? "

"The last will that I knew of was made about four months ago—just about the time that Mr. Chennault thought about selling out to World Wide Investigations That's the only one I know of."

Vallon asked : "Where is it ? "

"It's with Pritchards—his lawyers," said Marvin " Their address is in Lincoln's Inn."

Vallon asked him what the number was. Then he said " O.K., Marvin. I'll let you know if I want you."

When Marvin had gone he dialled the number. He said " My name's Vallon—John Vallon. I was Mr. Chennault's manager. Now I'm running the business for Mrs. Chennault. I understand he made a will about four months ago."

Pritchard said : " I was going to get in touch with you about that thing to-day, Mr. Vallon. The will made four months ago doesn't matter. A will quite recently made cancels that."

"I see . . ." said Vallon. "Why were you getting into touch with me about it ? "

"You're the sole executor, Mr. Vallon."

Vallon said nothing. He held on for a minute ; then " What's it worth, Mr. Pritchard ? "

Pritchard said : " Roughly his estate, excluding the money paid rather quickly by the Acme Agency who, as you probably know, Mr. Vallon, bought the business for ten thousand pounds on a verbal agreement, and who will probably be taking it over towards the end of this month, is worth about thirty-five thousand pounds. There's another one hundred thousand dollars in America and some property here in the country that hasn't been valued, but which I should say is worth quite a little bit."

"I see . . ." said Vallon. "Who does he leave his money to ? "

Pritchard said : " To some relatives in America. And there's quite a sum left to Army, Navy and Air Force funds in the United States. You yourself are a beneficiary, Mr. Vallon. Mr. Chennault's left you ten thousand pounds duty free—he evidently thought a lot of you—in memory of a long and good friendship."

"What does Mrs. Chennault get ? " asked Vallon.

Pritchard said : " I'm afraid this is rather sad and

137

startling. Mr. Chennault's left her the equivalent in English money, when it's worked out, of five dollars."

" What were the terms of the first will ? " asked Vallon.

Pritchard said : " Everything was left to Mrs. Chennault under trust, and three trustees were appointed. He made a few small bequests to other people, but practically everything went to her."

" All right, Mr. Pritchard," said Vallon. " I'm sending round for a copy of the will. Perhaps you'll let me have it. Keep the original. I'll get in touch with you about probate in a day or two. Is that all right ? "

" Perfectly all right," said Pritchard. " The estate's in order. It's all quite simple and straightforward."

Vallon said : " Thanks a lot." He hung up.

He sat back in the chair, looking at the ceiling, thinking about Joe Chennault. After a little while he rang through on the office phone and asked for Lipscombe.

When Lipscombe came in, Vallon said : " Sit down and listen, Lipscombe. Did you know that Mr. Chennault was making a new will ? "

Lipscombe nodded. " He drafted it in this office, in his own handwriting. I took it round to Pritchard the lawyer for engrossing. The next day Mr. Chennault went there and signed it. I was one witness and Pritchard's clerk the other. He told me to say nothing about it to anybody. I suppose the lawyers have advised you that you're the sole executor, Mr. Vallon ? "

Vallon said : " Yes, I've heard about that. And of course Mrs. Chennault knows nothing at all about this ? "

Lipscombe shook his head. " How should she know ? Nobody knew except Mr. Chennault, myself and Pritchard."

Vallon asked : " In the will he made before this last one he left practically everything he had in trust for Mrs. Chennault. Did she know about *that* ? "

Lipscombe nodded. " She knew about that will. She probably thinks she's got the lot, plus the twenty-five thousand which she thinks World Wide Investigations were paying for the business. You understand, Mr. Vallon, she knows nothing about the quick sale made under the verbal agreement with Acme."

Vallon said : " I suppose, as you were in on everything, you were a witness to that verbal agreement ?"

"Yes, sir," said Lipscombe. " I was."

"All right. We'll probably be handing over to them at the end of the month. You'd better take two or three days off, Lipscombe. Give yourself a rest."

"You won't be wanting me, Mr. Vallon ? "

Vallon said : " I don't think so."

Lipscombe got up. He had his hand on the knob of the door when Vallon said : " Wait a minute, Lipscombe." He went on : " You know the lay-out of the Mandrake Club. Is there a garage there ? "

Lipscombe nodded. "It's at the back of the club—a lock-up shed. It takes two or three cars, I should say."

"I suppose you wouldn't know what car Gale drives ? " asked Vallon.

"No," said Lipscombe. " I don't know which one it is, but it's one of the cars kept in the garage. That point never worried me."

Vallon said : " Go down to Chertsey. Arrange to be there somewhere about six-thirty or a quarter to seven this evening. Go round to the Mandrake and find out if Gale's there."

"Very well, Mr. Vallon."

"On your way out of London," said Vallon, "get the number of the call-box in Jermyn Street. There's one near the cocktail bar there. At six fifty-five precisely ring me at that box and tell me if Gale's there. I'll be waiting for the call."

Lipscombe said. " All right. We'd better check our watches."

They checked their watches.

" Don't be early or late . . . six fifty-five exactly " said Vallon. " It's important."

Lipscombe said he understood. He went out of the office.

Vallon lighted a cigarette. He looked at his strap-watch. It was twelve o'clock. He put on his hat ; walked through the communicating door into the secretaries' room ; through that into Marvin's room.

He said : " Marvin, I may be here to morrow and I may not. I'm not certain. If by any chance I don't turn up you'd better take over here. Understand ? "

" I understand, Mr. Vallon."

" If you do have to take over," Vallon went on, " you'd

139

better have a talk with Lipscombe. Tell him that I told you to ask him for all the private information he's got about this business and the stuff he's told me. You'll need to know it. And there's another thing, send round to Pritchard this afternoon, and get a copy of Mr. Chennault's last will. When you've got it, put it, with a compliments slip, in an envelope addressed to Mrs. Chennault. Post it to-night so that she gets it to-morrow morning."

Marvin said : " Very well. Is there any chance of your not coming back, Mr. Vallon ? "

" How do I know ? You'll find out. So long, Marvin."

He went through the door into the passageway, past the lift ; walked slowly down the stairs. He got into his car and drove to the bar in Jermyn Street. He ordered a double rye whisky. The pain in his stomach had come back. He drank the rye ; then a little water. He went out ; walked to the call-box farther down the street. He dialled Dolores Chennault's number. She answered the telephone.

He said : " This is Johnny. I've got to see you, Dolores. I have some very important information that you ought to know about."

" You mean about Joe ? You've found out something ? "

He said : " I've found out plenty. I've got to see you, but I can't see you before seven-thirty to-night. Will you be in then ? "

" Of course, Johnny." Her voice was surprised. " What's it all about ? Do you mean that you've found the man who killed Joe—if he *was* killed ? "

Vallon said : " I wasn't thinking about that. It's something quite different but very important. I can't talk to you on the telephone. I'll see you at seven-thirty to-night."

" All right, Johnny. I'll be here. How's the pain ? "

He visualised her smiling acidly into the transmitter.

He said : " Not too bad. It comes and goes like everything else. It could be worse. I'll be seeing you, Dolores."

He hung up ; walked back to the bar.

.   .   .   .   .

The alarm clock beside Vallon's bed went off with a jangle at five-fifteen. He woke up. He lay looking at the ceiling. He had a headache. He swung himself off the bed ; took a couple of aspirin tablets ; drank a little whisky. The pain in his stomach had stopped. He thought maybe it had moved to his head. He thought life was like that. When you got rid of one pain you got another one. You always had something to think about—something to keep you amused.

He took off his shirt and under-vest ; went into the bathroom ; turned on the cold shower ; held his head beneath it. He stood there until the back of his neck felt numb. Then he brushed his hair ; put on his clothes ; went downstairs ; started up the car and drove to the Jermyn Street bar.

He drank a rye whisky ; started to eat a sandwich ; pushed it away after a few bites. At six-fifty he walked along to the telephone box. He went inside ; held the door open with his foot so as to get some air ; leant against the side of the box, smoking a cigarette. After three or four minutes, Lipscombe came through.

" I'm speaking to you from the station," he said. " I've been able to get a little information. Gale's been here and he's got an appointment at nine-thirty to-night, so he's likely to be back. The two cars in the garage both belong to him. One's a big American car ; the other an Austin twenty. Is that what you wanted, Mr. Vallon ? "

" Thanks a lot, Lipscombe. O.K. Now you can go and have a rest."

.   .   .   .

It was five-and-twenty past seven when Vallon got out of the car outside the apartment block at Hendon. He walked across the courtyard ; went up in the lift ; rang the bell. He waited, his hands in his jacket pockets, a dead cigarette stub hanging from the corner of his mouth.

Dolores Chennault opened the door. She was wearing a black lace negligee. Her hair had been freshly done. Vallon could see, peeping from beneath the hem of her wrap, a small high-heeled, satin slipper. He thought that Dolores certainly knew how to make herself look attractive—when she wanted to.

She said : " Hallo, Johnny. What's the matter ? You look like death. Aren't you well ? "

Vallon grinned at her. " I'm all right. Maybe things are catching up with me a bit."

She said : " Come inside, Johnny. You need a drink. What's all the excitement about ? When you came through

141

earlier to-day I thought there'd been a fire-call or something."

He followed her into the drawing-room; closed the door quietly behind him.

He asked: "Don't you ever get excited, Dolores?"

She shrugged her shoulders. She moved slowly to the sideboard; began to mix drinks.

She said: "I'm going to give you a very dry Martini. You need it. As for getting excited, what's the good of it, Johnny? Getting excited never gets you anywhere. I should think you ought to know that. I don't think you've ever been excited in your life about anything"—she looked over her shoulder; smiled at him wryly—"except perhaps one thing."

Vallon was standing in front of the fireplace. He asked: "What thing?"

She yawned. "Remember when you came here and told me about that new girl of yours"—she looked at him mischievously—"the one who walked out on you? I thought you seemed a little bit excited then for the first time since I've known you." She turned her head; continued mixing the drinks. "But even that didn't last, did it, Johnny? It must have been a new experience to have a girl walk out on you."

He said: "Maybe. They tell me experience is good for everybody." He threw the cigarette stub into the fire-grate behind him; lighted another. "It does me a lot of good to hear that you don't think a lot of being excited. So you're learning control!" He laughed. "It's about time, Dolores."

"Listen, Johnny, what are you so damned acid about?" She came towards him; a Martini in each hand. She gave him one. She asked: "What's the trouble now? Or is it something nice for a change?"

"It's not so good, Dolores. Go and sit down and take it easy. This is one of those times when it's going to be good for you to take your weight off your feet."

She drank some of the Martini. "So I'm due for another shock?"

He nodded. "You're due for a couple of shocks. First of all I want to talk to you about Joe. Do you know something? That boy was taking us all for a ride—especially

142

you. Joe wasn't half as big a mug as you thought he was. That deal with the World Wide agency is no good. It just doesn't matter a thing."

There was a moment's silence. She said : " What the hell are you talking about, Johnny ? I know that the deal with the World Wide agency was fixed. The draft contract was settled. Even the date that they were to take over was all arranged."

He nodded. " You're perfectly right, Dolores. The draft agreement was settled, but it was only a draft ; it wasn't signed. For some reason best known to himself Joe decided that he didn't like it. He decided that he wanted to take a run-out powder on you. So do you know what he did ? He didn't bother to say anything to World Wide, and I suppose they waited for him to sign the agreement. In the meantime he made a verbal agreement with the Acme agency, in front of a witness ; took ten thousand pounds off them for the business. And that was that. He never told anybody. He didn't want to at that time."

She looked at him. Vallon realised with almost a feeling of pleasure that her self-satisfaction was badly shaken.

She said : " Well, if he wanted to do that, he did it. I'd like to know why."

Vallon finished the Martini in one gulp. He put the glass on the mantelpiece behind him. He said : " I'll tell you why. Joe was wise to you. He wasn't playing it your way any more. He knew what was going on."

She smiled dryly. " Oh, yes, Johnny . . . meaning exactly what ? "

Vallon said : " Meaning that he wanted to know what you were at. Remember Lipscombe ? "

She nodded. " He's Joe's oldest operative. Joe was fond of him. He worked for Joe in China."

" That's the one," said Vallon. " Joe wanted to know what you were doing, so he put Lipscombe on your tail. I'll tell you something else. He didn't fall for that line about Perdreau as much as you may have thought he did."

She said : " I wish to God I knew what you were talking about. What are you doing, Johnny—being a little theatrical and dramatising the situation ? If you are, go on giving yourself a good time. But all this doesn't make sense to me. It sounds like riddles."

143

" Like hell it does," said Vallon. " Tell me something, Dolores. Joe used to keep two appointment books—one at the office and one in his room here. He kept one here so that he could know what he was doing if he decided not to go to the office on any given day. Where's his appointment book—the one he kept here ? "

She shrugged her shoulders. " I don't know. I expect he took it away."

" Don't give me that," said Vallon. " You know damned well what happened to his appointment book. You burned t."

She laughed. " Now I know you're crazy. So I burned it. Maybe you'll tell me why."

Vallon said : " You looked at Joe's appointment book and you found an afternoon when he hadn't any appointments at the office. So you told him the story about Perdreau. You were the dear little wife who had slipped up and were sorry for it ; who'd allowed a not very nice man to make love to her and was getting a little scared of him, and who told her husband all about it. That's what you did, didn't you, Dolores ? You told Joe all about the Perdreau affair. You told him you were scared of Perdreau. You told him Perdreau was making a damned nuisance of himself. You asked him to see Perdreau. Joe asked you when he'd be in town and how he could get at him. You gave him the date —the date when Joe hadn't got an appointment at the office. You asked him to see him privately. You didn't want Perdreau to make a scene. Joe fell for that one, didn't he ? He rang up Perdreau and made a date for two-thirty on the afternoon he died. He told Perdreau to come round and come in through the private door in the corridor. Perdreau went. Why shouldn't he ? You were all washed up as far as he was concerned. In point of fact, I don't think Perdreau would have had anything at all to do with you except that he was good and annoyed. He was annoyed because Pierce Gale tried to make his girl—the Ansteley woman.

" But he went round and saw Joe, and when Joe talked to him Perdreau told him it was all over ; that there was nothing on between you and him. And Joe believed him. Joe believed him because he was no push-over and he knew when a man was telling the truth, and Perdreau *was* telling the truth."

144

She said : " Isn't this all frightfully exciting ? I wonder why I did that, Johnny ? "

Vallon grinned. " You wouldn't know, would you ? You'll know before I'm through with you. But you did it for the same reason that you burned Joe's appointment book here ; for the same reason that you sent that suit of clothes away. That's probably burned too. You remember the suit I mean—the one he was wearing when he died—the one that had the cigarette burn on the waistcoat." He smiled at her. " It was that cigarette stub stuck on that burn—a cigarette of a brand that Joe never smoked—that set my mind working. So all the evidence is destroyed. There's no suit with a burn on it. There's no appointment book ; the appointment with Perdreau won't be in the book at the office. You know that Perdreau is supposed to be the only man who saw Joe on the afternoon that he died. So even if suspicion were to fasten on somebody, there'd still be a red herring, and in this country a jury have to be certain beyond all reasonable doubt that a murderer has committed a murder. The prosecution have to prove that he did it. He hasn't got to prove that he didn't do it."

She sat back in her arm-chair, looking at the half-filled glass of Martini.

Vallon said : " You'd better finish it and give yourself another. There's a lot more to come, baby. I've an idea you're not going to like it either."

She smiled at him. Vallon thought that, whatever she was and whatever she wasn't, she had a hell of a nerve.

She got up ; went to the sideboard. She poured a whisky and soda. She said : " I think this drink is better to receive shocks on. It's more stimulating. Go on with the story, Johnny. You don't know how you're intriguing me."

He said : " I'm going on with it. The trouble with you is that you're inclined to be stupid, Dolores. You want too much of everything. You thought you were all set for your American trip. You thought you'd got the twenty-five thousand that World Wide were going to pay for the business, and you thought you'd got something else too, didn't you ? You and your boy friend were going to start life in a big way out there. You'd have a lot of capital behind you. That's where you made a big mistake. You're not

145   K

going to have any capital behind you. You're not going to have a goddam thing."

He put his hand up. "I'm wrong. You're going to have something. You're going to have five bucks, baby. And how do you like that one? That's what Joe thought of you."

There was a long silence. She stood half-way between the sideboard and the arm-chair, looking at him. Her eyes were narrowed. Then she moved slowly back to the arm-chair; sat down. Vallon noticed that, disturbed as she was, she still managed to show the right amount of leg in the process.

She said in a very soft voice: "Tell me about the five bucks, Johnny."

Vallon said: "You know about the will Joe made—his original will? He'd left everything he had in trust for you —the money he had in America; the property he had here in the country and his liquid cash assets. Well, it's not as good as that, baby. He cancelled that will. He made another one. He left you nothing. He left most of his money to American Service charities. He's left you five bucks, and he left an executor who's going to see that his wishes are carried out."

" Really . . . ? Who's the executor, Johnny? "

" I am," said Vallon.

She began to laugh. He thought it wasn't a very nice laugh. She said: " Is this damned funny, or is it ? "

Vallon said: " You're telling me! You know, Joe always had a sense of humour."

She drank the whisky; put the glass on the floor beside her chair. " So," she said, " I'm all washed up. There's no money from the World Wide sale. Joe's kept me out of his will and left me five bucks. All right . . . the laugh's on me. So Acme are going to take the agency over ? "

He nodded. " At the end of this month."

She said: " That means you'll be out of a job, Johnny, doesn't it ? "

" Yes, I'm glad. I've got a feeling I've outgrown it. Maybe I'll start something on my own."

She raised her eyebrows. " Yes, Johnny . . .? With what ? "

He looked out of the window. " Joe left me ten thousand pounds duty free. I think he thought I might start something. Maybe that's why I'll try and do it."

There was another silence. She said : " Well, that's that. Where do we go from here ? "

Vallon said : " I don't know. The question is where you go from here." He went on : " Both of you—you and your boy friend—have made one very large-sized mistake."

She raised her eyebrows again. She said sarcastically " Not another ? "

Vallon nodded. " Hipper," he said. He thought for a moment, framing his words carefully, making the lie a good one. " Hipper always thought he was all right. Hipper thought that his own position in this business was assured ; that he was safe anyway. The way he thought was this : Here he was, an operative employed by a detective agency. He was sent out to find evidence of misconduct and to secure that evidence when he'd found it. He did that. He also found out something else. He found definite evidence of collusion, so he worked it out and came to the conclusion that he might play this game to his own advantage. So he had a talk with your boy friend, and your boy friend who's got a brain, evolved a lovely idea. You know what it was, don't you ? And in order to make that idea successful ; in order to make it stick, he passed a certain document to Hipper. But what you didn't know was that Joe had Lipscombe on your tail.

" Lipscombe had seen Hipper coming to this apartment. So then Joe had Hipper watched. Then he found Hipper was having appointments with your boy friend. Joe put two and two together without making twenty-seven out of it. He knew that Hipper must have some important evidence, and that he wouldn't let it out of his possession. He knew it would be on Hipper. So he waited until one day in the office Hipper went into the washroom to wash his hands and left his coat hanging in the staff-room. Joe went over to his coat and got the document. He guessed what was going on. He knew the case that Hipper had been working on. He guessed it was a collusive case, and he guessed what Hipper was playing at.

" Just before his appointment with Perdreau Joe put that document in the bottom right-hand drawer of his office desk. You or your boy friend—or both of you— guessed that he'd got it. You knew that it meant the end of your little scheme. Whatever happened, at any

147

price, whatever it cost, that document had to be regained. So somebody went round and waited until Perdreau left the office. They were probably on the other side of the road watching the main entrance, and they went up and in through the private door in the corridor and asked Joe for the document.

" But Joe wasn't playing. So an automatic pistol was produced with a silencer on it, and a blank cartridge was fired at Joe. That fixed him. Then the drawer with the document in it was burst open and the murderer walked away. Nobody saw him come in ; nobody saw him go out. There's no evidence against him. Joe dies of shock and everything in the garden is lovely, and if it had been like that it would have been very nice for you. But it's not like that."

She said quietly : " Isn't it, Johnny ? Why isn't it like that ? "

Vallon told his star lie. He said : " Look, you know Hipper, don't you ? You know the sort of man he is. You know what people like Hipper do when they're in a corner."

She said : " You mean he's talked."

Vallon nodded. " I mean just that. He's talked. His type always does. That means that we've exchanged one set of circumstantial evidence for another set. But Hipper's circumstantial evidence is just as good as anything else. It's good enough to fix the pair of you."

She said nothing. She sat, her hands folded in her lap, looking at the carpet in front of her.

Then : " All this is very exciting. Where do we go from here, Johnny ? " She paused. " Once upon a time you didn't dislike me."

Vallon said : " Once upon a time I didn't dislike anybody much. But this is different. You're trying to make me find an out for you, aren't you, Dolores ? You think you're entitled to that." He shrugged his shoulders. " Maybe I'm going to do it, *if I can*. And I'm not going to do it because I like you. I'm not going to do it because I like anybody. I'm not even trying to do it because I dislike myself."

She asked : " Then why ? "

Vallon said : " Joe. Joe is the reason. I know what Joe would expect me to do. As far as I can I'm going to do it."

148

He picked up his hat. " You be around to-morrow. I'll call through to you and tell you when I'm coming. If you're lucky there might be an out—if you're lucky." He went to the door. " So long, Dolores. I'll be seeing you."

She said : " Just a minute, Johnny. I rather like you in your new part. Are you being Sir Galahad or what ? What's the thing about doing what Joe wanted you to do ? It doesn't look as if I was very popular with Joe at the end, does it ? "

Vallon said : " I know what Joe wanted. He knew I never take tips. I know why he left me that ten thousand pounds. Maybe you can guess. Good night."

He closed the door softly behind him.

.   .   .   .

Vallon parked his car in St. James's Square ; looked at his strap-watch ; began to walk towards Jermyn Street. He wasn't quite certain where he was going or what he intended to do when he got there. He wasn't certain about anything. That, he thought, was one of the difficulties of life. When something turned up—something that was very important to a lot of people—you were never quite certain what you were going to do. You knew what you *ought* to do and then kidded yourself that possibly something else might be better ; something that wasn't going to cause quite so much trouble.

He thought, with an inward cynical smile, that this was the reason why people went about asking other people s advice. They wanted somebody to put them off what they knew they ought to do. They didn't need the advice. Anyone, confronted with *any* situation, always knew what he— or she—*ought* to do. But it was goddam seldom that they got around to doing it. The line of least resistance was always so much more attractive or seductive !

Almost automatically he turned into the cocktail bar in Jermyn Street. This place, he thought, was almost his second home. Simultaneously, he realised that he did not like his own home—his rooms in Kensington. He didn't like the place because, anyhow, it wasn't any sort of home. If you had a home there ought to be a woman in it— the right sort of woman. Somebody that you wanted to go back to and not get away from.

He went into the bar; sat on a high stool; ordered rye whisky. He thought he was drinking a damned sight too much; that maybe if he stopped drinking the pain in his stomach would also stop. He thought that maybe he'd rather have the pain. When you didn't drink your brain became orderly and quiet and you felt things more. If you carried a certain amount of alcohol inside you you numbed everything considerably. You could think all right, but you didn't *feel* quite so much.

He began to think about Dolores. That one, he considered, was in a hell of a spot. *Anyhow*, she was in a hell of a spot. If she'd known what Gale intended to do or if she hadn't, her position was just about the same. If enough circumstantial evidence could be produced or framed against Gale, it was good enough to take her in too. If Gale swung for the job she'd probably be in the same boat. Vallon remembered the Thompson-Bywaters case. Dolores, he thought, was probably in the same spot as that woman had been.

And if she hadn't known what Gale intended to do she was, in one way, in a worse spot. Because nobody was going to believe her. Nobody unless . . .

He put down his glass and concentrated. If Dolores hadn't known what was in Gale's mind; if she hadn't guessed afterwards when he, Vallon, had told her that Joe had been murdered; if she *hadn't* known and did this and that she could still be all right.

A girl came into the bar and sat on the high stool next to him. He looked at her casually. She was pretty and had a good figure. Her coat and skirt were well-cut—even if the skirt was a trifle short. Her stockings were sheer and her patent pumps had been expensive. They *had* been. Now, he noticed, there was a slight inclination on the part of the sole of the left shoe to part company with the upper. You could only notice this when she was sitting, as she sat now, with one foot tilted on the bar-rail at an angle.

Vallon saw, casually, that her mouth was mobile and her nostrils well-cut. He thought maybe she'd hit a bad spot too. Why not? Lots of people did . . . all the time.

The bar-tender brought the drink she ordered. She fumbled in her handbag; then looked at the man. She said : " I'm sorry . . . I've come out without any money. You'd better keep the drink."

Vallon winked at the bar-tender. He said to her : " It's my birthday, so if you don't mind I'll pay for your drink. I've been buying everybody drinks all evening so one more isn't going to mean all that. Besides which, I'm an extremely nice man who doesn't often buy drinks for charming women whom he doesn't know."

He smiled at her. Almost in spite of herself she smiled back.

She said : " I'm not in the habit of cadging drinks, but I'll drink to many happy returns of your birthday. Thank you ! "

" Those two speeches constitute an introduction," said Vallon. He drank a little rye.

He began to think about Hipper. It was a certainty that Hipper didn't know. He didn't know a thing about anything, which was the reason he'd been so uppish and sure of himself the last time they had met. If Hipper got into touch with Dolores and she told him, he'd be scared stiff. He would never stop running. Not until he hit something. If he knew, he'd have the pants scared off him.

The girl said : " Thank you for my drink. It was delicious." She spoke softly and enunciated her words well.

Vallon smiled at her sideways. He wished she wouldn't interrupt his train of thought. Then he remembered that most of his life some woman or other had been interrupting his train of thought.

He said : " A drink always tastes like that when you want it badly. I'm going to have another. You too. I told you this was my birthday and one drink is no good to anybody on somebody else's birthday."

He ordered the drinks.

" Really . . . I'm not used to drinking," she said.

" Neither am I," said Vallon. " I practically never touch the stuff." He scowled at the bar-tender, who had turned away to hide the expression on his face. " It doesn't agree with me next morning but it's very nice while you're drinking it—or just after."

The bar-tender brought the drinks. Vallon said to the girl : " Well . . . here's to you ! "

He drank some of the rye ; brought his mind back to

Hipper. He wished he'd kept a closer tail on Hipper. Just now—just at this moment—Hipper might be damned useful—especially if he didn't know anything. He could be very useful. Hipper might be the means of swinging this thing the way he, Vallon, wanted it swung . . .

The girl said : " I'm feeling so much better now. I was depressed this evening and——"

" I know," said Vallon. " I'm a mind reader. I know all about it. You're worried about two things."

She looked at him seriously. She thought he was a very strange, rather attractive man. She thought she didn't dislike him at all.

" How did you know ? " she asked. " And what two things . . . ? "

" Money and a man," said Vallon. He laughed at her. " There are only three things ever worry people . . . health, money and a man—or a woman. Depending on your sex. You look very healthy so I gather you're worried about the other two things. You must be worrying about a man. You're too pretty not to be. What's he like ? "

She smiled. " Really you're rather amazing. Perhaps you've second sight. I'm very fond of him but I don't trust him . . . much."

" Of course not," said Vallon. He signalled quietly to the bar-tender for more drinks. " Women who are crazy about a man never really do. That's why they're crazy about him. Haven't you ever noticed that all the nice women fall for men who aren't quite so good ? That's because they've got something. See what I mean ? The very good and trustworthy guys never have it. If they had they wouldn't be good and trustworthy . . . see ? "

She nodded. " I think you're right. You've made up my mind for me. I had a wire from him this morning asking me to go off with him and get married. I didn't know what to do ; whether to do that or go back home. Now I know I shall go back home."

Vallon nodded. He thought he knew what Dolores had done. Directly he had left her she'd telephoned through to Gale. She'd told Gale plenty—or asked him plenty. Now, as far as Gale was concerned, the fat would be in the fire.

And what was Gale going to do ? That, Vallon thought

was even more important than what Hipper would do. *I*
he knew.

The girl got off the stool. She finished her third drink.
She said: " Good evening to you and thank you for your
kindness. I hope you have a very happy birthday."

"Thanks a lot," said Vallon. "And now you're going
home ? "

She nodded. " I *think* so . . . I'll think it over very
seriously."

Vallon said: " You don't have to think about it. You're
not going home and you know it. But you're trying to kid
yourself that you'll think it over. Actually, you're going to
join your boy friend. I hope he makes you a good husband."

" I hope so too. But I still think I might go home."

"Why not ? " asked Vallon. "Thinking never hurts
anyone."

She smiled at him ; went out of the bar.

The bar-tender said: " I didn't know it was your birthday, sir."

"Of course you didn't," said Vallon. He paid for the
drinks. "How should you ? Even *I* didn't know it. Not
until recently."

He got off the stool. He said: " My mother was a very
secretive woman. She never let any of us know when we
were born."

He walked out of the bar ; down Regent Street ; into
St. James's Square. He started up the car ; drove into
Piccadilly ; turned westwards.

He thought he'd been everywhere else ; that he might as
well go to Chertsey.

.   .   .

It was just after nine o'clock when Vallon parked his car
in a lane near the Mandrake Club. He switched off the
lights ; lighted a cigarette. He walked down the lane ;
turned into a field ; crossed the field. He approached the
club from the back.

In the dusk the place looked romantic. The club con-
sisted of an old house with a long, low out-building added
on to the back of it. There were some lights in the front
and at the side, but the back of the place was in half darkness.
The lawn at the back of the house was well-kept and on the

right-hand side Vallon could see the converted shed—the place that Lipscombe had told him was used as a garage.

He walked towards it, keeping to the side of the lawn in the shadows of the hedge that surrounded it. There were folding doors to the front of the shed; a small door at the side. It took only three minutes for Vallon to get it open. He went inside. By the dim light that percolated through the two high, small windows, he could see the shapes of the two cars—a big American car—showy, ostentatious—the sort of car Vallon thought that Gale would like to impress people with; the other a twenty horse-power Austin.

Vallon opened the driving door of the American car. He got behind the wheel; looked into the glove box. He wasn't certain what he was looking for, but you never knew and, anyway, he hadn't anything to do. At the back of his mind was the idea that he'd come down to this place to see Gale. Or had he? He didn't know. He felt a peculiar vagueness of mind, as though he were being carried forward into an almost negative state of affairs by some motive other than his own volition.

There was nothing in the glove box. Vallon got out of the car; opened the boot at the back. That, too, was empty. Underneath in its recess was the tool chest. There was a flashlight in it. He switched it on; examined the tools. They were all big tools. There was none of the small implements usually found in a tool case. This gave him an idea. He closed the boot; went to the front of the car; opened the door.

He sniffed appreciatively. In the car was a faint smell. He recognised it. It was Fougère—a man's hair lotion made by Pinaud. Vallon grinned to himself. It was the sort of lotion a man like Gale would use. Maybe he had a bottle somewhere in the car. The odour of the perfume was strongest near the passenger seat. Vallon pulled up the leather-sprung cushion. Underneath was a tool box and a half-used bottle of Fougère.

Vallon opened the tool box; stood with the flashlight directed on the wood-lined cavity, smiling. Staring up at him were a .38 Colt automatic with a silencer on the barrel and Joe Chennault's home diary. He took them out; put the diary in his left-hand jacket pocket, the pistol in his hip-pocket. He replaced the seat; switched off the light.

He didn't even think that Gale was a fool for keeping the diary and the gun. Why shouldn't he? Gale knew when he'd put them under the seat of his car that there would never be any suspicion of murder. He knew what the death certificate would be. He knew that Chennault had died of shock. But he thought he was the only person who knew that the shock had been produced by the effects of a blank cartridge fired from an automatic and not the shock produced from an attack of angina. Probably, thought Vallon, he'd intended to get rid of the diary; to throw the gun away. He'd intended to do that sometime, but just hadn't bothered. Why should he?

Vallon went out of the shed. He closed and re-locked the door behind him. He walked across the lawn and into the little coppice at the end of it. He sat down on a fallen tree-trunk.

He thought that finding the diary let Dolores out. If she'd known the use that Gale had made of that diary she'd have destroyed it, which he had accused her of doing. She hadn't destroyed it because she hadn't even thought of it. She hadn't even known that Gale had taken it. Vallon could bring a picture to his mind of the scene which had occurred in the flat—some scene in which the participants had been Gale and Dolores. She'd told him that Chennault knew about Perdreau; that she'd told him about Perdreau.

Vallon could understand why she did this. Maybe Dolores, who was quick and sensitive, had an idea that Joe wasn't feeling so good about something. So she wanted a red herring to take his mind off Gale. So she did the obvious thing. She concentrated it on another man—on Perdreau. She told Joe about Perdreau, and when she saw Gale she told him what she'd done; that she'd fixed an appointment; that Joe was going to see Perdreau privately. She knew that Joe intended to do this on a clear afternoon, because she'd seen the note he'd made in the diary. There was nobody else coming to see him. The very fact that he was seeing Perdreau would cause him to inform the outer office that he didn't want to be disturbed.

Gale had taken this opportunity to look at the diary. He'd got the date and the time of the afternoon when Joe was going to see Perdreau. Then he pulled a fast one and said nothing to anybody about it. Dolores Chennault believed that Joe had died of angina. She'd probably disbelieved Vallon when he'd told her that he thought that Joe had been murdered. Now that he'd put the idea into her head that Gale had killed Joe; suggested to her that she'd been a party to it, she'd be in a hell of a sweat. He knew that immediately he'd left her she'd have phoned Gale; told him. Now what would Gale do? Vallon thought he could find the answer to that one.

He got up; walked along the winding path through the coppice; came to the open field, on the other side of which his car was parked. He stood in the shadow of a tree as he saw the parking lights of a car stop at the opposite end of the lane. He waited. He saw the gate on the other side of the field open. A man began to walk across the field. Vallon thought that this was really very funny.

Hipper came slowly and solidly across the field. As he turned into the pathway, Vallon came out from behind the tree.

He said: "Hallo . . . pal!"

Hipper stopped; spun round. "Well, I'll be damned I'm always meeting you. I wonder what's eating you now?"

Vallon said: "You'll know. You're still feeling pretty uppish, aren't you, Hipper? You won't in a minute. Have you ever seen an air balloon when somebody sticks a pin in it?"

Hipper said: "What the hell do you mean?"

"Come with me and I'll tell you." Vallon moved along the path towards the fallen tree.

Hipper, walking a little behind him, muttered: "What's all this damned nonsense about? I don't understand."

Vallon sat down on the tree-trunk. He lighted a cigarette. Hipper stood still in front of him, his hands in his trouser pockets. Vallon noticed his fat, round stomach with the cigarette ash in the folds of his waistcoat.

He said: "What's the betting I could tell you what you came down here for to-night, Hipper?"

Hipper said: "All right. What did I come down here for?"

"You came down here to see Gale. You came down here to tell him that you'd searched high and low but you couldn't find the letter—the one you lost. Remember? But you weren't worried too much about it, because you were going to tell him that it didn't really matter; that Querida Gale knew she'd written it; that she knew it existed; that she wouldn't know you'd lost it. So you and Gale were in just as good a position as you were before. There was no reason for him to tell her that the letter had been lost."

Hipper said nothing. He stood, his feet planted wide apart, looking at Vallon. But his face had lost its casual, easy expression. He looked a little concerned.

Vallon went on: "It's my bet that if you told Gale that you couldn't find the letter, he'd agree, as I have just suggested, that the letter didn't matter. He could bluff Querida Gale just as well without it. But if he said that, Hipper—and he would say it—he would be lying."

Hipper said: "What the hell do you mean?" His voice was a little unhappy.

Vallon said: "Gale's got the letter, you bloody fool. He killed Joe Chennault to get it. How do you like being an accessory before and after a murder, Hipper? They'll have to have a nice strong rope for you. You're so heavy. You might break a normal one. I bet you don't feel so good now, stupid." Vallon sat, grinning wickedly, drawing on his cigarette.

"What is all this stuff? What are you trying to tell me?" asked Hipper.

Vallon said: "Why don't you take your weight off your feet, Hipper? Sit down on the end of the tree here. I'll tell you a little story. You were the operative put in by the Chennault agency to find the evidence against Gale in his wife's divorce action. You knew damned well there was evidence against Gale. All right . . . you'd got that evidence. But the woman wasn't Miss Evangeline Roberta Trickett. It was a woman called Claire Ansteley. Right?"

Hipper said nothing.

Vallon continued: "You're a guy who's always played it off the cuff, Hipper. If you can play it both ways with safety you will, and this was one of the times when you thought you could play it both ways with safety. You knew Claire Ansteley is what is usually called a nice woman, and you knew Gale would want her name kept out of this. So you had a talk with him. He probably gave you a few quid to forget about Ansteley; to arrange to find another co-

157

respondent. As a matter of fact," said Vallon casually, "I wouldn't mind betting you found him Miss Trickett. I bet you've had contacts with Messrs. Sulkin & Frash before now in some of the divorce cases you've handled for the firm. So that was that. You and Gale contacted over this business. He goes off with Trickett and you get the evidence and Claire Ansteley's name is kept out of it. How am I doing, Hipper?"

Hipper said : " Go on . . ." He took a carton of cigarettes out of his pocket, extracted one and lighted it. Vallon could see that his fingers were shaking a little.

" I expect," said Vallon, " that you asked Gale a question —just between friends—a question that has intrigued everybody. You asked him how he liked giving up the five thousand a year that he was getting from Querida Gale while he was married to her ? And he told you the truth. He said he was going to sell out for forty thousand pounds ; that on the day the decree nisi was pronounced he was going to get forty thousand pounds for being a good boy and allowing himself to be divorced and for losing five thousand a year. He said Mrs. Gale had given him a letter to that effect.

" And then you got a brainwave, didn't you, Hipper—a hell of a brainwave ? I must say it was very clever. You told Gale that if he liked to give you that letter, all you had to do was to wait a week or two after the decree nisi was pronounced—but before it was made absolute—and then send the letter to the King's Proctor and tell him that you'd found it in the course of your investigations ; that as a responsible citizen you could not be connected with a collusive divorce case. You knew exactly what would happen. The decree nisi would be rescinded. Gale would still be the husband of Querida Gale, still getting five thousand a year while he was her husband, plus the forty thousand pounds for which he'd taken her. I wonder how much he agreed to pay you out of that sum, Hipper."

Vallon paused.

Hipper said nothing. He sat, the cigarette still between his fingers. He was breathing heavily.

" You and Gale," went on Vallon, " must have thought you were on a damned good wicket. You were too. You were absolutely safe. Your story could always be that you'd done your duty. Gale liked it because he was going to get his forty thousand pounds, and his allowance of five thousand a year would have to continue under the deed until such time as Mrs. Gale got a fresh divorce to go through. And the court wouldn't allow that to happen too quickly after the evidence of collusion in the first case. They'd have made her wait at least a year, perhaps two. They get very funny about things like that, you know. And *you* ought to know.

"So as the time comes for the petition to be heard you begin to put the screw on Querida Gale, just in case you can do a little extra blackmailing yourself. But still you're perfectly safe because you're pretending to be her friend and adviser. You go down to see her and you don't tell her anything except that you believe Gale is going to make trouble over the divorce. When she asks you what trouble you don't know. But she gives you twenty-five pounds and you promise to go and see her again if anything happens ; if you get any information that you think might be useful to her. That's what you were at when I met you at the fair at Paignton. Well ? "

Hipper said : " Well, supposing you're right, what about it ? Isn't it right for a detective employed by a responsible agency to produce evidence of collusion in a divorce case if he has reason to believe it's going on, and wasn't it the decent thing for me to do to see Mrs. Gale and to tell her there was probably going to be some trouble ? " Now his tone had become a little more truculent.

Vallon said : " You're breaking my heart, Hipper. What a nice man you're making yourself out to be. But your trouble's got to come. You're in a very nasty spot, my friend."

" What spot ? " asked Hipper. " Why am I in a spot ? I haven't done anything."

" That's what you think. I've got a very different story," said Vallon. " You lost the letter. Gale gave it to you for safe keeping, because you were the person who had to produce it *after* the decree nisi ; after he'd got the forty thousand pounds from Mrs. Gale. Now that letter was dynamite, wasn't it ? You wouldn't even put it in a drawer or lock it up. You carried it about with you all the time. You carried it about in the breast pocket of your coat. But there are some things, Hipper, we get so used to doing that we don't even notice when we're doing them, and one of those things was that you used to hang up your coat in the staff-room when you went to wash your hands. Joe Chennault wanted to have a look at your coat. Do you know why?"

"No . . ." Hipper spoke very quietly. "Tell me why Joe did that."

"His wife was up to something," said Vallon. "So he put Lipscombe to watch her. It's a stone certainty that some time or other Lipscombe saw you going up to her apartment, or talking to her. He must have. He reported this to Chennault. Chennault knew that there was something on between you and his wife. Chennault also knew that Gale had visited her at her apartment. He also knew that you were the operative who handled the Gale divorce. He knew there was some funny business going on somewhere. Joe was a pretty quick man, you know. He had a fine, intuitive brain. He was a man who had hunches and very often they were right. I ought to know.

"So that morning while he was standing in Marvin's room with the door open talking to Marvin, he saw you hang up your coat and he saw you go into the wash-room, and whilst you were washing your hands he went through your coat and found that letter. You came out of the wash-room. You put your coat on. Some time afterwards you missed that letter. But you had no idea that Joe Chennault had taken it. You thought it might have fallen out of your pocket. You thought a dozen things. You've been looking for it ever since. Right?"

Hipper said nothing.

Vallon drew on his cigarette. "It's a nice story, isn't it? It's all beginning to take shape, Hipper. All the little pieces of the jig-saw puzzle are beginning to fit in. So now what's the next act? Would you like to know what the next act is? And this is very funny. This is what people call the hand of fate. Joe's got an idea that there's something going on between his wife and Pierce Gale. He knows that Querida Gale is divorcing Gale. He knows that you were the operative employed by his agency to get the evidence and that somehow you're mixed up with them. And then he gets this letter. So he guesses the whole story.

" He guesses there's a blackmail racket on against Mrs. Gale between you and Pierce. So he looks in his diary and he finds that the best afternoon to have a talk with Pierce Gale is the afternoon which is reserved to talk with Perdreau. So he telephones through to Gale and asks him to come and see him. He guesses he'll be through with Perdreau by three o'clock. He probably asks Gale to come up between three-thirty and four, and because he thinks it may be a little tough he sends me an urgent message to my apartment telling me to be with him before four o'clock."

Vallon shrugged his shoulders. " I wish I'd been there," he said. " Joe would have been alive now. So on this afternoon Perdreau goes there at two-thirty making a very nice red herring for Pierce Gale. Gale arrives at three-thirty or a quarter to four, or whatever time the appointment was made for. He wonders what the hell Chennault wants to see him about. He wonders if by any chance Chennault has an inkling as to what's going on. This man Gale's no push-over. They tell me he has a brain. It may be that he also had an idea that you'd double-crossed him. He may even have thought that you'd get the wind up because he thinks you're a scared rabbit, Hipper. And he may have thought you'd got so frightened that you'd handed the letter back to Joe Chennault. I bet you never thought of that one, did you, Hipper ? "

Hipper said nothing. He tried to light his cigarette. He couldn't get the lighter to work. Vallon said : " Don't worry about smoking for a minute. What I've got to say is much more interesting than any cigarette.

" So he goes along to see Joe Chennault. Joe's told him to come in by the private door for a very obvious reason. Chennault was working for Mrs. Gale in the divorce action. He wouldn't want anybody to know that he was seeing the respondent in that case. So he told Gale to come in by the private door, and he kept everybody out of his office.

" Gale knew that Chennault was a sick man. He knew that he hadn't long to live. He knew that any shock would kill him. So he went prepared to pull a strong-arm act. He took with him an automatic pistol with a silencer on it, loaded with a blank cartridge. He kept the appointment.

" Then Joe tells him. Joe tells him he's got the letter. Joe tells him he's wise to the whole business. He also probably tells him that he's running around with Dolores."

Vallon stopped talking. He smiled. He said : " You know, Hipper, Joe Chennault—angina or not—was a hell of a man. I served with him before his heart got so bad. He wasn't the sort of fellow to take anything from Pierce Gale. He told Gale just what he was going to do with him. He told Gale he was going to send him inside. He told Gale that when the court discovered that the husband of Querida Gale was a common blackmailer, they'd discount the evidence of what Chennault would describe as a forged letter from her, and give her her divorce. See ? You begin to understand ? "

Hipper nodded. His face was livid.

" So then Gale pulled the big act," said Vallon. " He brought out the gun and told Joe that unless he handed that letter over he'd give it to him. Joe told him to go to hell. He probably thought he was bluffing anyway. So Gale squeezed the trigger ; the wad hit Joe and the shock killed him. But the wad burned a little hole in Joe's waistcoat. So Gale stuck a cigarette stub on to the hole so that it would appear that when Joe slumped forward over the desk the stub fell out of his mouth and was caught in the fold of his waistcoat. The only thing is," said Vallon, " it was the wrong cigarette. You know Joe only smoked ' All American.' "

There was a silence. Somewhere, inconsequently enough, an owl hooted.

Vallon said : " That sounds nice, doesn't it—the owl hooting ? I mean you won't hear it where they're going to put you, pal. Because you see you're going to break over this job. The letter was in your coat pocket. You were in this thing from the start. And you know what the law says, don't you ? English law says that when people are connected together to commit a felony and as a result of that felony a murder is committed by one of them, with their common knowledge, all of them are responsible for the murder. And how do you like that, Hipper ? "

Hipper said hoarsely : " You've got to prove all this. How do you know that Gale went to Chennault's office ? If nobody saw him there ; if nobody saw him go in or come out, nobody can say that it was Gale who killed him ; Perdreau might have killed him. There's no evidence."

Vallon grinned. " There wasn't any evidence, but there

is now. Look . . ." He produced the automatic from his hip pocket ; he put his hand in his coat pocket ; brought out the diary. "I've just been over Gale's car in the garage. I found them under the passenger seat. He hadn't even worried to get rid of them. Why should he after the death certificate ? He was probably going to keep them as mementoes."

Hipper's face sagged. He sat, his shoulders hunched forward.

Vallon said : " Put the cigarette in your mouth, pal." He produced his lighter ; lighted it. " Look, maybe if you do what I tell you I'll find a way out for you, not because I like you, not because I think you're worth it, but just because that's how I want it. Are you going to do what you're told, or do I turn you in ? "

Hipper said : " What the hell ? I didn't know anything about this. I didn't know a thing. Maybe you're right about the first part, but——"

Vallon interrupted. " I know all that. But it isn't going to save you, baby. You tell that story to a jury and see if they believe it."

Hipper spread his hands hopelessly. " What do I do ? "

" You get up," said Vallon. " You get into that car of yours and you go home. You stay there till I send for you. Do what I tell you and you've got a chance. Do anything else but what I tell you and you'll hang."

Hipper got up. " If it's like that they'll have to hang her too. They'll have to."

Vallon said : " Why not ? But what's that got to do with it ? Are you going to play ball ? Are you going to do what you're told ? "

Hipper said : " All right. You win." He got up from the tree-trunk. He moved a few steps. He turned. " Damn you, Vallon."

Vallon said : " That's O.K. by me. And damn you too. Good night, sweetie-pie."

Vallon sat motionless for a few minutes ; then he got up from the tree-trunk and stretched. He felt tired ; worn out. The pain in his stomach was working overtime, he thought. He wondered where he could get a drink ; decided he couldn't ; that in any event he had to think out what he was going to do.

He found he had a little difficulty in concentrating. Driving about the countryside; living on Bacardi whisky and cigarettes was no sort of way *not* to feel tired. He thought, vaguely, that sometime or other he must try a different diet.

He lighted a cigarette, sat down again on the tree-trunk and tried to make up his mind. Dolores Chennault, he considered, was out of the murder rap. She hadn't known what Gale had planned; she hadn't known that he'd killed Chennault. She had only just got the idea after his last conversation with her, and even so she probably didn't believe it. Not if she was fond of Gale.

The fact that he, Vallon, had accused her of burning Joe's private appointment diary, had probably decided her that the whole thing was nonsense. If anyone had killed Joe it must be Perdreau. That is what she believed.

But it wouldn't save her. The evidence surrounding Joe's death, if it came to light, implicated her and Hipper. The three of them would be for the high jump, although she and Hipper were innocent of anything to do with the killing.

The idea came to Vallon that he would go into the Mandrake Club and have a showdown with Gale. He dismissed it immediately. It didn't make sense. Not at the moment. If he guessed right, Dolores would have telephoned Gale and given him the story and then Gale would have had to do something about it. And pretty quickly. She would have told Gale about Joe's will and not having any money. She would certainly have told him that, because no matter what other faults she might have Dolores was honest enough about money. She'd feel that she ought to tell him that.

And that would have settled Gale's mind once and for all. There was only one thing for him to do and he would do it and he'd do it right away.

Vallon looked at his strap-watch. It was nearly ten o'clock. He got up from the tree-trunk and stretched himself again. That didn't help. He was so tired that nothing helped, and the idea of another trip to Devonshire appalled him.

He shrugged his shoulders. Once on the main road he could do it in four and a half hours. He could get a drink anywhere between now and eleven o'clock. If he were lucky he might even be able to buy a bottle to keep going on.

He walked slowly through the coppice, across the field to the lane where his car was parked. He slid into the driving seat ; reversed the car, turned it. He drove on to the main road.

He put his foot down on the accelerator. He thought that his big job was going to be to keep awake. Four and a half hours driving, at speed, isn't easy for a man who was as tired as he was.

He drove on, his sleepy eyes on the road, yawning, talking to himself to keep awake.

CHAPTER FIVE

MITSOUKO

1

IT WAS ten minutes past three when Vallon stopped the car on the grass verge opposite the entrance gates of Ladycourt. He got out of the driving seat slowly ; turned off the lights ; sat on the near-side wing. He lighted a cigarette and thought that nothing tasted so awful as tobacco when you were tired.

He got up ; stretched ; walked slowly across the road, through the entrance gates, into the courtyard of Ladycourt. As he approached the wide Tudor doors he saw the crack of light showing through the side window of the drawing-room.

So she was up ! Vallon grinned. He pulled the handle of the door-bell. He waited, leaning against the door-post, the cigarette hanging out of the corner of his mouth, his hands in his jacket pockets.

The door opened. Querida Gale stood, framed in the open doorway, her figure illuminated almost theatrically, he thought, by the light of the stained-glass hall light.

He pushed himself away from the door-post. He said : " Well, Querida . . . how's it going ? "

" Come in, Johnny. My God . . . but you look awful ! What's the matter . . . what's wrong ? "

He went into the hall. He waited while she closed the

door ; followed her into the drawing-room. A small fire was lit. He thought the room seemed cosy and attractive.

Vallon said : " The matter with me is Bacardi, whisky and no sleep. I've forgotten the last time I went to sleep. I've been driving around this goddam country until I'm seeing double. And I've got to drive back to-night. I must be in London by the morning and the idea doesn't appeal to me a hell of a lot."

She said : " I'm going to give you some tea and you've *got* to eat something. You must. You look like death."

" I feel like it. But never mind about the tea just now. What about Gale ? "

She said : " Sit down and put your feet on this stool. Johnny . . . I'm damned frightened of Pierce. He telephoned me through at ten o'clock to-night. He told me that the letter I'd given him—the one about paying him the money— had somehow got into the hands of Hipper. He said Hipper wanted twenty thousand pounds for it ; that he must have the money. He said that I must find it ; that he was coming down here to-morrow night ; arriving about mid-night and that somehow I'd got to have the money. He said if I hadn't got it by then, Hipper was going to send the letter to the court ; that the divorce would never go through. He said if I didn't give him the twenty thousand pounds to-morrow night he was getting out ; that I'd still have to pay him the allowance ; that I'd never see him again ; that I'd never be divorced."

Vallon grinned. " And you believe that ? " he asked. " If you do, you must be a mug."

" I don't know what to believe," she said. " All I know is I'm terrified of Pierce. You don't know what he's like when he's in a bad spot. You just don't know, Johnny . . ."

" Don't I ? You'd be surprised. I know plenty about that egg. He stops at nothing—not even murder. He's a nice guy . . . but you've got to take him in small doses."

She said : " I knew you'd come down, Johnny. I *knew* you'd be here."

He looked at her. She was wearing a French blue velvet house-coat with a wide, deeper blue sash. He thought she looked pretty good. He thought Gale had been a damned fool to lose a woman as good as Querida Gale *could* have been—with the right man.

She asked: "What am I to do, Johnny . . . ? Shall I give him the money? How do I know what he'll do if I don't?"

"How do you know what he'll do if you *do*?" Vallon smiled at her. He leaned his head against the back of the chair. She thought that any moment he would fall asleep.

"Go and make me some coffee," he said. "Black coffee with a little brandy in it. Just do that."

"All right, Johnny." She went out of the room.

He began to think about Gale. Gale was a hard man. If he were in a corner he'd do the obvious things. *All* the obvious things. Pierce Gale was not the type who would stand being pushed around. Vallon thought he could take a chance on that.

She came back with the tray. She gave him the black coffee. It was hot, strong, and the brandy put a bite into it. He sat up and sipped it.

He said: "Has Gale got a boat down here? I bet he has. D'you know anything about a boat?"

"Of course." She went to the mantelpiece; took a cigarette from the silver box; lighted it; gave it to him. "I gave him a boat. A sixty-foot launch—*The Syriad*. She's moored in the basin at Torquay. He often used her to go to France. Why, Johnny . . . ?"

"Never mind," he said. "It doesn't matter."

He drank some more coffee. Now he knew why Gale had planned to arrive late next night. After the interview with Querida he was going to get out. He'd collect the money —or such of it as was available—and blow before the trouble started.

"Have you friends in the country? Somewhere where you can stay?" he asked.

She nodded. "Of course . . . I have a friend in Kent. But . . ."

"To-morrow early," said Vallon, "you pack some things and get out. Understand? When Gale gets here to-morrow night you're not going to be here. It isn't going to be at all healthy for you if you're here. He's going to be in a very bad temper and you're not going to give him any money. Even if you were here, and gave him the money he'd still double-cross you. That boyo would two-time his own mother. He's like that. So you're not going to be here.

Go to Kent and when you're there telephone Marvin at Chennault Investigations and give him your address and telephone number. I'll get in touch with you. Understand ? "

" I understand, Johnny," she said. " Why don't you eat something ? Let me give you some food."

" I'd like that," he said. " If you know how to cook eggs and bacon I could eat that."

She smiled. " I even know how to do that," she said. " I won't be long."

He gave her time to get to the kitchen. Then he went to the telephone at the end of the room. He sat down, dialled Trunks, gave Trant's number. He waited impatiently. He sat, drumming his fingers on the telephone table.

Trant's voice came over the line. He sounded sleepy. Vallon could hear the yawn.

He said : " Wake up, Trant . . . this is dynamite. So there can't be any slip-ups. Are you listening ? "

Trant said : " O.K., Mr. Vallon. I can still hear even if I am half-asleep ! "

" To-morrow morning, at half-past nine," said Vallon, " you telephone Detective-Inspector McNeil at Scotland Yard. You make an appointment to see him at ten-thirty. You tell him it's a murder job. Have you got that ? "

" I've got it," said Trant. " So things are moving, Mr. Vallon ? "

" They're exceeding the speed-limit," said Vallon. " All right, when you've made that appointment you go round and you see Hipper. He's at his home. You know the address. And he's scared stiff. He's anybody's meat. I've given him plenty to think about and he's so steamed up about being sucked into this business as an accessory before and after that he'll eat dirt for anybody. See ? "

" I see," said Trant. " I'm ahead of you, Mr. Vallon."

" You tell Hipper that you know everything—the whole book," Vallon went on. " You tell him that if he wants to keep out of the big thing he's got to talk about the little thing. You tell him he's got to make a statement about the collusive divorce, the letter to Gale and the plot to blackmail Mrs. Gale. You take him round to the Yard at ten-thirty. He talks to McNeil. But he doesn't mention Dolores Chennault . . . see ? There's no need for him to bring her into it at all. He tells McNeil all about the conversations he had with Gale, and the letter and all that nonsense ; but he doesn't say anything about losing the letter or Joe Chennault finding it . . . see ? He just says he's lost the letter. Are you still with me ? "

" Yes," said Trant. " I've got it. He admits to the original plot to blackmail Mrs. Gale, but he says nothing that's going to implicate him in any way in the other business."

" Right," said Vallon. " That's the idea. Tell him if he does that he'll be safe. He's turning King's Evidence against Gale—make him understand that. Lead him to believe if he does that the police will leave him out of it and go for Gale on the blackmail charge. Understand ? "

" I've got it," said Trant. " Is that all ? "

" No," said Vallon. " After he's made the statement to McNeil about the letter, the collusive divorce case and the blackmail lark ; tell McNeil to get rid of him. When he's gone give McNeil the whole story. Tell him that Gale killed Chennault and that I can very nearly prove it. Then tell McNeil I want to see him. Bring him round to my rooms in Kensington at about half-past twelve to-morrow. Tell him I'll give him the whole works. Have you got it all now ? "

" I've got it," said Trant. " I won't let you down, Mr. Vallon."

" You better hadn't," said Vallon. " So long, Trant."

He hung up the receiver ; went back to his chair.

She came in with the tray. She put it on a small table. Vallon looked at it. The sight of the food made him feel ill.

He said : " I'm sorry you've had all this trouble. I couldn't eat. I'll have some more coffee and a spot of brandy in it."

She poured the coffee. " How long do you think you're going to be able to go on like this ?" she asked. " You must eat."

He smiled at her. " Why ? " he asked. " And I don't have to go on like this much longer. I think that everything's very nearly nicely sewn up—one way or another."

She stood in front of the fire, her hands held towards the flame. He noticed the sparkle of her rings in the firelight.

He poured out more coffee.

She looked at him sideways. " Johnny, what's going to happen to Pierce ? What is the end of all this business going to be ? What will he do ? "

He shrugged his shoulders. " Search me . . . ! But people like Gale usually manage to make their own heavens and their own hells. This time it looks as if he's bitten off a bit more than he can chew."

" Be careful, Johnny," she said softly. " Pierce is a dangerous man. He can be a desperate man."

" So what," said Vallon. " Everybody's desperate sometime. And the bigger they come the harder they fall."

She smiled at him. " You've got your nerve, and you're full of confidence." She turned and faced him. " You're an odd type, Johnny, but you're a very attractive person. I expect a lot of women have told you that ? "

He nodded.

" Plenty," he said. " And look where it's got me. I'm a millionaire, I'm happily married to a lovely woman, and I've got forty-three children and a future ! " He grinned at her. " I'd like to be a chicken farmer on some little farm where it's so goddam quiet you can hear yourself think. As for being full of confidence, I'm full of a mixture of alcohol that's nearly blowing my top, black coffee and near-fright."

He got up. " It's nearly five o'clock. I've got to be on my way. If I tread on it and don't fall asleep on the way I can make it by ten o'clock. Just now there's nothing on the road."

She came over to where he was. She stood close to him, looking up into his face.

" When all this business is over, Johnny," she said, " when it's all settled one way or another, there's still a lot of time left for you and me to be happy. We *could* be, you know. Or aren't you interested ? "

He said : " It's nice of you, but I'm not. At the moment I'm not looking forward further than a day and if I did, my sweet, I wouldn't be looking forward to a future with you."

He picked up his hat. He said : " So long, Querida."

When he was at the door she said : " Johnny . . . do you want anything ? Some money ? And aren't you going to kiss me ? "

He laughed. " I wouldn't know what to buy if I had some money. . . . And I'm tired of kissing women. Everything

170

starts with a kiss and very often the pay-off is a lemon. From now on my middle name's ' Hermit.' "

He went out. She stood looking at the door.

Then he came back into the room. He said : " I suppose you wouldn't know the name of a perfume. It's a light, flowery sort of scent. With an odd name. I suppose you wouldn't know ? "

She said : " What sort of odd name, Johnny ? Can't you explain a little more fully ? "

He shrugged his shoulders. " It's an oriental sort of name," he said. " It reminds you of Japan or somewhere in the East. . . ."

" It wouldn't be ' Mitsouko ' would it ? " she asked. " ' Mitsouko ' by Guerlain."

" For God's sake," he said. " That's it . . . ' Mitsouko ' . . . Thanks a lot . . . So long. . . ."

She stood motionless until she heard the front door close behind him. Then she went back to the fire. She said quietly : " Good luck, Johnny . . . good luck. . . ."

Then she lighted a cigarette. She went up to her room ; began to pack a suitcase. Half-way through she began to cry.

She sat down on the bed. She thought the trouble with life was if you asked for too much you got nothing, and if you asked for nothing . . . She thought of Vallon. She could hear his voice saying : " And if you ask for nothing you get that, too, baby. To hell with it anyway."

She got on with the packing. She found you could pack and cry at the same time quite easily. It was no effort at all.

2

It was just after ten when the doctor opened the door of his consulting-room.

He said : " I thought it was you. I recognised your car from the window." He stood looking at Vallon. " You're in a hell of a state, aren't you ? Aren't you ever going to listen to sense ? " He smiled. " Has anybody ever told you about a nervous breakdown ? When did you eat last, Johnny ? "

Vallon said : " I forget. I've been keeping going on alcohol. It's easy and it doesn't take any digesting.".

The doctor said : " Come in. Let's have a look at you."

After a while : " You've got to take a pull at yourself. You're in a bad shape. You've a good constitution, but you're worn out. Nobody could go on the way you do. And you've got to cut this whisky out. It's poison for you, especially if you don't eat."

Vallon said : " Look . . . I didn't come here to listen to a lecture. Pep talks are normally very nice, but not just now. I want some help, see ? "

" I see . . ." said the doctor. " What do you want—a prescription for heroin or a medical certificate entitling you to four bottles of whisky a day. Which ? " He grinned cheerfully at Vallon.

Vallon said : " Listen, I've been working, see ? I'm on a case. It's one of those things. If I start something I have to finish it, and I've nearly finished this. But I've got to keep going for another twenty-four hours. Now, what can you give me for that ? "

" I suppose you feel that your legs are folding up under you ? " asked the doctor.

" Something like that. I also feel as if my stomach belongs to a man in Nova Scotia, and as if I've no backbone."

The doctor drew his prescription pad towards him. " Listen, Johnny. I'm going to give you some Coramine. Perhaps it'll counteract the effect of some of the whisky you've absorbed, and it'll keep you going for a bit. But you're not going to have much. And there's no more after this. What you really need is food and sleep, and then food and more sleep. And no liquor and no cigarettes."

Vallon said : " That sounds like heaven to me. Give me that prescription, you quack ! " He put the prescription in his pocket. At the door he said : " You're not really a bad egg. . . . So long ! I'll see you at the graveside ! "

.   .   .   .

Vallon was lying on his bed, looking at the ceiling, when he heard the front-door bell ring. He swung his legs off the bed ; brushed his hair ; went downstairs. On the way down he looked at his strap-watch. It was just twelve o'clock. He thought that Trant was pretty good. He always kept to time.

When he got to his sitting-room, McNeil and Trant were there.

McNeil said: " Hallo, Johnny. What's all this nonsense about ? "

" Take you weight off your feet, copper . . ." Vallon grinned. " It's a long time since I've seen you. Remember that last thing ? "

" I remember," said McNeil. " You ought to have been a policeman—except you're not honest enough."

" You're telling me ! What do you think about this lark, Mac ? "

McNeil said: " By what I've heard I don't like it at all. Trant here brought Hipper along to the Yard this morning, and Hipper's made a statement. That was easy enough. It's quite obvious that a collusive divorce action was arranged between Mrs. Gale and her husband, in consideration of which he was to receive a sum of money the day after the decree nisi was pronounced. Well, that isn't a criminal act ; that's an affair for the Divorce Court authorities to deal with. But the blackmail, and the use of the letter as a lever, is criminal. I put Hipper in another room and had a talk with Trant before I spoke to him.

" I played it your way, Johnny. I allowed Hipper to think that making this statement would let him out on the blackmail thing ; that we were going after Gale on a charge of blackmail."

Vallon said: " Fine. And what do you think about the other thing—the murder thing ? "

The detective-inspector shrugged his wide shoulders. " I don't think anything at the moment. By what I can hear from Trant, Chennault had an appointment at two-thirty on the afternoon he died with the man Perdreau. Nobody saw Perdreau go into the office ; nobody saw him come out. If we try to hang a murder charge on to Gale the defence is going to say that Perdreau could have done it, unless we can prove conclusively that Perdreau was out of the office and Gale was in it at the time of the killing. That visit of Perdreau's makes it very convenient for the defence.

" Then there's the fact that nobody saw Gale go into the office and nobody saw him come out," he concluded.

Vallon said : " I know. But there was a hell of a motive for him killing Chennault. He had to get the letter."

The detective-inspector nodded. " The motive's there all right. But you can't hang a man on motive. You know the law as well as I do, Vallon. A jury has to be satisfied beyond reasonable doubt. There're too many ' ifs ' in this case. There may be circumstantial evidence, and circumstantial evidence is as good as any other evidence if it's the right sort, but if Gale has an alibi for that afternoon, he'll get away with it."

Vallon said : " Supposing I told you that I'd got Chennault's private diary. This was the diary he kept in his own house. Supposing I told you that on the day in question there are two entries in the afternoon—one at two-thirty for Perdreau, and the second one at three-fifteen for Gale. I can prove that I found that diary under one of the seats in Gale's car, and what do you think was with it —an automatic with a silencer over the barrel."

" Now you're beginning to talk," said McNeil. " But even if you are beginning to talk, you're only beginning. You've got to prove that that was the gun that fired the wad that caused Chennault to die. While ballistic experts can check up with a bullet, I doubt if they can check up with a wad. Gale can say that he never knew the gun was in his car. He can say that somebody planted it on him. He can say that Perdreau planted it there. See what I mean ? Don't think I'm being difficult . . .."

Vallon said : " I see what you mean. You're dead right. If you're going to bring a charge, you've got to make it stick. And there's a new angle. I think Gale's wise to something. He's beginning to smell some rats—maybe because he hasn't seen anything of Hipper."

The police officer asked : " What's he at now ? "

" Last night," said Vallon, " he expected to see Hipper, and Hipper didn't turn up." He grinned. " He turned up all right, but he didn't see Gale. I had a little meeting with him instead. So while I was on my way to Paignton, he got through to Mrs. Gale. He told her a cock and bull story about Hipper having put the screws on him and saying that unless he had twenty thousand pounds he was going to send that letter to the court, in which case there would be no divorce for her. And he also said unless she cashed out the twenty thousand pounds to-night he was going to get out and leave her in the air, because nobody would know where he was."

McNeil said : " I see. So he's getting out ? "

" That's what he wants to do," said Vallon. " Look, I think you could hang this murder rap on to him if he did a little talking. I have an idea as to how he might do a little talking. I'm a disinterested party and my evidence might clinch it if I knew what he'd done ; exactly how he'd done it."

McNeil nodded. " That, with the gun, the appointment book and Hipper's story, might make it stick," he said.

" All right," said Vallon. " Now, I've got an idea. Listen to me, Mac. This is the way we play it, and I'm certain of this. Play it my way and you'll get him."

McNeil said : " I'll try anything once. Let's hear your big idea, Johnny . . ."

.   .   .   .

Vallon got off the bed at three o'clock. His head ached and his tongue felt like the covering of a plush sofa. He went downstairs ; drank a cup of tea. Then he telephoned to Dolores Chennault.

When she came on the line he said : " Hallo, Dolores. . . . This is Johnny. I'm coming out to see you. I want to talk to you."

" All right, Johnny. What is it this time ? Has somebody murdered someone else, or is this just another of your false alarms ? "

" You'll be able to judge for yourself," he said. " I'll be with you in half an hour or so."

When he rang, she opened the door of the flat. She was dressed in a neat black coat and skirt ; an amber-coloured silk blouse. There were dark circles under her eyes. She looked unhappy.

He followed her into the sitting-room. He said : " You're looking tired, Dolores. Maybe you're worried."

" Does that mean anything ? " she asked. " People do get tired, you know, and everybody's worried sometime or other. Look at you—you look as if you've been dragged through a hedge backwards. What's the matter with you, Johnny ? Have you got some other bee in your bonnet ? "

175

He sat down in an arm-chair. She stood, leaning against the sideboard, looking at him with sombre eyes.

He asked: " Have you heard from your boy friend, Gale ? I bet you haven't ? Do you think you're likely to hear from him ? "

She shrugged her shoulders. " How should I know ? And what in hell has it to do with you, Johnny ? Why don't you mind your own business for a change ? "

He grinned at her. He lighted a cigarette with a hand that was not too steady. He said: " Don't worry. You're not going to hear from Gale. He's had it. You won't be troubled with him any more. Maybe you ought to return thanks for that."

She said seriously: " Johnny . . . what do you mean by that ? "

" Just this . . . I take it that you telephoned Gale after I saw you last time. You told him that the deal with the World Wide Agency for the purchase of Chennault Investigations was off. You told him that Acme had bought the business for a paltry ten thousand. You told him that Joe had cut you out of his will and left you five bucks. Isn't that right ? "

She nodded. " So what ? "

Vallon said: " That was good enough for him. He's planning to get out. But you know that boy. He's not going before he's collected from someone or other. Your little trip with him to South America is off. It's one thing for a boyo like Gale to be going to South America with a good-looker like you and about fifty thousand pounds, and another thing to have to tote an expensive woman, with no money, around the place. What did you expect him to do ? "

" Well . . . what's he going to do, Mr. Know-All ?" she asked acidly.

" I went down to see his wife last night," said Vallon. " He's trying to work the black on her. He telephoned her yesterday that Hipper had found the letter he lost—the letter from her to Gale promising him forty thousand when the decree nisi was through. He told her that Hipper was asking twenty thousand for the letter ; that he had to have the money right away. Gale's going down there this evening to collect it ; after which he's going to duck so as to be out

176

of the way if somebody tries to pin this murder thing on him."

She shrugged her shoulders. "So you're still talking about that nonsense. I tell you Pierce never killed Joe. Why should he? I never believed it and I never will. Joe just died and *you* thought up the rest of that fairy story. Anyhow, where is Pierce going to duck to?"

"He's got a boat down at Torquay in the basin," said Vallon. "A sixty-foot motor launch. His wife gave it to him. He's often made trips to France in it. He's taking that way out *after* he's collected from his wife for the letter. He's going to leave you flat and get away with twenty thousand pounds. That's what *he* thinks."

She said nothing. She moved over to the window; stood looking out.

Vallon went on: "It's tough for you, Dolores. You've tried damned hard to be loyal to this man; to believe that he was alright. He isn't. He's a louse and a killer. Even if I understand why you don't believe it."

She turned towards him. "So you see *that*, do you Johnny? Tell me why."

"I made two mistakes when I talked to you before," said Vallon. "I accused you of sending Joe's suit away—the one with the burn on the waistcoat—because you wanted to destroy that evidence. I was wrong. You sent that suit away before you began to believe that I was right about Joe being killed. Afterwards when you thought there *was* something in the idea you preferred to think that Perdreau might have done it—anybody but Gale. I was wrong about the suit."

He lighted a fresh cigarette from the stub of the old one. "And I was wrong about something else. I was wrong about Joe's diary. I accused you of having burned it. You hadn't. You couldn't have burned it because you didn't even know where it was." He grinned at her. "I bet you've been plenty busy looking for it since I last saw you, haven't you, Dolores?"

She nodded. "I've looked everywhere. It's gone. I can't find it."

"You bet you can't," said Vallon. "Because I've got it."

She raised her eyebrows. "Where'd you get it, Johnny?"

Vallon said : " That can wait for a minute. When I talked to you before I suggested to you that you'd told Gale about the appointment Joe had with Perdreau. I expect that's true. But you didn't tell him for the reason I thought. You didn't tell him because you wanted to help him kill Joe. You didn't even *know* that he was going to kill Joe. Perhaps *he* didn't at that time. Perhaps he only thought of it after you'd told him that you'd seen the appointment with Perdreau written in Joe's private diary in his room here."

Vallon stretched out his legs and rested his aching head on the cushion behind him.

" I think he got the idea after that," he said. " So he got in touch with Joe and made an appointment for the same afternoon. He knew that Joe would prefer to meet both your boy friends on the same day—privately—without any interference. He was right. Joe told him to come up at three-fifteen and use the private staircase and door to the office. That suited Gale perfectly.

" But afterwards he got a brainwave. He realised that if Joe had put the appointment with Perdreau down in his private diary, it was on the cards that he might also write in the appointment with Gale. He was dead right. Joe did write it in. It's there—' 3.15 *p.m. Pierce Gale re D.*' I've seen it."

She moved a little. " Oh, my God . . . ! "

" You're telling me," said Vallon. " So Gale has to get the diary and have a look. He comes here one day and he goes into Joe's room while you are out or busy and grabs the diary. He puts it in his pocket, probably intending to look at it afterwards. He wouldn't want to be caught by you in the act of examining it. You might get ideas. See ? "

" I see . . ." Dolores' voice was quiet and steady.

" I found the diary with the appointments with Perdreau and Gale in it, and the automatic with a bulb silencer on the barrel which Gale used to kill Joe. I found them under the seat in Gale's car. I've got them. That evidence just about fixes Gale . . . don't you think, Dolores ? "

She leaned against the wall. Her face was ashen.

She said : " You've been pretty clever, Johnny. But then you always were. Joe used to say that it would be safer for anybody to kiss a rattlesnake than to start something with you. He used to say that you never gave up. He said once that you were the most consistent bastard he'd ever known."

Vallon grinned. "And I'll bet he was smiling when he said 'bastard' . . . But he was right. I'm an old-fashioned type. I like to see things through to their logical conclusion."

She smiled sadly. "So you're an old-fashioned type, are you, Johnny? That's a new one. And what's the logical conclusion of all this? I don't suppose it's going to be very pleasant for anyone."

"It's going to be goddam unpleasant for Gale," said Vallon. "It's going to be a nice piece of rope and an eight-foot drop. They'll probably allow him an extra two feet. They tell me he's a very big strong man. One of those attractive types."

She shrugged her shoulders. "*If* they get him. If you knew Pierce Gale you'd know that no hangman is going to get his hands on him. He's not that sort."

Vallon said: "That's what they all say. But they usually believe that they've got a chance to beat the rap. So they go carefully. But perhaps he's the exception that proves the rule."

There was a long silence. Then she came towards him. She stood in front of the chair in which he was slumped, looking down at him.

She said: "Johnny, what's going to happen to me?"

He shrugged his shoulders. His eyes were serious. "You're in a spot. Joe's left you in the ditch. He's cut you out of his will, and you won't have a penny piece to play with. Have you any money?"

She nodded. "I've a few hundreds. Bits and pieces that I've saved out of money Joe gave me."

"What about South America?" Vallon asked.

She laughed. "It's not much good going there on what I've got. Besides . . . will they let me go? Perhaps I shall be dragged into this thing. Perhaps I'll have to give evidence."

He shook his head. "You won't. Hipper has already made a statement to the police. He's talked about the collusive divorce, the blackmail, and the letter. But not about you. Up to the moment you don't come into this. If you behave yourself and keep quiet there's no reason why you should . . . *if* you're lucky."

179

She said : " Johnny . . . I've never felt more like behaving myself and keeping quiet. I think I'm sick of everything . . . including myself."

He put his hands on the arms of the chair ; dragged himself to his feet. He smiled at her. " Me too . . ." he said. " Maybe it's a good sign. Maybe everybody's growing up—or something."

" You'd better have a drink," she said. " You look like the wrath of God. Why don't you go to bed and sleep ? "

" For the same reason that pigs don't fly," said Vallon. " They can't. One of these fine days I'm going to bed for ten years. And I'll have a little brandy. Just to keep the cold out."

She went to the sideboard ; mixed the drink ; brought it to him.

He asked : " What's the telephone number of the Mandrake Club at Chertsey, Dolores ? "

She told him.

He said : " I'm going to make a phone call to your ex-boy friend. I'll do it from here. I think I'm right in believing that you're going to mind your own business from now on, aren't I ? That you're going to give a very good imitation of a good girl ? "

She laughed. " You're right. I've had it, Johnny. I wish Joe was back here. I wish I'd been different. I wish a million things. I don't wonder he thought I was a cheap heel . . ."

Vallon drank a little of the brandy. He didn't like the taste of it. Maybe, he thought, that was the Coramine.

He brought out the lie pat. " Perhaps Joe didn't really think *that* badly. In fact I know he didn't."

She laughed bitterly. " No ? What about the five bucks he left me ? "

Vallon said casually : " When I told you that, I didn't tell you *all* the truth about his will. I only told you some of it. The day after he made that will, Joe gave a further instruction to the lawyers, and confirmed it by a letter. There was another ten thousand he was sitting on. He had that up his sleeve in a separate banking account. He said in the letter that, if in the opinion of his executor you merited it, you were to have the ten thousand. Well . . . I'm the executor, and I think that if Joe were here now he'd

180

want me to see you got it. I'll see the lawyers to-morrow and fix it."

"That makes it easy, Johnny. I've friends in South America. I'll start some sort of business. I'll try and forget all this."

"You will," said Vallon. He grinned at her. "The truest thing in the world is that trouble passes and time fixes everything."

He went to the telephone. He asked the operator for the Chertsey number. After a minute he asked to speak to Mr. Gale.

She stood by the fireplace watching him. Her eyes were worried.

Vallon said cheerfully: "Is that Mr. Gale? Good! My name's Vallon—Johnny Vallon. I'm running Chennault Investigations. A client of ours, Mrs. Querida Gale, has given me certain instructions that I'd like to discuss with you, Mr. Gale. It's in connection with your telephone call to her yesterday. I've been asked to settle the matter with you on certain terms. I'd like to see you as soon as possible. O.K. . . . I'll be with you between five-thirty and a quarter to six. Good-bye."

He hung up.

She said: "For God's sake be careful, Johnny. Gale is no push-over. He can be tough. I don't know what you've got in your mind, but——"

He interrupted: "Of course he's a push-over. Killers always are. If they weren't, they wouldn't be killers."

He picked up his hat. "So long . . . Dolores . . ."

She moved a little. "So this is it. . . . This is good-bye, Johnny?"

"Yes," said Vallon. "This is it. Remember what I told you, and don't stick your neck out. Don't lean out of any high windows, or do anything I wouldn't like to see photographed!"

He grinned at her. "So long . . ."

She watched the door close. Then she walked to the window; watched him get into the car; drive out of the courtyard.

.   .   .   .

When Vallon walked through the entrance doors of the

181

Mandrake Club, Gale was standing over by the cloakroom in the shadow.

The foyer of the club formed a large square. It was thickly carpeted, with handsome settees placed here and there. On the left was the corridor leading to the restaurant and dance floor. On the right, in the corner, was the door leading to the cloakroom. Next to it was a wide flight of stairs leading to the upper regions. The place was well-furnished; had an air almost of opulence.

Gale came out of the shadows. He moved quickly across the hall; came into Vallon's line of vision.

Vallon looked at him quickly. Gale was tall, very broad-shouldered. His round face was bronzed with sun and open air. He wore a thin, black pencil-line moustache. He looked good-natured; capable and in the best of physical shape.

He said pleasantly: " Mr. Vallon? You wanted to see me ? "

Vallon yawned. " Yes . . . I wanted to have a talk with you. You'll probably consider it urgent business."

Gale said: " Of course. Come upstairs to my room. Perhaps you'd like a drink ? "

" No thanks," said Vallon. " I never touch the stuff. It doesn't suit me."

He followed Gale up the stairs.

They went into a room on the first floor. It was large; well-appointed. It possessed an air of efficiency. Gale sat down behind the large desk; motioned Vallon to a chair opposite.

Vallon sat down. He said: " I don't think either of us wants to waste a lot of time. So I'll get down to cases."

" Why not ? " Gale smiled. " I like getting down to hard tacks. It saves a lot of time and temper. I understand you run Chennault Investigations ? "

Vallon nodded. " I've been doing that ever since Joe Chennault died," he said easily. " I used to be staff manager. I knew that he was particularly interested in your wife's divorce suit but I didn't know why. Since I've seen the files and since Mrs. Gale talked to me on the telephone last night, I've been getting quite a lot of ideas." He smiled amiably at Gale.

"Ideas may be good—or not," said Gale. "Let's hear about them."

Vallon yawned again. He covered his mouth with his hand. " I'm goddam tired," he said. " You must excuse me for yawning. I just can't stop it."

Gale said a trifle impatiently : " Let's hear about the ideas. We won't bother about the yawns."

" All right," said Vallon. " Well, last night Mrs. Gale telephoned me. She told me you'd been through to her on the telephone ; that an operative of ours—a man called Hipper who had worked on her divorce case—was trying to do a little blackmail on the side. It seems that Hipper has in his possession a letter she wrote you which proves collusion between her and you ; that he's asking a lot of money for it. She said that you thought he ought to be paid so as to stop any trouble, and that you were going down there to-night to collect the money. She asked me what I thought she ought to do."

" I see. . . ." Gale's tone was still easy and pleasant. " And what did you tell her she ought to do ? "

Vallon stifled another yawn. He took out his cigarette case ; selected a cigarette ; lighted it. He took plenty of time in the process. Gale began to drum with his fingers on the desk top.

" It isn't much good being impatient," said Vallon. " Impatience isn't going to get either you or me anywhere." His tone was insolent.

Gale repeated : " What did you tell her she ought to do ? "

Vallon said : " I told her the best thing she could do would be to draw the money—just in case. I thought it might be a good thing to do to pay off Hipper. She said she'd do that. Then I said I'd come and see you and have a little talk. I thought it might be a good thing if you and I understood each other."

" There isn't anything to understand," said Gale. " The position is simple. This man Hipper somehow became possessed of the letter my wife wrote to me guaranteeing me a certain sum of money after the divorce went through. Obviously, that letter's an extremely dangerous weapon in the hands of such a man. He's got to be paid off. Once the letter is back in my hands everything will be perfectly simple and in order."

Vallon said : " As easy as that ? "

Gale shrugged his shoulders. " What else is there to do ?

Personally, I don't mind a lot either way. But if she wants the divorce to go through she'll have to satisfy Hipper."

"No, she won't," said Vallon. His tone was airy. "Where's the letter now? Who's got it?"

"Hipper's got it. He'll hand it over to me when I give him the money."

"Don't tell damned lies," said Vallon quietly. "You know Hipper hasn't got the letter. You know you've got it. So do I. You give it to me, and we'll talk business."

Gale said: "You must be crazy."

"I'm not a bit crazy," said Vallon. "I'm full of common sense. You'd be surprised. I had a little talk with Hipper this afternoon and scared the pants off him. He said you had the letter. He said you were in this thing together. So I thought you and I might do a little deal, Gale."

"What deal?" Gale asked. "What deal should I do with you?"

Vallon said: "I like money as well as anyone else. This is my proposition, and believe it or not you're going to like it because you've *got* to like it. See . . . ?"

He drew on his cigarette. "The proposition is this. First of all you're going to give me the letter. That's the first thing. Then, when I have the letter, you can start off and see Mrs. Gale. You can tell her that Hipper will hand it over for twenty thousand. She'll give you the money. Then you come back and see me and you give me ten thousand—we'll cut fifty-fifty. We won't bother about Hipper. What the hell does he matter anyway?"

Gale leaned back in his chair. He looked at Vallon. His eyes were very blue and very fierce. He flicked angrily on the desk top with the fingers of his right hand.

He said: "Supposing, for the sake of argument, that I had the letter. Supposing I had. Why should I hand it over to you instead of beating your ears off?"

Vallon yawned again. He said casually: "Don't try any strong-arm stuff with me, Gale. Keep that for the women you spend your time pushing around. You don't scare me a bit. If you want to know why you're going to hand over that letter I'll tell you. Are you listening?"

"I'm listening," said Gale. "And make it good or I'm going to throw you out of this office, and it's going to hurt a lot."

Vallon said : " Talk big while you've got the chance, Gale. I've got you where I want you, and you're going to do as I say—and like it. I said I'd make a deal with you. I will. Here's the deal. First of all you give me the letter. Then you go down to Devon and collect the twenty thousand from Mrs. Gale. Then you come back here and give me my cut. When you've done that—if you're *very* good—I'll give you something you'd like to have."

" What ? " asked Gale.

Vallon stretched. He got up. He stood, close to the desk, looking at Gale. He repeated : " When you give me the ten thousand I'll give you back something you'll like to have. I'll give you back Joe Chennault's private diary with the appointment with you in it, in his handwriting ; an appointment with you on the day he died. I'll give you that. And *if* you're very good I'll give you back the automatic you killed him with ! "

There was a silence. A little hissing noise came from Gale. He asked : " If you have these things where did you get them ? "

" From under the seat of your car," said Vallon. He grinned. " You just don't know what a busy little bee I've been," he concluded.

Gale said : " Goddam you, Vallon. How do I know you'll keep your word ? "

" You don't. You have to take a chance. But work it out for yourself. I don't do myself any good by turning you in . . . do I ? I don't make anything out of that. And I like money as well as anybody else . . . see ? You pay me the ten thousand to-morrow and I hand over the diary and the gun. You've got to take my word for that."

Gale said in a low voice : " And what about the letter ? "

" I'm going to sell that." Vallon was grinning. " I'm going to hand that back to Mrs. Gale for what I can get. That is if she's got any more spare cash handy. If she hasn't she'll have to sell something."

Gale got up. He was smiling. " You win. You're a man after my own heart." He put his hand into the breast pocket of his coat. He produced an envelope. " Here's the letter," he said. " I'll meet you here to-morrow with the money. I'll give you your cut and you'll hand me the things you mentioned. Is that a deal ? "

185

Vallon said : " That's O.K. by me. I'll be on my way. I'll be here at twelve o'clock to-morrow and we'll fix everything. Good night, Gale . . ."

He walked out of the office.

Gale sat for a long time looking at the desk. Then he shrugged his shoulders. He thought to himself he'd been right in planning to get out while the going was good ; while there was lots of time.

He smiled. The punk Vallon, he thought, was a fool. He'd left it a little too late. Querida would part with the money. She never expected to be given the letter to-night. She expected Hipper to hand it over to Gale when he was paid. And by to-morrow he, Gale, would be a long way away. Everything, he thought, was still O.K. If you missed it one way, you picked it up another.

He lighted a cigarette ; went down to the garage ; got out his car. He thought it was a pleasant evening for driving. He whistled softly to himself.

.   .   .   .

Darkness was falling when Gale pulled up the car outside the inn at Stockbridge. He went inside ; bought himself a whisky and soda ; drank it ; went into the telephone box in the hall. He asked for a Torquay number ; waited impatiently.

A woman's voice came on the line. Gale said : " Well, honey. . . . Is the boat all right ? "

She said : " Listen, Pierce . . . there's something damn' funny going on down here. I got the stuff aboard this morning . . . like you said. She's full of gas and everything is O.K. But——"

" But *what*, Rita ? " asked Gale impatiently. " What's the trouble now ? Can't you fix anything without a lot of baloney and talk . . . ? "

" You *listen* . . ." Her voice was shrill. " I was going to tell you. I went down to the harbour to-night to take a couple of bottles of liquor aboard. O.K. Well, there were a pair of cops standing just where *The Syriad* is moored. There's something damn' funny going on, Pierce. I don't like it. Those cops are waiting for something. Maybe it's us."

" The hell with it," said Gale. " It's your imagination.

I'll be with you in a few hours. You've been dreaming. So long, Rita."

He hung up. He thought she must be crazy. But he was worried.

He dialled operator; asked for the Ladycourt number. When the maid answered he said : " I want to talk to Mrs. Gale. It's urgent. This is Mr. Gale."

" She's not here," said the prim voice of the maid. " She left this morning, sir. She's gone off for a holiday. She didn't leave any address."

Gale slammed the receiver back on its hook with a curse. He walked quickly out of the hotel ; got into his car ; started the engine. Out on the main road across Salisbury Plain he put his foot down on the accelerator.

What the hell was happening ? Querida away when she was supposed to be waiting for him . . . police officers stationed on the quay watching *The Syriad* . . .

He thought of Vallon. The skin of his face stiffened. It was as if a cold hand had been laid across his neck.

Vallon . . . Vallon . . . God . . . what a fool he'd been !

He'd given Vallon the letter—the letter from Querida Gale to him about the money. And Vallon had Joe Chennault's diary and the automatic.

God dam it, he'd given Vallon the last bit of evidence he wanted . . . the letter. . . . Vallon had enough to send him to the gallows !

The wind whistled by the car. It was half-way across the Plain that the police car came out of the side turning. Gale could hear the gong behind him ; saw the blue police lights on the top of the car.

He began to sweat. He trod on the accelerator. His speedometer needle stood at eighty-five.

He looked behind him. They were still there . . . and gaining every moment . . .

3

At eleven o'clock Vallon went into Joe Chennault's office and sat down at the desk. He rested his elbows on the desk, his head in his hands. He thought that he felt like something the cat had brought in.

Anyhow, now he could get some sleep. Whatever happened; whoever did what, to-night he was going to sleep; maybe this afternoon; maybe any time now.

The telephone jangled. Vallon started; grinned to himself. He took off the receiver.

It was McNeil. He said: "Well . . . we got him. It looks as if you were right, Johnny."

Vallon asked: "What happened?"

"The police car picked him up near The Wallops on Salisbury Plain," said McNeil. "So he thought he'd make a run for it. Where the hell he thought he was going to run to, I don't know. But he was scared. The boys tell me that he got up to nearly ninety when he crashed. He was so busy looking in the driving mirror to see if they were gaining on him that he didn't see the lorry in front until it was too late. His car was telescoped. He was killed instantaneously. Just as well perhaps."

"I got the letter from him," said Vallon. "The letter I told you about; and I've got the gun and the diary. I'l hand them over to you sometime."

"If you like," said McNeil. "But it doesn't really matter . . . now. By the way, you were right in all your guesses. The Torquay C.I.D. picked up a girl named Rita Elvast. She was going with him to France, in the motor-boat. Apparently, he telephoned her from Stockbridge and she told him that a couple of officers were on the quay, watching the boat. That must have shaken him quite a bit. Then he put a call through to his wife at Ladycourt, and the maid told him that she'd gone off, on holiday; that she wouldn't be back for some time. That must have shaken him some more. And when he saw the police car coming after him on the Plain, that finished him off. He knew it was all over bar shouting, and I suppose he thought his one chance was to make Torquay and chance getting the boat away somehow."

"I see," said Vallon. "Well . . . thanks a lot, Mac. I suppose it is all over now bar shouting?"

"Yes," said McNeil. "It will be accidental death. We shall state at the inquest that the police car was picking him up on a charge. That's all. Come in and see me some time. 'Bye, Johnny."

"So long . . ." Vallon hung up. He thought: So that's that!

The office telephone tinkled. The girl on the office exchange said: "There's a lady on the line for you, Mr. Vallon. A Mrs. Gale."

"Put her through," said Vallon.

Querida Gale came on the line. She said: "Good morning, Johnny. I'm at Cary House, near Sevenoaks. I shall be here for a week."

"Listen," said Vallon. "And take a pull at yourself. You don't have to worry about Gale or the divorce or anything. He was killed in a car smash last night on Salisbury Plain. Trying to evade arrest. A police car was after him."

There was a long pause. Then she said: "I can't even pretend I'm sorry, Johnny."

"You're telling me! Well . . . so long, Querida . . . Keep smiling."

He hung up. He got up; picked up his hat; went into Marvin's room.

He said to Marvin: "I'm going home. I'm going to sleep for a few years. You'd better get ready to hand over to Acme. They'll be coming to take over in a week or so. If you want me, you know where to get me."

Marvin said O.K. Vallon put on his hat; went out.

.   .   .   .

At twelve-thirty Vallon came out of the cocktail bar in Jermyn Street. He thought he was losing his taste for rye whisky; that he didn't like it much; that it wasn't even putting the pain in his stomach to sleep.

The sun was shining. He thought Regent Street looked attractive. He wondered what he was going to do. Maybe, he thought, he would get in touch with Strype in New York and find out if there was some sort of job for him there.

He opened the car door; got into the driving seat; started the car. He turned left into Piccadilly; began to drive towards Knightsbridge.

He felt very odd. The pain n his stomach was there, but it wasn't too bad. He felt a little light-headed and faint. He thought that maybe he would go home and go to bed. Except that the idea was boring. He had a peculiar feeling of being keyed up to something.

He thought that life was an odd sort of lark. Nothing

189

ever happened according to plan ; all sorts of things happened for abstruse reasons that didn't matter a damn. The truest thing was that you never knew what was waiting round the corner. He wondered what would be waiting round the corner for him. He thought that maybe it wouldn't be so hot ; that it was even wasting its time—waiting.

His mind wandered to Joe Chennault—who knew all the answers now ; to Dolores Chennault ; to Querida Gale. He wondered what the girl Rita Elvast was like—the girl who thought she was going to France with Gale. Maybe she'd missed a lot of trouble. She didn't know how lucky she was ! The joke was she probably didn't think so.

He thought about Madeleine. He wondered where she was ; if he would ever see her again.

And he thought it was damned funny that Querida should be able to give him the name of the perfume . . . Mitsouko . . . Madeleine's perfume.

He stopped the car outside the perfumery shop in Knightsbridge. He stumbled a little getting out. He thought he had never been so tired.

He went into the shop. He said to the girl behind the counter : " I want a flask of perfume called ' Mitsouko.' It's by Guerlain."

She said : " I'm very sorry but we haven't one in stock. We are delivering the last bottle we have to a customer who's had it on order. And I don't even know when we shall have any more. Can I show you something else ? "

Vallon said : " No thanks . . ." He went out of the shop ; got into the car. He sat behind the wheel ; lighting a cigarette and thinking it was a damned shame about the perfume.

A boy came out of the shop. He carried a delivery basket, and he put the basket in the frame carrier on the handlebars of the bicycle that was parked a few feet in front of Vallon's car. Then he mounted the bicycle and rode off. He was whistling.

Vallon started up the car and followed. He went after the boy when he turned left into Seville Place. The boy stopped outside a house. He took some bottles out of the carrier and went inside. Vallon got out of the car and opened the basket carrier ; looked inside. On top of the packages was a parcelled box. It was labelled " *Mitsouko*."

Vallon felt for his note-case. He took out a five-pound note and put it in the carrier. He took the package labelled "*Mitsouko*"; put it in the side pocket of his jacket. He got back into the car; drove to his rooms in Kensington. He left the car outside; went up to his sitting-room. He sat down in the big arm-chair and took the package from his pocket. He sat there, looking at it, turning it in his hands.

It was addressed to: "*Miss Madeleine Thorne, Chestnut Court, Lowndes Square.*"

Vallon said to himself: Jeez . . . ! Is this funny or is it funny. . . .

He put the package into his pocket; went downstairs. He pushed himself into the car; began to drive towards Lowndes Square. His head was aching and he thought he wasn't seeing very well.

When he arrived, he walked up the stairs unsteadily. He kept his finger on the bell-push for quite a while. He hoped somebody would open the door quickly.

She opened the door. She wore a dog's tooth tweed coat and skirt and a cream silk blouse. Vallon thought she looked marvellous.

He grinned at her. He said: "I'm from the perfumery shop. I've a flask of perfume for Miss Madeleine Thorne." He leaned against the side of the door.

She said quickly: "For God's sake, Johnny . . . what's the matter? You look like death. Come in."

He stepped into the hallway and she closed the door behind him. He stood, swaying a little, in the middle of the hall.

He said: "You listen to me. Somebody killed Joe Chennault. Joe was my boss in China . . . you remember? Well, I had to do something about it. See? I was fond of Joe. That's why I stood you up for our appointment at the Hungaria. I couldn't help it. Not this time. When I came here they said you'd gone."

She said softly: "I told them to. What's the matter with you, Johnny. Are you ill?"

He said: "I've been driving around this goddam country for days. I'm all right. The prescription is sleep, more sleep, food, no liquor and no cigarettes—and some more sleep." He grinned at her weakly. "I've got an idea I've been worrying a little about you too," he said. He moved over to the wall and leaned against it.

She came towards him. She put her arm round his shoulder. "You're going to lie down. This way, Johnny."

In the bedroom she said: "Take your shoes off and lie on the bed. And don't worry about anything."

Vallon sat on the bed. He began to tear the paper off the perfume package. He said: "It's damned funny how I got this scent . . . it's damned funny . . ."

He pulled the stopper out of the flask. Then he fell on his side. He lay there, his legs hanging over the side of the bed—sound asleep.

She stood looking at him. Then she lifted his legs on to the bed; took off his shoes. She went into the drawing-room.

She sat down in front of the telephone table. She thought for a moment. Then she picked up the receiver. She said to the girl on the switchboard: "Please put me through to a firm of lawyers in Lincoln's Inn Fields called Swithin & May. I want to speak to Mr. May."

When he came on the line, she said: "Mr. May . . . I want to be married. Will you tell me about getting a special licence. Yes . . . his name's John Vallon . . . yes . . . yes. . . Very well, I'll expect you at three o'clock."

She hung up; went back to the bedroom.

Vallon still held the perfume flask. The stopper was out and the perfume had soaked into the bed. The room reeked of "*Mitsouko*."

She opened the window; took the bottle from his hand. Then she went into the bedroom on the far side of the sitting-room. She came back with an eiderdown. She put it over him.

She sat down on the cushioned stool in front of the dressing-table. She sat there, watching him.

She began to smile. She said softly: "Johnny . . . you heel . . . you lovely heel . . . !"

THE END